TWIN FLAMES

By Faith Prince

CHAPTER 1

Saria

I tumble down the vortex, spinning round and round. Bold colors zoom past: streaks of ocean blue, a splatter of blood red, a beam of gold. My heart pounds in my throat. Silver ribbons encircle my arms: slick, cold, suctioned to my skin like tentacles. A scream erupts in my throat, but I can't hear myself over the roar of the whirlwind.

A slingshot propels me into space. I zip alongside a trail of gold glitter, like I'm one with a shooting star. If I wasn't terrified, I'd be awestruck.

But I'm not on a carnival ride and this portal doesn't lead to Disney World. I'm catapulting into Aurelia, the supernatural realm and homeland of witches. The Descendants of Xaphan, better known as DOX, opened the portal with the intention to wage war on Aurelia. If they win, they'll enact their radical terrorist agenda to take over Aurelia and make humans their slaves.

I didn't dive into the portal to protect Aurelia from the oncoming invasion. My twin sister Zoeli would be the one to do that. I'm Saria: powerless, afraid, and useless in battle. In fact, as soon as I hit the ground, I plan to run as far away from the warzone as I can.

There's only one reason that I made the arguably stupid decision to jump into the portal: Zoeli. The last time I saw my twin sister, we were both prisoners in Nightingale Dungeon. Since then, I was released and she escaped. My sister's still at large. I don't even know if she's alive. Still, I'm holding onto hope that I'll find her somewhere in Aurelia, and bring her home.

Not a moment passes that I don't miss her. I wasn't always good to her. I've done some things that I'm ashamed of. Despite all of that, when we were imprisoned in Nightingale Dungeon, she was my protector. When I couldn't withstand the freezing temperatures, Zoe held me to her chest, her warmth seeping into my trembling bones. As we both wasted away, she handed me her ration of stale bread, a smile plastered on her sunken cheeks.

But my sister did more than care for my physical needs. Zoe kept me sane. There were nights when the cockroaches who skittered across the floor made their way under my skin. The dungeon bars closed in, caging my brain, locking out every memory from before my imprisonment. This was it: concrete floors, ice-cold chills, the guard's sneers and groping hands. Terror, hunger and pain. I teetered on the edge of madness, wondering if death was the better choice.

In those moments, I curled up next to Zoe. My twin spoke in a soft voice, her breath on my cheek. Suddenly, I was a child again, running through a garden of wildflowers. Then, I was exploring the woods in our backyard, climbing the tallest trees, my little legs stretching from bough to bough. Perched on a branch, I watched the sun dip below pink cotton-candy clouds. On the trek home, as we ducked under brush, Logan appeared by my side. His skinny arms held branches aside, preventing them from tangling in my hair. When we came to a grassy clearing, I reached for the sky. A blue jay alit on my wrist. Logan's jaw fell open, his hazel eyes widening with awe.

With every word, Zoe replaced the dungeon's horrors with sweet memories from home. She stroked my hair as she talked, never stopping until my breathing steadied and my limbs ceased to shake.

I need to find her.

Arms clasp around my waist. I jolt. "Sari, it's me." Electric blue eyes meet mine. For a moment, I can't find my breath. I study him: pitch-black hair, ghost-white skin, chiseled jawline, massive shoulders. He looks like he stepped off the cover of GQ's jacked and goth edition. If Redvers Castigan could show up in photographs, modeling agencies would call him off the hook.

"You found me," I breathe. I wrap my arms around him, his back muscles hard beneath my palms. When we jumped in the portal, we were holding hands. Somewhere in the whirlwind, we lost each other.

Thud! We hit the ground, stirring up a cloud of brown dust in the moonlight. I squint, struggling to see through the fog. Red sprawls out over me, shielding me with his colossal frame. "We have to get out of here," he whispers in my ear.

I rise up, Red's arm around my shoulders. About a dozen Aurelian soldiers, marked by royal blue army uniforms, hold crystals above their golden-nightingale adorned helmets. An otherworldly mist floats around them, gleaming, sparkles reflecting on their gold belts.

DOX militants, dressed in black and gray camouflage fatigues, fire their machine guns. When bullets enter the mist, they stop mid-air and clatter to the ground, missing the Aurelian soldiers' flesh by mere inches. Smoke burns in my nostrils.

"Let's go," Red murmurs, leading me away from the conflict. I wobble on stiletto heels. Looking down, I cringe at the ridiculous outfit that Talon forced me to wear. I look like the naughty maid in a porn movie.

We speed walk: slow enough to not draw attention, but fast enough to work up a sweat. I suck in a deep breath. *Zoe, I'm coming.* We're a stone's throw from disappearing into the thicket.

"Where ya going with the nimwit?" The brute voice sends chills down my spine. Three DOX soldiers step out in front of us, blocking our way. One crosses his arms over his puffed-out chest. He stares at Red, waiting for an answer.

Red raises his hands. "Look, man, I'm with you guys." He points to the DOX patch sewn on his military jacket. "I'm just following Talon's orders. I'm taking her where he told me to."

"Hmph." The soldier grunts. He runs his fingers over his acne-inflamed chin. "Where's Igor? He was in charge of the nimwit."

"One of those Fawley bastards killed him," Red says. I drop my gaze, worried that my expression might give us away. Red's lying. Igor is dead. That much is true. Someone drove a dagger into Igor's neck. But it wasn't someone from the Fawley agency. It was Red. "Talon told me to keep an eye on them, and if anything happened, I was to take over."

"I never heard Talon say that."

Red shrugs. "It was just between us. He spoke to me in private."

The soldier narrows his eyes. "What's your name again, sir?"

"They call me Red. Who are you?"

"I'm Brock Van Houten. I've been working closely with Talon on this whole operation. If you're one of Talon's top guys, how come I've never heard of ya?"

"I like to stay under the radar." Red steps aside, his arm snug around my shoulders. "If you'll excuse me, I have to go. I have a delivery to make."

"Not so fast." Brock grabs my wrist. His fingers press on my bones. "It's best for you to leave the nimwit with us."

"I disagree." Red squares his shoulders. "Talon is expecting me. Now, if you'll move out of my way—"

"I wasn't asking." Brock jerks me away from Red. Pop! My shoulder rips out of its socket. I yelp in agony. Black spots dance in my vision. I try to wiggle my fingers, but they don't move. Tears burn in the corners of my eyes. "The nimwit stays with us until I hear otherwise from Talon himself."

More hands reach for me. One clamps my upper arm. Another snags my bun, lurching me backwards. Brock's eyes wander up my fishnet stockings. "She's not bad looking for a nimwit. We could have some fun with this one." He chuckles.

"You can take her," Red says. I swallow hard. Why would Red say that? A tear slides down my cheek. I will not be Talon's slave. I won't be degraded and tortured by DOX. Never again.

I try to pull away. Pain radiates from my shoulder injury. The soldiers tighten their grip. It's no use. They're so much stronger than me. They drag me down the path.

"Over my dead body," Red finishes. He punches Brock in the nose. Crack! Brock releases me, his hands flying to his face. Blood drips down his fingers. Red jump-kicks him in the head. Brock drops to the ground, a foot-sized dent in his forehead.

Another soldier raises his fist. Red captures his arm mid-swing and twists it around. "Ahhh!" The soldier shouts, his forearm dangling at an unnatural angle. Red's silver dagger glints in the moonlight. He plunges the blade into the soldier's gut. He crumples in the dirt.

Behind Red, the last soldier is poised to pounce. Red spins around. With one swift motion, he cuts his throat. He collapses on top of his comrades, blood pouring from his neck.

"Red." I stagger to him. I'm dizzy from the rush of adrenaline and woozy from all the blood. I fall into his arms. He holds me.

"I hope you knew that I wasn't going to let them take you. I just needed the element of surprise."

"I know," I murmur into his chest.

"We need to get out of here," Red says. "And fast." He crouches down. "Climb on my back." I wrap my arms around his neck and my legs around his waist, gritting my teeth as pain sears in my shoulder. "Hold on tight."

And we're off.

Red sprints through the forest like a cheetah hunting prey. He can run like a predator because he is one.

The speed loosens my bun. My long hair unravels, sailing loose and wild behind me. I wonder if this is what it feels like to fly. I feel a pang of longing for the birthright that was taken from me. After my mother married a human, the

Aurelian government authorized the curse that stole my immediate family's shapeshifting power. I'll never be able to fly as a crow.

The forest thickens. Leaves graze my cheeks. Branches scratch my arms. Red doesn't slow down. I breathe in the heady scent of pine, moss and damp earth. It almost feels like home. In another life, these woods might've been my terrain: paths worn down by my footprints, my initials carved into these trees. If our family wasn't banished from Aurelia, I might know these woods like the back of my hand. Instead, this world is a mystery, each turn leading to more of the unknown.

A while later, Red comes to an abrupt stop. "I think we're in the clear. No one seems to be around." Even though he ran at least five miles with one hundred thirty pounds on his back, Red isn't out of breath. The undead don't require oxygen.

My stiletto heels sink into the mud. I groan. I can't wait to toss these wretched shoes in the trash, but for now they're all I have.

Red takes my wrist. "Your shoulder is dislocated," he says. "We need to put your bone back in place." He lifts my arm. Pain, sharp and intense, explodes like gasoline in a fire. Even as I bite my lips, a hitched sob escapes. Red's brows draw together. "Sari, I'm so sorry. I'm a fool. I so seldomly experience pain. I forget about your human vulnerabilities." Red rests his palm on my injury. Blue tendrils emerge from his fingertips. A cool, soothing sensation slides under my skin.

"What's that?" I breathe.

"Let's call it a local anesthetic." Red raises my arm. This time, the motion is painless. Pop! Red expertly repositions my shoulder. "With some rest and time, it'll heal right up."

"Thank you," I murmur. "Although I'm not sure if rest is possible in our situation."

"Sari, I must rest." Red checks his watch. "There's less than an hour before sunrise. I already feel my body slowing down."

"Oh." I swallow hard. The same way he forgot about my susceptibility to pain, I forgot about his to the sun. Our life experiences are nothing alike. He's a creature of the night; I adore the sun on my face. He drinks blood; I am the blood he drinks. Can two beings who are so different be together? It would be a challenge, for sure. But not impossible… right? "Is the sun in Aurelia, er, as dangerous for you as the sun on earth?"

"It's the same sun," Red says. Twigs crunch under his boots. "The same moon, too."

I look up. A half-moon twinkles above a canopy of leaves. "How can it be?" Back home, the moon hangs outside our living room window. I wonder if my mom is awake, staring outside, thinking of me. The two of us, a world apart, gazing at the same moon.

"I need to find a safe place for you to stay while I rest," Red says.

A cold wind rustles my skirt. I shiver and rub my arms. Red shrugs off his jacket and slips it over my shoulders. It smells like him. I wrap it tighter around me. "Can I stay with you?"

"Sari, if I could keep you next to me, that's what I'd do, but I doubt you'll be comfortable six feet underground beside a stiff body."

I raise my brows. "I guess that depends on what's stiff."

"Get your mind out of the gutter." Red pokes my side.

I giggle to keep it lighthearted, but in my mind's eye, I see Red's twinkling eyes replaced by a vacant stare, cold and alone, buried deep in the earth. I shudder. This vampire stuff takes some getting used to.

Red and I reach a fork in the road. He looks down one way, and then the other. He shrugs. "Your guess is as good as mine. You lead the way."

It's a gamble. DOX militants could be in either direction. To the left, I peer into an endless tunnel of trees and bark. A white light materializes in the darkness. Thousands of rays stretch from its center, illuminating the forest. It's so bright I have to shield my eyes. Boom! A gigantic tree topples over, barricading the trail with its wide array of leaves and branches. The light is gone as suddenly as it appeared.

"What the hell was that?" I ask.

"I have no idea," Red whispers. Looking at the downed tree, I'm reminded of the time a tree fell on me. Last year, I was hiking with my friends when a storm hit. A bough impaled me in the chest. Later on, I discovered that it was a magic attack executed by Talon's associates.

My heart beats double time. "We're not going that way." I turn around, hoping that whatever cast that white glow doesn't follow us.

"I was hoping we'd get lucky and find an abandoned shed or tree house, but we're running out of time." Red snaps a bough off a tree. "We need to build a shelter for you. We'll use sticks for the frame, and then cover it with leaves and moss."

"Okay." I swallow hard. It won't be that bad, I tell myself, as I gather leaves. After all, I love the woods. As a kid, I often fell asleep outside, swinging in a hammock, lulled into oblivion by the medley of songbirds and whistling winds. Another time, I slept on the freezing cold floor of an abandoned shed. I cuddled with a litter of stray kittens, determined to use my body heat to rescue them from hypothermia. Still, I wasn't alone in an unfamiliar land under siege by supernatural terrorists. Once Talon hears about my escape, he'll be furious. If DOX militants recapture me, I can't even fathom the obscene forms of torture they'll put me through.

I weave through trees, plucking leaves as I go. Nearby Red arranges sticks in a triangular shape. I'm an idiot. I never should've jumped into the portal. My recklessness may cost both of our lives.

I suck in a deep breath. I imagine Zoeli: cross-legged on our front porch, strumming her guitar, her cat Batman curled up beside her. If I can bring her home, it'll all be worth it.

I yank a cluster of leaves off a branch. Through the brush, purple mist swirls over a black cauldron. I push the branch aside. Wrinkled hands drift through the lavender haze. Eyes closed, an old woman sways, her cotton nightgown billowing in the icy breeze.

Her lips peel back, showing yellowed horse-like teeth. An ear-piercing cackle slices the night. I wince, hand clasped to my chest.

Eyes still closed, the woman beckons me, her gnarled fingers curling in and out. "There you are. I've been expecting you. Come to me, little crow."

CHAPTER 2

Zoeli

Damian! I soar over Nightingale Palace, my wings beating against the wind. Terrorist troops approach from every angle. Hundreds of militants march up the mountain, guns raised, boots stomping on the ground.

Zoe, thank God, I've been freaking out wondering if you're okay. Aurelia is under attack. Being telepathically connected to my ex-boyfriend is annoying, but can be advantageous at a time like this.

Don't worry about me. I can handle myself. Where are you? The palace is surrounded.

I'm hiding out in a panic room with my family. The walls are fortified with katium. I'm safe. How do you know what's going on at the palace?

I have a front row seat, right in the middle of the action.

Are you crazy? Get out of here. Fly as far away as you can.

And miss all the fun? I focus inwards, finding the root of my power. It releases easily, coursing hot in my veins.

I swoop down, my talons extended. A bright blue fireball hits a DOX scumbag in the chest. He drops to the ground, eyes rolling back in his head. One less morally corrupt slimebucket left in the world. You're welcome.

I speed away before anyone can identify who initiated the attack. I perch atop an oak tree, planning my next move. From a nearby treetop, a hawk shoots red lasers from its beady eyes. Several DOX soldiers return fire. The hawk takes off, narrowly escaping a fatal blow.

I duck behind a leafy branch. Even the side I'm fighting for wants me dead. As a crow, I'm less likely to be recognized, but I have to be careful. I scan the battlefield for an opportunity to strike.

I dive towards the enemy. Blue lightning bolts shoot from my claws. I nail two DOX dirtbags in their heads. They crumple to the ground. If they survive, they'll suffer severe brain damage. Although in their case, the difference may be negligible.

I fly up the castle walls, weaving through ribbons of color emitted by the Rock of Vitality. I perch on a turret, surveying the scene below. Combat boots pound the bejeweled roads surrounding the palace.

I remember the first time I saw this place, how I marveled over its magnificence. Now, its stained glass windows and opulent archways are riddled by bullet holes. Blood pools on sapphire-adorned walkways.

Just beyond the palace, Mount Zamus, Aurelia's infamous volcano, is more active than usual. Red sparks shoot out of the crater, exploding like fireworks in the sky. Lava boils over. It drips down its sides, glowing red, like it too, is angered by the invasion.

Another troop stomps over the collapsed palace gates. Long platinum-blonde hair shines beneath the half-moon. Licinia. She thinks she's so tough with her hybrid witch-vampire powers, but the last time we met I smashed her face in. I look forward to the pleasure of doing it again.

Licinia looks like a vampire queen in a skintight black catsuit. A black crystal crown glistens on her head. A black lace cape flies behind her. Streams of red magic surge from the spikes of her crown. Red fog encircles Licinia and the tall man beside her. Talon. My evil great uncle. He wears a black three-piece suit and a crisp white shirt. His thick gray hair is slicked back, not a strand out of place.

Licinia and Talon stroll onwards, unperturbed as countless bullets and missiles, both magical and not, are fired in their direction. The red mist easily dissolves every kind of projectile aimed in their direction. Even I have to admit, they look badass. If I wasn't disgusted by them, I'd be impressed.

The militants draw closer to the palace. Hundreds of Aurelian knights, guards, and soldiers assemble, blocking the entrance. On the front line, soldiers open fire. The repetitive blast of machine guns rattles my bones. A grenade explodes.

Just ahead of Licinia and Talon, a man leads their troop. At first glance, he's unremarkable: average height, mediocre build, basic haircut. His face is so ordinary that I might have met him in the grocery store line or doctor's office waiting room, and then promptly forgotten his existence.

The man raises his palm. His eyes blaze red, like a demon's. Dozens of Aurelian soldiers fall backwards, limbs splayed out on the grass: limp, lifeless. More shots are fired. The man is pummeled by bullets and blasts of magic. Unfazed, he forges ahead, his army jacket in tatters. A knot tightens in my stomach.

This is bad. Very bad.

What the hell are you doing? I told you to get out of there!

The man's eyes are a dull brown color again. Maybe the massacre will stop. Then, he flicks his fingers. Rows of soldiers drop to the ground. The man smirks as he tramples over a stiff body. Blood trickles from the fallen soldier's eyes.

Only a short flight of stairs separates the terrorists from the palace doors. Licinia's struts ahead, chin held high, tossing her platinum blonde hair over her shoulders. Talon pats her on the back, his lips curved into a smug smile.

There's a guy who's killing everyone. I've never seen a power like this. He looks like he could take out your entire army by himself.

Goddamn it. Zoe, stay away from him.

No shit. I may have guts, but I'm not stupid.

A fully armored knight is the last one standing. He wields a sword in one hand, a shield in the other. The impossibly powerful man's eyes glow red. The sword flies out of the knight's hands. Mid-air, the sword flips around and slices the knight's neck. His severed head rolls on the front step. Licinia kicks it aside.

A few blasts of magic knocks the front door off its hinges. DOX militants cheer and clap. Fists pump over their heads.

Licinia, Talon and the impossibly powerful man enter first. Hundreds of DOX militants follow, pouring into the palace like maggots spilling over a rotting corpse.

Damian, they went inside. Licinia, Talon and countless others.

In my mind's eye, I see the impossibly powerful man kicking down the door to Damian's bedroom. He confronts Damian, eyes burning red. Damian keels over, the mischievous sparkle gone from his eyes. I picture him: sprawled out on the floor next to the bed we used to share. Blood drains from his chiseled features. I watch as his full lips turn blue. Lips that will never curl into that goddamn arrogant lopsided grin again. As much as I loathe to admit it, that smile looks sexy on him.

I swallow hard, a lump rising in my throat. Throughout our relationship, Damian repeatedly lied and cheated on me. He's full of excuses and never takes responsibility for his actions. I have no regrets about walking out. If I could go back in time, I'd leave him sooner.

Yet the thought of anything happening to him is like a knife twisting in my chest. As much as I hate him, part of me still loves him.

I love you too, Zoe.

You weren't supposed to hear that. I grumble. This telepathic connection is a pain in my butt.

I know how bad I messed up. I'm sorry.

I've heard that so many times. I don't believe you anymore. His empty promises and sweet talk are nothing but band aids on bullet holes. They won't stop the bleeding. Not anymore.

If you let me, I'll show you that I mean— Damian cuts off abruptly.

I can't catch my breath. It feels like someone knocked the wind out of me. Damian! Are you okay?

They're here. They're banging on the other side of the wall.

My heart crashes into my breast bone. Stay safe.

My talons dig into the palace's stone walls, my mind spinning with a dichotomy of conflicting emotions. Part of me is determined to never get back together with Damian. The other part yearns for his touch.

Running away was my only choice. I thought that separation would break his hold over me, but even after months of no contact, my feelings flood back the moment I hear his voice.

Sometimes I wonder if we met when we were too young. Maybe in time, Damian will evolve into a better man: less self-centered, more compassionate. Late at night, when I crave his arms around me, I imagine a man who looks like Damian: same bedroom eyes, chiseled features and dreamy smile, but unrecognizable in every other way. A man who's true to his word. A man who's kind to those who society labels as beneath him. A man who stands up for what's right, even when it doesn't benefit him. In my wildest dreams, this man shows up on my doorstep, unafraid to shout from the rooftops that he loves a half-breed.

I know it's just a silly fantasy. True change takes years of self-examination and introspection. I doubt that Damian's ego would allow him to put in the work.

Yet, I still hoped that one day he'd become the man I need and deserve.

Now I might never find out.

CHAPTER 3

Saria

The moonlight shines on the old woman like a spotlight. Straggly gray curls frame her withered face. "Hey there, little birdie bird. Come to me." Her neck jiggles as a cackle erupts from her throat. Goosebumps run down my arms.

In a flash, Red's by my side. "Who are you?" He demands.

"Oh, lookie here, it's the vampire boyfriend. When I told Zoeli about your little love affair, she thought I was lying."

I step forward. "You know my sister?"

Red slips his arm around me, pulling me back. "You still haven't told us who you are."

The woman slaps herself on the forehead. "Oh, dear me, where are my manners?" Something crackles inside her cauldron. Purple sparks shoot into the air. "I'm Edith. It's a pleasure to meet you both." Her eerie green gaze shifts from me to Red.

"What are you doing out here?" Red asks.

"I live here." Edith gestures behind her. "If you come out from behind those trees, I'll show you my home."

While Red regards Edith with suspicion, I'm more focused on the fact that she knows my sister. "Do you know where Zoeli is?"

"I'm not sure, my dear, but I can help you find her."

"You can?" I take another step towards Edith.

Red pulls me closer to him. "Excuse me, Edith. Can we have a moment?"

Her lips twist into a sly smile. "Certainly." Edith spins around, almost losing her footing before she steadies herself on a tree trunk. She staggers away, disappearing from sight.

"Sari." Red wraps his arms around my waist. "I don't know about this. It might be a trap." He leans down to whisper in my ear.

"You're good at reading people. Are you getting a bad feeling?" Red's extrasensory perspective is usually on point.

Red's brow furrows. "I didn't have enough time to get a good read on her." He pauses. "It seems awfully convenient, don't you think? Why is she wandering around the woods in the middle of the night? How does she know who we are?"

"I see what you're saying, but we don't exactly have a lot of options here. I'm hungry, tired and cold. You're running out of time before the sun comes up. We don't know where to go or what to do. This woman says that she can help us find Zoeli. I think we should at least hear her out."

Red's breath tickles my neck, his cheek pressed against mine. "You're right. I'm just so scared of something happening to you while I'm asleep."

"We'll talk to her. If you get a bad vibe, we're out of there. Okay?"

Red nods. His fingers lace through my hair, stroking my scalp. His lips are inches away from mine. As much as I want to kiss him, I remember the sting of his rejection all too well. After the most euphoric night of my life, Red called the next day to tell me that it was a "mistake."

I turn away from him. "Let's go." My stiletto heel catches in a tree root. I stumble forward, my arms spiraling through the air. I'm seconds from face planting when Red catches me. He grabs my hips and pulls me against him. Fire races through my veins. I hate how bad I want him, even at a time like this. "Thank you," I breathe.

"No problem." His lips are too close to mine again. I pull away, but my legs are wobbly. He puts his arms around my shoulders, steadying me. We walk side by side.

We duck through boughs and brush. I bat away branches that scratch my cheeks. In a small clearing, Edith's fingers flutter over her cauldron. Eyes closed, purple mist whirls around her. A few yards away, puffs of smoke rise from a small cottage's chimney.

Edith's hooded green eyes open. "You've decided to join me," She rasps, an uncanny smile further wrinkling her cheeks. "The little crow and her vampire love." She guffaws like it's all a big joke.

My cheeks redden. I wish she would stop using the L-word. Red never said that he loves me. We're not together, and he's made it clear that we shouldn't be.

"Come with me." Edith leads the way to her cottage, her nightgown swaying behind her. She tugs open a creaky wooden door. "Welcome to my home."

I peer through the doorway into a tiny kitchen. Floral wallpaper decorates the walls. A steaming cast-iron pot sits atop an old-fashioned range. Edith hobbles into the kitchen. She stirs the bubbling concoction on the stove. A mouthwatering aroma wafts out of the pot. "When I found out you were coming, I made chicken noodle soup." My stomach grumbles.

"Who told you we were coming?" Red wipes his boots on a doormat that says **BEWARE OF THE CAT.**

Edith ladles soup into a ceramic bowl. "My dear friend Betty." She cradles the bowl, carrying it to a circular table. She places it on a red-and-white checkered placemat. "Come in, little birdie. You're hungry. Eat your soup." She croons in a sing-songy voice.

A chill slithers down my spine. I'm starving, but this woman gives me the creeps. I catch Red's eye. He nods and gestures me ahead. The door slams shut behind us with a bang!

I plop into a wooden chair. I breathe in the heavenly scent of chicken noodle soup. My bowl is filled with carrots, celery, pasta and fresh chicken. I dig in.

Red slides into the seat beside me. "Who's Betty? How did she know we were coming?"

Edith wears a proud smile. "Betty knows everything. You just have to ask her the right questions."

"This is delicious." I gulp down another spoonful of chicken broth. "I love homemade soup."

"I'm glad you like it, little crow." She turns to Red. "I'm sorry that I don't have anything suitable for your tastes. I did notice a few squirrels frolicking in the yard earlier."

Red rests his chin on his palm. "I'll be alright, thank you. I'm surprised you let me in, knowing what I am. Most witches fear that I'll make them my dinner."

Edith waves a gnarled hand. "Most witches are fools. We're going to need vampires on our side to have any hope of winning this war." She raises one silver brow. "Besides, I doubt my old blood is very appetizing." She cackles.

I get the distinct feeling that someone is watching me. Hairs raise on the back of my neck. My heart rattles against my rib cage. It's just my paranoia again, I tell myself. After everything I've been through, it's a wonder that I haven't lost my mind. Still, I can't shake the feeling.

I spin around. Green eyes meet mine. I gasp. A black Persian cat leaps, his claws extended like tiny knives. He swipes my cheek, slicing the delicate skin.

Edith flies to her feet. "Edgar! Bad kitty! That's not how we treat our guests." She rummages through the oak cabinets and retrieves cotton balls and a bottle of rubbing alcohol. "May I, dear?" I nod. The scratches sting as Edith applies the disinfectant. "That grouchy cat." Edith mutters under her breath. "That'll heal up in no time. I added a little something extra to the alcohol." Edith winks at me. "And you!" She points at the cat. "No treats for a week." Edgar releases a low growl. "If you keep it up, it'll be two weeks." Edgar points his tail straight up, turns around and prances away, chin held high. "Fresh little bastard." Edith shakes her head. "I'm sorry about that, dear." Edith's gaze shifts to the window. "It's going to be light soon. We'd better start digging. Redvers can sleep right outside my window where I can keep an eye on him. You, little birdie, can sleep on my couch."

In the yard, Edith and Red dig a grave below Edith's bedroom window. "I can help," I protest, reaching for Edith's shovel.

She pulls away. "Nonsense. You have a shoulder injury. You need to rest."

I sigh. I know she's right, but I hate feeling useless. I walk over to where Red uses his shovel to rip through the dirt like butter. "Do you feel comfortable with this?" I whisper. "Me staying here, I mean?"

Red nods. "She's a bit odd, but I don't sense any malicious intent. You'll be safe and warm here."

Edith hums while she works. For an old woman, she sure is making a dent in the earth. "I'm impressed, Edith," I say.

"This isn't my first time burying a body." Edith cackles.

I giggle uneasily. She's joking, right?

Ten minutes later, Red's resting place is ready. He climbs in and lays down. Edith spears the earth with her shovel and hurls dirt on top of him. I use my feet to push mounds of dirt into the grave. Dirt falls and splatters on his pants.

"My husband Everett was buried around here. If you see him down there, let him know that he still owes me an anniversary dinner. He had some nerve keeling over the night before our fancy reservation." Edith chuckles.

"I'll relay the message," Red calls from below. I kick another heap of dirt onto him. It lands on his face, hiding his porcelain-white skin. I swallow hard.

About an hour later, Edith and I are sweaty and out of breath. Red is six feet under. Even though I know that he'll awaken at dawn, burying him still felt wrong. With every shovelful of dirt, my blood pressure rose, panic swelling in my chest. I never imagined a time that I would bury someone alive. Except, of course, Red isn't alive. At least, not during daylight hours.

"Let's go in," Edith puts her hand on my back. "You need some rest, too."

Inside, Edith leads me to the bathroom. I wash my face and change into one of her tent-like flannel nightgowns. It's not flattering, but it's a thousand times better than the degrading maid costume Talon forced me to wear.

Back in the living room, Edith places a pillow and a blanket on a blue couch with white polka dots. "I don't have a guest bedroom, so the couch will have to do."

"It'll do just fine. Thank you for dinner and allowing me to stay in your home. I'm so grateful."

Edith waves her palm. "It's nothing. In due time, I'll have much more to thank you for." As I settle on the couch, Edith pulls a tiny chain that turns off the floor lamp. I stare at a wall clock shaped like a black cat, it's tail swinging like a pendulum. It's 6:30 am. Outside, the sky is brightening.

On the other side of the room, Edith pulls the floral curtains closed, covering a singular window. Darkness engulfs the room, only a tiny sliver of light sneaking between the drapery. "Goodnight, little birdie. We both must get our rest."

"Goodnight, Edith." The floorboards groan with every footfall, and then a door screeches shut. I stretch out, happy to have a full stomach and a soft place to sleep. I close my eyes and drift away.

A noise startles me awake. It's ever so light: tap, tap, tap. Is someone knocking on the window? I try to open my eyes, but my eyelids are so damn heavy. It's probably just a dream…

Clunk! Something clatters to the floor. I jolt up, eyes wide open. I'm sure that I didn't imagine that one. It takes a moment for my vision to adjust. I make out shapes in the darkness: a fluffy tail, long-stemmed flowers strewn across the floor, and a glass container lying on its side.

I shake my head. That nasty cat knocked a vase off the counter. I better clean up this mess. It's the least I can do to repay Edith for her hospitality.

Tap, tap, tap. A shadow moves on the other side of the living room curtain. Someone's outside, rapping on the window. I freeze. Maybe this is a nightmare. I bite the inside of my cheek until I taste blood. Ouch. I'm awake.

Tap, tap, tap. It's probably just a squirrel or chipmunk. Tap, tap, tap. A cold sweat drips down my back.

I tiptoe across the room and throw open the curtain. My jaw drops, clenched fists clutching floral fabric.

From the other side of the glass, a pair of brown eyes stare back at me.

CHAPTER 4

Damian

Mom strides back and forth across the safe room. "Has anyone gotten in touch with Fallon?" She takes several steps and then she has to turn around again. It's a small space; she paces like a caged lion.

"I sent her a text ten minutes ago. She hasn't responded to me." I check my phone again. The text is still unread.

Mom wrings her hands. "I've been calling for hours and she doesn't pick up."

"Will you sit down? You're driving all of us mad." My father pats the seat on the couch beside him.

"Sit down?" Mom shoots him a glare that could kill. "Our country is under attack. We don't know where our daughter is. And you want me to sit down? We should be out there fighting with our people!" Mom thrusts her arm towards the door.

"Taya, I know you're upset, but Fallon is probably off with her boyfriend, Tim or Tom or whatever his name is."

"It's Tad," Mom hisses. Although he's far from dad of the year, I can't really fault my father on this one. My sister changes boyfriends more often than her underwear. "And you obviously haven't been listening because I already called him and he has no idea where she is. Our people are being slaughtered! Our daughter could be dead right now!" Mom's voice rises into a shrill crescendo.

Elric, my father's close friend and advisor, sits behind an antique desk, his bony fingers tapping away at a keyboard. He tugs on the end of his long silver ponytail, his thin lips twisting into a frown. "It's reported that DOX is defeating our army, almost entirely due to one ruthless monster. He has a demon's glowing red eyes, but a vampire's thirst for blood. He's fed on countless men, shredding their throats and draining them dry. One of his finger flicks has taken down our most powerful men, killing them instantaneously. Even though he's been shot at least a dozen times in vital organs, he hasn't slowed down a bit." Elric swallows, his Adam's apple poking out of his skeletal neck. "Everyone's terrified. They're calling for us to surrender before more are killed."

"Absolutely not!" My father slams his fist on the table. "They'll have to kill every last one of us before we'll give our land to terrorists!"

"It looks like they're doing just that." The glow of the computer screen illuminates Elric's grayish skin. "According to the latest reports, there are over one million casualties, both civilian and military, and that number rises by the minute."

Colson perches at the edge of a blue velvet armchair, his face ghost-white. "Has anyone gotten in touch with my parents? My phone's dead." His heels bounce up and down.

"Aurelian officials evacuated your parents, Kelvin and Marjorie Nightingale, from their home and escorted them to the Refugium Bunker, where they are being protected along with many other people of importance," Elric says.

"And Atlas?" Colson's voice trembles on the name. Being eleven years older, Colson's almost like a second father to his little brother.

"He's with your parents. They're all safe," Elric reports. Colson releases an audible breath.

Staring at the computer screen, a deep crease materializes on Elric's forehead. "Your majesty, they've infiltrated the palace."

The announcement comes moments after Zoeli told me the same. I open my mouth, feigning surprise. If my father knew that I was in contact with Zoeli, he'd disown me. If he knew that I helped her escape from his dungeon, a move that both humiliated him and caused a public uproar about his fitness to be king, he'd probably murder me. Of course, my death would be made to look like a tragic accident. It would require precise planning, a job far too complex to be done alone. My father has men for this type of purpose: criminals he pardoned who owe him a favor, advisors who are knee deep in criminal activity and can be blackmailed into just about anything. They'd be discreet. They'd be meticulous. Afterwards, my father would kneel beside my grave, eyes downcast, wearing a perfectly practiced forlorn expression. The grieving father is a great photo opp. It would be all over social media for weeks. Sympathy points up the wazoo.

My father clenches his fists. "We have the strongest military that Aurelia has ever seen. How could this happen?"

"Your majesty, we didn't anticipate their strength and numbers. We also didn't know about this… creature—"

"What the hell is wrong with our intelligence? Who dropped the ball?" My father's face reddens as he stares at Elric, waiting for an answer.

"I'm, um, not sure, your majesty."

"Well, someone has to take the fall for this. How about the director of national security, Preston Alcott? I've been wanting to can him ever since he made a snide comment about how much my new throne cost."

"Hmm," Elric taps a finger on his chin. "Everyone loves Alcott. He's too popular. How about Charles Olsen? Ever since he took over the terrorism task force, the problem's gotten worse."

Mom throws her hands in the air. "Are you two seriously discussing PR right now? You're more worried about assigning blame than the people who are dying. DOX is inside the castle as we speak! Our servants, cooks, and knights are all in danger!"

"Taya, honey, relax." My father's voice is smooth as velvet. He taps on the metal wall behind him. "This shelter is one of a kind. We melted ten tons of steel and combined it with fifty pounds of katium shavings. The mixture was then molded into this room, a space that's impenetrable by both bullets and magical force."

I close my eyes, trying to zone out my parents' argument. In my mind, I slide down the invisible string that connects me to Zoeli. It's become a habit at this point, reaching out, hoping for a flicker of her warmth or scent before she erects the icy wall that keeps me out.

It's a bit harsh, but I guess I deserve it

Today, it's different. Maybe it's because we were just in contact, or maybe it's from the stress of the battle. Either way, instead of hitting a wall, I glide into the recesses of her mind. I can hear her thoughts. *He's a goddamn liar...* She's still angry at me. I wince, feeling the sting of my betrayal.

So many damn excuses… I lurk in the shadows, hiding in the murky crevices of her psyche. I swallow, guilt going down like a jagged pill. What I'm doing isn't right. I should leave. I should respect Zoeli's privacy. But I rarely do what I should.

I need to hear her, to feel her, to know her. It's something beyond my control. Besides, in a way, it's kind of Zoeli's fault. If she hadn't been so damn determined to block me out, I wouldn't have to sneak around like this.

Even though I should hate him, part of me still loves him. My heart crashes into my chest. She still loves me. I knew it.

I love you too, Zoe. I blurt it out without thinking.

You weren't supposed to hear that. Zoeli's voice is closer now, the volume of intentional telepathic communication rather than the wispy whispers of her subconscious. I screwed up. I shouldn't have let her know that I was listening.

I know how bad I messed up. I'm sorry.

I've heard that so many times. I don't believe you anymore.

If you let me, I'll show you that I mean— Thump! Something smashes into the safe room wall. Clack! Clang! Bang! The walls shake.

Damian! Are you okay?

They're here. They're banging on the other side of the wall.

Stay safe.

A phone rings. Elric holds it to his ear. "Elric Hawke, court magistrate and chief advisor to the king. How may I help you?"

Wham! The blood drains from my mom's face. She points a shaky finger at a dent in the wall. "You said that we're safe here."

For a moment, worry lines stretch between my father's brows. Then, he throws his shoulders back, recomposing himself. "They can't get in, my dear." Slam! A larger dent emerges beside the first one.

"Are you sure about that?" Mom asks.

"Your majesty, I think you're going to want to take this call." Elric holds out the phone.

"Who is it?"

"It's Talon Crowe, your majesty. He has your daughter."

Mom snatches the phone before my father has a chance to respond. "Fallon? Fallon! Are you okay?" I hear my sister's voice on the other end, but I can't make out the words. Mom presses her palm to her lips. My heart beats so hard it vibrates in my ears.

"What's going on, Taya?" My father stands, his blue velvet cloak unfolding behind him.

Mom presses the speakerphone button. She holds the phone in trembling hands. "Come out of your hiding place or we'll slice your daughter's throat." Talon's voice booms through the speaker.

"Mom!" Fallon wails in the background.

"We're coming, sweetie." Mom moves towards the door.

"Hold on, Taya." My father grabs her arm. "We don't take orders from terrorists."

"They have our daughter," Mom hisses.

"I'm rather enjoying your office, Keifer." Talon muses. "The seat of your throne is plusher than expected. It's quite comfortable. I could get used to it."

My father snags the phone. "What do you want, Talon? If we come upstairs, will you guarantee my daughter's safety?"

Talon chuckles. "I cannot make any such guarantee. That will depend on your cooperation."

"I don't cooperate with terrorists."

"I see. Would you like to see your daughter alive again or not?"

For once, my father seems to be at a loss for words.

"Come up to your office. Bring your wife and your boy. No one else. I'm not the enemy that you make me out to be, Keifer. Once we sit down to negotiate, I think you'll find that we're not so different after all."

CHAPTER 5

Zoeli

Damian left his bedroom window open just the tiniest bit. I wedge my beak into the crack, pushing until it widens enough so I can squeeze through. Once inside, I slip under his closet doors, fly to the top shelf and shimmy inside the vent. I speed down the duct, my wings fluttering against the aluminum walls. After I escaped from the dungeon, I hid inside Damian's bedroom for months. While he went to school, social events and romanced his fiancé Caliah, I was locked inside his closet. After a few weeks, I was going stir crazy. To ease my boredom, I meandered through the ducts. I learned my way around the labyrinth, finding entertainment opportunities in both the servant's kitchen and the king's meeting room. I became invested in a love triangle between a waitress, a maid and a cook. I rolled my eyes as King Keifer sat at the head of the conference table, boasting more than strategizing with his team of advisors.

I know these ducts like the back of my wing. I glide through the maze, stopping when I hear voices coming from the king's office. I tiptoe over to the vent and peer through. Talon Crowe, my blood uncle, sits in the blue velvet throne at the head of a mahogany conference table. "They're on their way up," Talon says, running his fingers along the jewel-encrusted armrests.

Licina slides into a chair, her black catsuit squeaking against the brown leather. "How likely are they to go along with our plan?"

"Very," Talon smirks, tilting his head towards the back corner of the room. Fallon Nightingale, Damian's sister and Aurelia's only princess, is curled up in the fetal position, her back against the wall, knees held tightly to her chest.

The impossibly powerful man lingers nearby, leaning against the wall. Aside from his gore-stained t-shirt, I'm struck by how ordinary he looks. I could've passed him on a dark city street and not looked twice. Monsters aren't always grotesque creatures lurking in the shadows. Sometimes they're hiding in plain sight, blood scrubbed clean from beneath their fingernails.

The door bursts open. Queen Taya barrels in. Her gaze darts around the room. "Fallon! Fallon!"

"Mom!" Fallon lifts her head, mascara streaming down her cheeks.

Taya runs towards her daughter. "Not so fast." Talon holds up his palm. The impossibly powerful man's eyes blaze red. Taya freezes mid-step, like a mosquito trapped in a spiderweb. "You'll have time for a sappy reunion after our negotiation. Assuming that all goes well, of course."

King Keifer and Damian appear in the doorway. The man's eyes flare red again, and a hot crimson light cloaks the walls.

"Argh!" A guttural scream, a sound of pure agony, the last squeal of a dying animal, escapes from Taya's throat.

"What are you doing to her?" Damian pulls his arm back and opens his fist. In his palm, an orb of purple magic glows. Before he can launch a magic attack, Damian drops to the ground. He howls in pain. Besides him, the king's knees buckle. King Keifer's shins hit the floor, his hand clutching his chest like he's been shot.

I stare in horror, calculating my next move. I never imagined this day. Adulated across the realms for their tremendous power, wit and magical talent, the Nightingales have been brought to their knees by one man.

Call me a fool, but I can't stand by and do nothing. I have to find the right moment, catch him my surprise–

"Hadrien," Talon addresses the impossibly powerful man, interrupting my thoughts. "I told you to hold them, not hurt them."

Hadrien smirks. "Sorry, boss. I couldn't resist." The red veneer fades from the wall: dark crimson dissolving into burnt copper before it disappears altogether.

King Keifer sucks in a loud breath. "What the hell was that?" He loosens his collar, veins bulging in his neck.

"A warning," Talon responds. "So, you don't doubt what we're capable of."

Queen Taya jerks out of paralysis. Eyes glossy, she wobbles forward, catching herself on the wall. Her breaths come fast, chest rising and falling beneath her gray sweatshirt.

Damian stands up, brushing black waves out of his eyes. "Mom, are you okay?"

"Release my daughter." The king points his golden scepter at Talon. Everyone knows it's futile. The only scepter that could possibly challenge Talon and his crew, The Great Ancestral Scepter, was depleted in a previous battle.

"Sit down, Keifer." Talon gestures to the row of empty chairs. "We'll chat." He looks from Taya to Damian. "You two as well. Take a seat. Join the party."

Eyes narrowed, Keifer walks to the conference table, but his gaze stays glued on the corner. His daughter, Fallon, is balled up. Hadrien hovers over her, licking his lips. "Who the hell are you?" Keifer spits at him.

"My secret weapon," Talon responds. Satisfaction tugs on the corners of his lips. "A hybrid I never believed possible until I saw it with my own eyes. My friend Hadrien here has the power of three: a vampire, a demon and a witch."

Keifer pulls out a chair on the opposite head of the conference table. Taya and Damian sit on either side of him. "A vampire, demon and witch, you say?" Keifer's brow creases. "That's impossible."

"I thought so, too," Talon says. "But Hadrien here is an anomaly. Born to a demon and a witch, Hadrien's mere existence already beat the odds. While witch and demon DNA are typically not compatible, hybrids are not unheard of. However, it's well known that demons cannot become vampires. While both are creatures of the night and possess some overlapping abilities, they are entirely different species who aren't genetically congruent. But, in the year twelve hundred and twenty-two, Hadrien became fascinated with vampires."

"Did you say twelve hundred and twenty-two?" Keifer interrupts. "That would make him over a thousand years old."

"I sure did." Talon grins. "And as we both know, demons live an average of 666 years, growing weaker during the latter years of their lifespan. However, vampires are immortal, growing stronger with each passing year." Talon rakes his fingers through his thick hair, his silver skull ring glinting under the lights. "Where was I? Oh, yes, at the ripe age of twenty-two, young Hadrien was a talented sorcerer, trained in spell casting by his witch mother and dark magic by his demon father. Still, he yearned to be part of the vampiric race."

Hadrien clears his throat. "That's not quite right."

Talon raises his silver-gray brows. "Oh, it's not? Please correct me."

"I didn't seek companionship amongst vampires. I just like the taste of blood." Hadrien runs his tongue over his lips, licking his blood-stained fangs clean. "I also wanted to fly as a bat."

"I see," Talon says. "Is there anything else you'd like to clarify?"

Hadrien waves his palm. "Go on."

"As I was saying, my friend Hadrien here, was determined to become a vampire, something that many considered impossible. Hadrien traveled the world, tracking down vampires. He drank their blood, hoping that the changeover process would begin. It took him years to find the right match, the vampire blood that would morph his own, changing him over into a tri-breed: vampire, witch and demon. More than a thousand years later, he's one of the most powerful creatures to walk the earth. He possesses the powers of a vampire, but none of their vulnerabilities. Like a vampire, he grows stronger each year. He prefers but does not require sleep during the daytime hours. Although the sun does weaken him to a certain extent, it will not harm him. A stake to the heart won't kill him either."

King Keifer studies Hadrien, his eyes narrowed. "How come we've never heard of you? Where have you been for the past thousand years?"

Hadrien chuckles. "Where haven't I been?" He pauses, tapping his finger on his chin. "What time period? The Trojan war? Nazi Germany? I was right there, sinking my teeth in flesh. I'd never miss out on a good ole genocide." His lips twist into a disturbing smile. "But most of the time, I acted alone. In the darkest hours, I picked locks and slipped inside windows. Whole families slaughtered. Children stolen from their beds. Cold cases freeze over because they never find me. Just for fun, I lingered around my crime scenes, watching the cops fumble around, overanalyzing meaningless clues, while I stood right in front of them, unnoticed. When you look like this," Hadrien jabs himself in the chest. "They never suspect you. When I knock on doors and say that my car broke down around the corner, old ladies invite me inside and offer me a cup of tea. A piece of candy is all it takes for kids to climb right into my car." Hadrien releases a long sigh. "After centuries, it was all too easy. I needed a challenge. That's when Talon came around."

Talon smooths his silver hair, a smug look on his face. "I saved him from boredom. Now, here we are. It's been a very exciting day indeed, if I don't say so myself."

"The most titillating day of my life." Licinia purrs next to him, black nails with red tips stroking his shoulder. I cringe. Is there something romantic between Licinia and Talon? I knew that they worked together, but I never imagined there was more between them. It shouldn't really surprise me. Licinia will do anything for power.

Before he met me, Damian secretly dated Licinia. It makes my stomach roil. He claims that she had him fooled. He says that he was infatuated by her looks, and had no idea how evil she could be. While I'll admit that she's beautiful, only the blind could miss the ugliness inside her. Right now, Damian sits across from her, his head hung. He stares down at the table, pretending they've never met.

"What do you want from us, Talon?" Queen Taya's voice trembles, but she holds her chin high.

"Ah, getting right down to business," Talon faces the queen. "I like that about you Taya. What I want from you is for us to work together."

Taya snorts. "Bullshit."

Talon raises his brows. "I have no reason to bullshit you, Taya. My friend here," he nods in Hadrien's direction, "could snap all of your throats with a flick of his wrist. You, your husband, your son, your pretty little daughter." Talon points at Fallon, still curled up in a ball in the corner. Her big eyes widen, swollen and red-rimmed from crying.

"Why would you want to work with us?" King Keifer growls.

Talon takes a long breath. "If you'll hear me out, you'll understand why it's in both of our best interests. For some reason, you're wildly popular among the Aurelian people. Although there are some who protest against you, the vast majority of the Aurelian population adore the Nightingale regime. If I oust you and take over myself, there will be a public outcry and rebellion. While we're well equipped to handle that, and let there be no misunderstanding, we will if we have to, I'm trying to minimize the amount of blood shed. After all, a country is only as powerful as its people. I'd rather not wipe out most of the population, particularly not the skilled and talented individuals who may prove useful once they acclimate to the new leadership." Talon drums his fingers on the tabletop. "While I'm confident that over time, the people will adjust to my rule, the process will be much smoother if I have the king's public support."

"Public support?" Keifer repeats.

"When hell freezes over," Taya scoffs. "We don't support terrorists."

Keifer holds up his palm. "Taya, hold on. What exactly are you asking of us here? You said the king's public support. Are you saying that I would still be king?"

Talon puts his elbows on the table and leans forward. He knows he's got him. "Yes, you'll retain your title as king." He waves his arms towards Taya, "and queen." He gestures to Damian. "You'll still be the prince. Your family would remain in the Nightingale Palace."

"And how do you fit into this?" Keifer asks.

"This is a big place," Talon says. "I'll have to do a bit of remodeling. For instance, the servant's rooms are far too large. We'll cut their rooms in half and install bunk beds. There'll be plenty of space for all of us. My team and yours. We won't touch your rooms."

"You won't touch our rooms," Keifer echoes, smoothing his blue velvet cloak. "And what would your title be? Baron? Earl?

Talon smirks. "I'll be called the High Ruler. Capital on the H and R."

"High Ruler?" Keifer echoes. "But what does that mean?"

"It means whatever I want it to." Talon's grin widens, his white teeth gleaming. "The head honcho. The commander in chief. The emperor. But I prefer High Ruler. It has a nice ring to it, doesn't it?"

"And what about him?" Keifer juts his chin in Hadrien's direction.

"I don't care for titles or accolades." Hadrien leans on the wall, hands in his jean's pockets. "I just want to be assigned the fun jobs."

"He's our muscle." Talon beams at him, not making any attempt to hide his admiration for the other man. "If anyone disobeys, he'll put them in line."

Taya is shaking her head. "Absolutely not. This is not how we run our coun—"

"Ahem." Talon clears his throat. "Let me make something clear. If you don't agree to our terms, Hadrien will take care of all of you right now. If I'm not mistaken, a number of your friends and family are taking cover at a bunker nearby. They'll be next."

"You won't get in!" Taya exclaims. "It's impenetrable."

"I'm not sure about that," Talon sneers. "But even so, they can't stay in there forever. They don't have infinite supplies. Eventually, they'll come out for food and water."

"If we work with you, we'll still be the royal family, and our friends and family will be safe," Keifer says.

"That's correct." Talon adjusts his black tie.

Keifer stands up, extending his hand. "We have a deal."

Taya's mouth opens and then snaps shut.

Talon rises to his feet. With one hand, he shakes Keifer's. His other hand claps Keifer on the back. "You've made an excellent choice, my friend."

All the blood drains from Taya's face. Damian reaches across the empty seat to hold his mom's hands. His fingers interlock with hers.

Something bangs inside the duct. What the hell was that? I hope it wasn't loud enough for anyone in the king's office to hear.

Across the room, Hadrien's eyes narrow. His gaze zones in on the vent. I'm frozen on the other side, a row of flimsy metal shutters the only barrier between us. I have to get out of here.

Heart battering my ribs, I take off, zooming down the duct. Just around the corner, I find the cause of the bang. Another crow stands in the center of the duct, looking just as surprised to see me as I am to see it.

Who's that? I pause, examining the other bird. During my time amongst the crows, I've learned to distinguish between a shapeshifter and an ordinary crow. It's ever so subtle: the glint in their eyes, the shimmer in their wings.

The longer I stare, the more I wonder if my eyes deceive me. This is an ordinary crow. What are the chances of a regular ole crow finding their way into the ducts on a night like this? On second thought, I suppose it isn't too unlikely. All of the gun fires and explosions probably spooked the poor bird, and it wriggled into a small place to hide. That makes sense, right?

Either way, I have to get out of here before Hadrien or Talon find me. I zip past the bird and weave through the labyrinth of ducts, never slowing down until I'm soaring above the trees.

The sunrise makes the sky look like it's on fire. I beat my wings against the flames.

CHAPTER 6

Saria

I stare into the brown eyes on the other side of the glass, disbelieving. I must be dreaming.

A door creaks open and shut. Edith shuffles into the living room, floorboards squealing beneath her bare feet. Her gaze glides to the window. "Ah, yes!" She smiles, the skin around her eyes crinkling. "The slayer! I've been expecting her." Edith shimmies past me, turns the doorknob and pokes her neck outside. "Come on in, dear." A gust of cold wind rushes through the open door. Edith's nightgown blows against her legs.

Keisha wipes her black combat boots on the welcome mat. Dark bags hang like half-moons beneath her eyes. It's obvious that she's been trekking through the woods all night. Bits of leaves and branches are tangled throughout her curly hair. She's still dressed for battle: cargo pants, a black hoodie, a tactical belt stocked with wooden stakes, a tomahawk ax and a machete.

Her big brown eyes meet mine. A kaleidoscope of memories cycle through my mind: curling Barbie doll's hair, sprinting through sprinklers, wet grass wedged between our toes, laughing until our stomachs hurt, popping wheelies on our pink bikes, ribbons flying from the handlebars, strolling through the mall, coordinating our outfits for the first day of middle school.

Tears well in my eyes. I swallow them down. Keisha's been my best friend since preschool. As close as we were, I never told her about my witch heritage. Magical law forbids speaking to humans about our craft. I never imagined that at the age of seventeen, Keisha would become a slayer intent on killing my kind.

I don't know if she's here to save me or to slaughter me. "Sar!" Keisha runs to me, her arms out, and scoops me into a hug. I bite my lips, but a few tears spill over. I cling to her.

"So, you don't want to kill me?" I ask.

Keisha pulls back, her eyes probing mine. "What? Are you kidding me? Of course not! Sar, you're my best friend!"

It's like a pipe burst open. There's no holding back my tears now. Rivers pour down my cheeks.

"Stop that!" Keisha swats me on the shoulder. "You actually thought that I might kill you? Have you lost your mind? You must have, running off with that goddamn vampire. I've been worried sick all night. I know you used to have bad taste in guys, but once you started dating Logan, I thought you'd turned a corner. What the hell are you thinking, Sar?"

"Red's not what you think," I say. "He's a good guy. But hold on, back up. How did you find me here? "Just last night, I was a prisoner of the terrorist group DOX. At the portal site, the slayers ambushed DOX. As the battle raged, Red sliced my captor's throat. A few minutes later, Keisha approached us, ready to strike.

"I watched you jump into what looked like the mouth of hell." Keisha puts her hands on her hips. "And like a damn idiot, I followed you. What are friends for?" She throws her hands up.

I can't help but laugh. "You're the best friend a girl could ever ask for."

"You owe me big time."

"You girls must be hungry." Edith pulls out a chair at the kitchen table. "Sit down. I'll whip up some breakfast."

Keisha and I sit down. Edith scurries around, humming as she cracks eggs into a bowl. "Who is she?" Keisha whispers.

I shrug. "Her name's Edith. We just met, but Red's good at reading people and he said she's alright. She offered me a place to stay, and she said that she can help me find Zoeli."

"Zoeli?" Keisha's eyes widen. "She's here? In this… world?"

I take a moment to appreciate how brave my best friend is. She leaped into a glowing hole in the earth, not even knowing where it would take her. All to rescue me. Even if we don't make it out of here, she's a goddamn hero. "This world is the magical realm," I explain. "The homeland for witches. It's called Aurelia."

Edith comes in, balancing plates of scrambled eggs and buttered toast on her palms. She places one in front of each of us. I take a bite. "Delicious," I say.

Edith scuttles back into the kitchen, returning moments later with another plate and three coffee mugs. She plops down in a seat. "I'm so hungry I could eat a horse." Edith chews like a cow: mouth open too wide, half-chewed food visible on her tongue. I stare at my plate, trying to hide my disgust. I don't want to be impolite.

"Thank you for cooking," Keisha says.

"It's no trouble at all." Egg dribbles down Edith's pointy chin.

"And for inviting me in," Keisha adds. "I didn't expect a witch to be so, you know, kind to me, being that I'm a slayer and all."

"Why's that?" Edith asks.

"I mean…" Keisha's voice trails off. "Aren't we natural enemies?"

"Nonsense." Edith waves a mangled hand. "Slayers and witches aren't enemies. Slayers are summoned during times when the balance between good and evil goes awry. Slayers fight evil, whether supernatural or otherwise."

Keisha taps her fingernail on the table. "Mr. Fawley told us that all witches and vampires are evil. He said that our job was to kill them on sight."

"This Mr. Fawley is sorely mistaken." Edith shakes her head. "There's many reasons someone might reject the righteous and choose the path of the devil: a difficult upbringing, an insatiable ego, a defect of the brain or the heart. But whether one is born a witch, human, vampire, or even a demon, is almost never a factor."

"That's not what Mr. Fawley taught us." Keisha's brow furrows. "How am I supposed to tell, then? How will I know if someone's evil?"

"You'll know, dear," Edith says. "It's what you're meant to do. Trust your gut. Oftentimes, we suppress our instincts and do what we're taught rather than what feels right. Most of the time, that's where we go wrong." As she eats, her lips make a smacking noise, saliva and crumbs gathering on her lips.

"Um," I start talking, hoping my voice will drown out the repulsive sounds. "After Red wakes, I want to try to find Zoeli. You said that you could help us. Do you know where we should look?"

"I don't, but Betty will. After breakfast, we'll ask her." Edith slurps her coffee.

I'm not sure who Betty is, but Edith sure seems to have a lot of trust in her. I scarf down the rest of my breakfast, eager to talk to Betty.

As soon as we're done eating, Edith rolls up her sleeves. She stacks the dishes up on her palm and tosses them into the sink. "I need to tidy up. You two go ahead and shower and get dressed. There's towels and shampoo in the bathroom. I also pulled some clothing from my younger days out from the back of my closet. I hope you find something you like." Edith slides yellow kitchen gloves onto her hands. The rubber snaps against her wrists.

As Edith scrubs bits of burnt egg stuck on the frying pan, Keisha's brow creases. "This might be a stupid question, but I don't get it. Doing dishes sucks. Can't you just wiggle your nose or something and this whole place would be spotless?"

Edith barks out a laugh. "If only it were that easy. Magic expends a lot of energy. If we use up all of our energy on menial tasks, there won't be any left for more important endeavors–like finding Zoeli. That's why some witches are keen on the idea of taking human slaves. No one enjoys spending hours mopping floors or prepping meals, but alas it's part of life."

"Do you need help with anything?" Keisha asks.

Edith waves a soapy glove. "Don't be ridiculous. You're my guests."

Keisha follows me into the living room and collapses on the polka-dot couch. "I'm exhausted."

I point to the hallway on the right. "The bathroom is down there. Do you want to shower first?"

Keisha's already laying down, her eyes closed. "You go first. I'm going to take a nap." She murmurs.

I walk to the bathroom, wood floorboards protesting beneath my toes. I lock the door behind me. A stack of plush towels and vintage clothing are piled on the toilet seat. I reach inside the shower and turn the dial all the way to the left.

As I undress, the tiny bathroom fills with steam. I inhale deeply, letting the water vapor soothe my lungs. As hot water beats down on my shoulders, I roll my neck, loosening up tense muscles. Edith's shampoo smells like lavender and tingles my scalp.

I spend so much time in fight-or-flight: sweaty palms, paranoid thoughts, lump in my throat, that I barely notice it anymore. For this brief moment, as streams of water massage my back and a divine scent tickles my nose, my heart rate slows down. I breathe easier. Airways expand. The tightness eases in my chest.

But intrusive thoughts still haunt me: that I'm too late and Zoeli's already dead, that Uncle Talon is crouching behind the shower curtain, waiting to strike. I do my best to ignore them. Everything is going to be okay, I tell myself, over and over again.

Beams of white light stream into the room. I squint, but it does little to block the glare. "What the…" My eyes sting.

I drop my gaze to the floor, step out of the shower and cover myself with a towel. The white glow illuminates the entire room. I can't see a damn thing. I wobble forward, unsure of my footing. I reach out, steadying my palm on the sink.

I cup my other hand over my eyes and lift my chin. A shining white orb floats right through the retro teal wall tiles, defying the laws of physics. Glittering rays radiate from its center like a starburst. It glides closer, changing shape, stretching taller and wider, curving along the sides, morphing into the body of a woman.

She stands in an ethereal glow. Amethyst eyes glitter. Dark brown waves cascade down her shoulders. Cherry-red lips in luminous skin.

I can't tell if she's real or if she's an apparition. I can see right through her translucent skin, teal tiles visible beyond her woman-like form. She's more mist than flesh.

She moves toward me, bare feet hovering above the floor. I raise my hands in defense, a scream erupting from my throat. I spin around, lunging towards the exit. I flail wildly in the fog, my hand miraculously finding the doorknob. I fling the door open.

Keisha and Edith stand on the other side. "My dear," Edith says, her brow creased with concern. "Whatever is the matter?"

I point behind me. "A ghost in the bathroom." As Edith hobbles past me, I turn back around. The bathroom is empty. There's no sign of the woman or the blinding lights. "I swear," I say. "She was just here."

Keisha's mouth forms a worried 'o.' She puts her arm around my shoulder. "Are you okay, Sar?"

"I don't know," I mumble. Did I imagine her? Maybe with all the stress I've finally lost my mind.

But no. Last night, I came across the same light in the forest. A few moments later, a tree toppled over. What does it mean? At least it means that I'm not insane. Red saw it too.

"Whoever it was, they're long gone." Edith says.

* * *

Twenty minutes later, Keisha and I are both showered and dressed like we're going to Woodstock in 1969. "I won't be camouflaged in this." Keisha pulls on a psychedelic tie-dye t-shirt.

"And I definitely can't run in these." My bell bottom jeans are so wide they're sure to snag on any rock or branch in the woods.

"The hippies weren't warriors," Keisha says. "They were all about peace and love."

"At least we look cute." I giggle. It's hard to imagine that just a year ago, looking cute in the latest fashions was a big concern. Looking back, I hardly recognize who I used to be.

I've made mistakes. I've been shallow and cruel. Back then, my greatest pain was not knowing who I was, and not knowing what I'm made of.

I never could've imagined the pain this past year would bring. My sister betrayed me and stole my power. My best friend became my boyfriend, and then I broke both of our hearts. I was jailed, released, kidnapped, and enslaved. My twin disappeared. I don't even know if she's still alive.

Most surprising of all, I fell in love with a vampire. Now my heart aches with every beat, knowing that we can't have a future together.

Yet, it's all made me stronger. I've shown bravery that I never knew I was capable of. I've damn near gotten myself killed to rescue those who I love.

I know what I'm made of now. I know who I am. They stole my shape-shifting power, but I'm still a crow. They took my crown, but royal blood flows hot in my veins, and with it, the strength and power of my ancestors who ruled before me.

If someone pushes me down, I get back up. Even without an ounce of magic to my name, I'm a badass woman.

"Follow me, girls." Edith leads us to the back of the living room and pulls aside a beaded curtain. "Welcome to my office." She cackles.

The room is replete with every witch resource imaginable. Floor-to-ceiling shelves are crammed with anything a witch could need for spell casting: herbs, candles, oils, potions, plants and crystals. There are thousands of books: lined up like a bookstore, labels designating genres such as history, spells, or potions.

Edith sits on a well-worn chair behind a glass table. A black velvet cloth hides an object in front of her. "Time to wake up from your nap, Betty." Edith lifts the cloth. The object underneath glistens beneath the ceiling light. It's some kind of magical object, a mishmash of crystals glued together: jade, bloodstone, amethyst and so many more kinds that I might be able to identify if I hadn't been denied admittance to Enchantments Academy. "Sit down, you two. It's time to talk to Betty."

"Betty?" I echo, mesmerized by the mysterious object. "Does she talk back?" I slide into a wicker seat. Keisha takes the seat beside me, brows raised, eyes wide.

Edith cackles. "She uses these to communicate." She taps a deck of plain black cards against the glass tabletop. "Betty, oh B-eee-tttt-yyyy. Wakey, wakey. Nap time is over." Edith coos like she's soothing a baby. She strokes the crystal with a gnarled finger.

Keisha and I exchange an alarmed look. Edith's been kind to me, but she might be off her rocker. Edith smiles, deep crinkles framing her green eyes. "Go ahead, Saria. She's ready for you."

"Um, what am I supposed to do?"

"Tell Betty your story. Talk to her. Ask her what you need to know." Edith nods at the crystal.

"Um, hi Betty," I say, feeling silly. "Do you know where Zoeli is?"

Edith sighs. "You'll have to do better than that. Betty's magic is energized by your emotions. Tell her about your relationship with your sister. Tell her how much you care about Zoeli. Tell her what it means to you to find her."

I clear my throat. "Zoeli's been by my side since the day we were born. Technically, I guess, since before we were born. The bond we shared was more than blood, and more than friendship. She's the other half of my soul." The lump in my throat makes it difficult to swallow. I put my hand to my trachea. "I wasn't always good to her. There was a time when I acted like I was better than her. But the truth is that I believed the opposite. Zoeli was always the stronger one. Even though I was the one with the magic, I struggled with insecurities and imposter syndrome." I bite my lip. "I did a lot of things I'm not proud of, but what I regret the most is hurting my sister. I didn't deserve her forgiveness, but she still gave it to me. When we were imprisoned together, I damn near lost my mind. I'm weaker than Zoe, physically and emotionally. When I was starving, Zoeli gave me her food. When I was freezing, she held me close and made me warm. When I was ready to give up, just shrivel into a ball and die, she'd somehow manage to make me laugh. When I was too mentally weak to remember anything but the pain and suffering, she'd talk about our parents, our goals, the people and places that I love. Without her, I'm sure that I wouldn't have survived.

"Zoe's not just my sister. She's my inspiration. Seeing her strength makes me want to be stronger. She's saved me so many times she doesn't even know. Now if she needs me, I'm going to be the one to save her." I shake my head. "Although I doubt that she even needs saving. Zoe's tough and she's smart. But still…" My voice trails off. "She's a wanted fugitive. Now that DOX invaded, the bloodshed and violence is only going to get worse. I need to know that she's safe. I need to be with my twin. And God willing, we need to go home. Together. Betty, please, if you know where Zoeli is, please tell me. Please."

Edith's eyes are closed, shuffling the deck of cards between her gnarled fingers. "She has your answer." Edith flips over a card and drops in on the table.

The number thirteen is scrawled at the top of the card. In the center, a hand-drawn grim reaper wears a black hooded cape and holds a scythe. At the bottom, one word is written in childish handwriting: DEATH.

Tears well in my eyes. I'm too late. Zoeli is dead.

CHAPTER 7

Zoeli

Coming back here was stupid. I was miles away from Nightingale Palace, soaring over the Azula sea, far from the violence and chaos. I should've kept going.

I kept imagining the scene in King Keifer's office playing out differently: Hadrien flicking one finger in Damian's direction, Damian raising his palms in defense just before his dismembered arms and legs scattered across the floor, black eyes rolled back in his decapitated head.

I turned around. Here I am, like a fool, in Damian's bedroom. It's the first time we've been face to face in months. "Zoe, I missed you so much." His voice is husky as he reaches for me. I can't look away; it's like a magnet pulls my gaze to his. He's like a black-and-white photo: creamy porcelain skin, wavy black hair, hypnotic black eyes.

Even as my brain tells me to step back, my body betrays me. I melt into his arms. I nuzzle against his muscular chest, his black t-shirt soft on my cheek. His hand cups my chin, lifting my mouth to his. His lips brush mine. When his tongue darts into my mouth, my brain shouts no, but my body screams yes. I picture us in the bed, legs intertwined, his black-and-white blurring until it becomes gray and I forget what's right and wrong. Damian's lips curl into a lopsided smile. "Mmm. I like that vision."

I smack his shoulder. This damn telepathy tells on me every time. I stumble back. "I can't do this."

"Yes, you can." Damian steps forward.

"I'm serious, Damian." I push him away. "I didn't come here to hook up."

Damian lifts one brow. "Then why are you here?"

"Because the most dangerous supernatural terrorist organization that ever existed just took over Aurelia. Hundreds, maybe thousands, of witches are dead in the streets. We need to make a plan. We need to save Aurelia."

Damian's forehead creases. "Zoe, everything is going to be okay. My father's still the king. I'm still the prince."

I blow out a puff of air. "And Talon will be the," my fingers make air-quotes, "High Ruler."

"Don't worry, Zoe. I'll take care of it."

"How?" I've heard that line before. "I need specifics. How can I help?"

Damian sighs and sits on the edge of his bed. He ruffles his hands through his hair. "I'm not sure. These things take time. I'll figure it out."

"While you figure it out, Talon will rewrite the constitution to allow human slaves. People will be brought here from the human realm, enslaved, tortured, and beaten. We don't have time to waste."

Damian presses his lips together. "Zoe, I don't think it's going to be as bad as you're making it out to be."

"You're right! It's going to be worse!"

"Listen. You're safe. I'm safe—"

"And that's all that matters?" I shake my head in disgust. I can't believe I allowed myself for one moment to believe that he was capable of change. All Damian cares about is himself. "I'm leaving."

Damian bolts to his feet. "Zoe, don't go. I said that I will figure it out. I got you out of prison, didn't I?"

"You did," I acquiesce. It's the one reason I still believe that he might be able to get something done. "And for that, I'm grateful. But I have to go."

Damian grabs my wrist. "Zoe, stay here. I'll keep you safe."

"And hide out in your closet again?" I guffaw. "I'll take my chances out there." I pull my arm away. Ribbons of blue wind around me, sparkling like blue topaz, as I morph into crow form. I soar out the open window, flying directly into the sun.

I fly over Nightingale City. It's chaos. Dead bodies are strewn in the streets. Family members scour through the bodies, searching for loved ones. Flames engulf a high-rise building. Black smoke billows in the wind. I hold my breath.

Fifteen minutes later, in the suburbs of Nightingale City, I perch on a windowsill, peering through the glass into a spacious kitchen. I don't even know if he's home. Even if he is, I can't be sure that he'll let me in.

He enters the kitchen, wearing nothing but boxers and a black undershirt, a mug in his hand. Silky white-blonde hair sweeps forward, covering his forehead. It's styled long on top, a tapered trim along the back and sides. His arms and legs are covered with images and designs, only small areas of pale skin untouched by elaborate tattoos. I can tell he works out: sculpted arms, defined biceps, powerful thighs. Dressed in his prison guard attire, I never realized how toned he is.

He refills his coffee cup while I gawk in the window like a peeping Tom. I better get out of here before he sees me. I'll come back when he's dressed.

He looks up. His strange eyes meet mine, blue irises so light that they almost blend into the sclera, black pupils floating alone in the white space. I freeze, hoping that he won't recognize me as a crow.

Kian crosses the room, unlatches the window and pulls it open. "Zoeli? Is that you?" Busted. If crows could blush, I'd be red as a tomato. "Come in."

As soon as I fly inside, Kian shuts and locks the window behind me. My heart rate quickens. I thought I could trust Kian, but if he tries to hurt me, I'm not opposed to blasting him with a beam of deadly blue magic.

Magic swirls around me as I become flesh and bone, wings to arms, black feathers to long black hair. "How did you know it was me?" I ask.

"Your eyes," Kian says. "Before I met you, I'd never seen a blue like that. Almost like the ocean on a sunny day."

"Oh," I murmur, at a loss for words. When I met Kian, he was a guard at Nightingale Dungeon, and I was a filthy prisoner with greasy hair. I never imagined that he noticed anything other than an unkempt nimwit and a heinous smell. Yet, he can describe the exact hue of my eyes.

Suddenly, I'm conscious of my midriff-baring black leather outfit. I've been a crow for so long, I forgot that I still had it on. The sexy ensemble I borrowed from Fallon's closet features skintight pants and a crop top.

Kian's gaze never lowers from my eyes. "Would you like some coffee?" He reaches into an oak cabinet and pulls out a mug decorated with moons and stars.

"Sure. Cream and sugar?"

Kian prepares a cup of coffee and sets it down on the kitchen table. "Thank you," I say as Kian places a box of pasties in front of me.

"Help yourself." Kian bites into a powdered donut. Sugar fills the gap between his front teeth. "I'll be right back."

I don't hold back. I inhale a blueberry tart and then devour another. Flaky layers of buttery croissant melt in my mouth. A cinnamon roll is gooey heaven sliding down my throat.

A few minutes later, Kian returns, dressed in jeans and a sweatshirt. He slides into the seat across from me. "Enjoying yourself, I see." He grins at the half empty box.

"You try living off worms and seeds for months," I mutter, popping another chocolate scone into my mouth.

"That sounds awful," Kian says. "Anytime you want some real food, feel free to stop by."

"You may live to regret that offer. I have a big appetite." I shove another donut into my mouth. "And after fighting DOX all night, I'm ravenous."

"Groceries aren't cheap. I might have to pick up extra shifts," Kian jokes. "It looks like we'll be fighting DOX for many more nights to come." Kian's lips settle into a firm line. "I led the Resistance into the streets last night. I wore a black ski mask, so no one would recognize me. We didn't have enough time to plan, and we didn't know what we were up against. We killed some of their men, but I also lost a few of mine." Kian's Adam's apple bobs in his throat. "Their deaths won't be in vain. The Resistance is stronger than ever. Even today, hundreds more joined. There's over a dozen factions now. We're working together, making big plans."

"I'm thinking about joining The Resistance," I say.

"You'd be a great asset to our team." Kian stands up. "Come with me. I'll show you our planning center." I follow him through the living room. Exposed ceiling beams and a stone fireplace give the space a rustic feel. We walk down a long hallway, passing three closed doors before he stops at the last. He reaches in his pocket. Keys jangle in his fist. As he unlocks the door, I study a painting hanging on the wall. The woman in the portrait is eerily beautiful: angular features, a willowy frame, long blonde hair blowing beneath a full moon. A strapless black-lace gown exposes her tattoos. Ink covers every inch of her shoulder and arms twisting around her fingers and wrists.

"Who's she?" I ask.

Kian glances over at the portrait. Pain flashes in his eyes. "My mom."

"She's gorgeous," I say.

"Yeah, she was." Kian says. I note the use of past tense, and decide not to press further. Kian opens the door and flicks on a light, revealing a long wooden staircase. As I follow him down, the overhead light flickers, taking us in and out of pitch blackness. "Damn bulb," Kian says. There's a loud pop, like a kernel of popcorn exploding.

It's so dark I can't see my hand, even as I hold it inches from my nose. Sweat drips down my back.

I can't believe how stupid I am. I'm a horror movie cliche, the dumb girl who walked right into the trap.

How did I miss it? Kian is a Nightingale guard, after all. He's on his own, and there's a huge price on my head. Maybe he just wants to claim his prize.

Or maybe he has more sinister plans for me.

CHAPTER 8

Saria

The grim reaper stares up at me, empty eyes drawn by an unsteady hand. I can't breathe. I fan myself with my hand, sucking in a strangled breath. It can't be true. I'd know if Zoeli died. Even a galaxy away, I'd feel it, like half of my soul being torn from my body. Right?

Keisha laces her fingers through mine and squeezes. It takes everything in me to not collapse on her shoulder and weep right there.

Edith flips over another card. It slides onto the glass table. I stare at the woman composed of scribbles: squiggly lines for hair, a backwards 'c' for a nose, multiple strands of u-shaped necklaces around her neck. A simple three-pointed crown sits on top of her head, adorned by diamond-shaped jewels. Underneath her, there's a caption in the same sloppy handwriting, QUEEN OF GEMS.

Edith places a third card beside the other two. The crescent has a face: an oval eye, curved brow, a line for a mouth. Beneath it reads THE MOON.

My gaze drifts back to the first card. DEATH. A tear rolls down my cheek. Keisha's palm makes circles on my back.

"My dear," Edith watches me with clear green eyes, her forehead furrowed. "Whatever is the matter?"

I gulp, the words caught in my throat. Realization dawns in Edith's eyes. She reaches across the table and takes my hand, her skin papery against mine. "Oh, dear, I should've said something sooner. I'm so familiar with the nuances of these cards that I forget that others might leap to conclusions."

My nails dig into my palms. "Are you saying that Zoeli is alive?" My voice cracks with hope.

"Yes, my dear. The cards have told you where to find Zoeli." Edith taps a wrinkled finger on the number 13 above the grim reaper. "Number 13," she says, her finger sliding to the next card. "Queen of Gems," Edith reads aloud. "Anyone who knows their stuff can tell you that the opal is the queen of gems." She points to the final card. "The Moon."

I shake my head, trying to decipher her meaning. Number thirteen? An opal? The moon? "I don't understand."

"13 Opal Moon Road," Edith says. "Kian Reynold's place."

"Kian Reynolds." I repeat. "The prison guard?" My time in Nightingale Dungeon is a blur, but I remember that Kian was nice enough, as far as guards go. He never spit at us. He even gave us a fluffy comforter once, which I'm sure was against the rules.

"That poor kid." Edith scratches her jaw. "His mother, Kinley, was a friend of mine. She was a powerful sorceress, even wrote her own spells, good ones, too, although she never received the credit she was due." Edith's face contorts, exposing her yellowed teeth. "Kinley was dead for over six months before I heard the news. By that time, I'd missed her funeral, so it was only right that I visit the Reynolds to offer my condolences. I went to their house with a basket of fruit. Kian answered the door…" Edith's voice trails off. "He looked like hell ran over: red cheeks, arms like toothpicks, puffy eyes like he'd been crying and hadn't slept in eons. He was gracious enough, even invited me inside for tea, but I couldn't stay long." Edith stares at her hands. "And then, only two years later, his sister disappeared. And then his dad. Very mysterious, both of their disappearances. That poor kid. He lost his whole family."

My mind races double-time. *That's so sad.* My thoughts ricochet. *What does she mean by disappeared?* Ideas ping off each other. *I can't imagine everything Kian's been through. Poor guy.* They whip back and forth fast enough to give me whiplash. *Maybe he killed them.*

First, Kian's mom died, then his dad and sister both vanished? I might be paranoid, but something seems off.

Zoeli isn't dead. Yet.

CHAPTER 9

Zoeli

I can hear Kian breathing in the dark, inches away from me. I raise my fists, ready to attack.

An orb of golden light materializes, illuminating the stairs like a flashlight. "Sorry about that," Kian says. "I should've changed that lightbulb a while ago."

I drop my hands, glad that Kian didn't turn and notice my offensive stance. Wearing socks and light on his feet, Kian soundlessly moves down the steps.

I stretch my shoulders back and roll my neck right and left, releasing the tension from moments before. My gut tells me that I can trust Kian, but that might be all those delicious pastries swimming around in there. Good chocolate can make me delirious.

I follow, but I keep a distance between us, still on guard. At the bottom of the stairs, Kian turns on the light. My jaw falls open as I step into the enormous room.

I weave through the rows of chairs, fingers grazing the cold metal. The walls are covered by various Aurelian maps. Most are marked up by black marker, arrows pointing this way or that, tracing paths to military bases and government buildings. "This is where we discuss and present strategies," Kian says.

We pass a conference table littered with stacks of papers, laptops, and blueprints. "Over here," Kian gestures to a station covered in crystals, herbs and potions, "is where we focus on spellcasting and magical weaponry."

He leads me to a table scattered with wires and electronic devices. "This is where we focus on human technology. We build rockets, missiles, and the likes."

Another workbench reminds me of my chemistry lab back in high school: beakers, test tubes, Bunsen burners and graduated cylinders. A collection of glass containers are lined up beside a slop sink. "This area is also dedicated to what humans call science. To me, it's just another form of magic." I pick up one of the containers and read the label: Hydrazine. "The Nightingales, and witches in general, think that human means are beneath them. They refuse to look into any of their war tactics, believing that magic always trumps anything man made." Kian shakes his head. "They're fools, and in the end, their prejudice and disdain for humans will be their downfall. By combining magic and science, we're working on a weapon of mass destruction that can blast the palace and its leaders into oblivion, while magically sparing the lives of innocents." Kian taps on the counter beside the sink. "We're getting close, but I'm not sure how much longer it will take. It could be months or even years. And how many more lives will be destroyed in the interim? I don't sleep at night. I stay up weighing the pros and cons, wondering if we should attack now, or wait until we have a more powerful and precise weapon."

I walk the perimeter of the room, marveling over the work that's been done. It's obvious that hundreds of thousands of hours have been spent down here: studying, experimenting, sketching, brainstorming. The contrast between Kian's preparation and work ethic, and Damian who will quote, "figure it out," is vast. *Damian did break you out of jail,* a small voice reminds me. He's not a lost cause. Maybe he'll come around.

Kian points to an intricate map of Nightingale Palace including all of the secret passageways and underground tunnels. "As a Nightingale guard, I'm in a unique position to gain access to places that most don't even know exist."

I study the pathways. I recognize a few from the time I spent navigating the ducts. I memorize the others, burning them into my brain. "If I'm going to be part of The Resistance, I won't sit back and take orders. Before I do anything, I'll need to know why. I'll need to see the bigger picture, the pros and cons, and understand the potential for civilian casualties."

Kian nods. "Understood."

"I don't know much about wars or military strategy," I admit. "But I want to learn."

"What would you like to know?" Kian asks.

"Everything." I lift my chin. "I want to know everything that you know."

"Everything that I know," Kian repeats, his brow furrowing. "I've been studying this for years."

I shrug my shoulders. "I have time."

Kian stares, his black pupils examining my face, as though gauging how serious I am. "Well, then you better sit down," he says, lips curving into a small smile.

I slide into a metal folding chair as Kian picks up a piece of white chalk. He writes on the board: Lesson 1.

* * *

I climb the basement stairs, soaking up the information flooding inside my brain. In the last few hours, I learned about military tactics including ambushing, frontal assault, and flanking. Kian didn't just recite the facts. For every technique, he drew diagrams. We analyzed mock scenarios, solved problems, and determined the best decisions in any given situation.

I asked a million and one questions. I'm sure nine hundred and ninety nine thousand of them were stupid, but Kian never made me feel that way. He took care to answer them all, confirming that I understood before moving on.

"I'm hungry." Kian opens the door at the top of the stairs. "Would you like to stay for dinner?"

"Sure." After months of eating beetles for dinner, he doesn't have to ask twice. Kian gathers ingredients from the refrigerator: a package of chicken breasts, eggs and shredded mozzarella cheese. Beyond the windowsill I perched on earlier, a crescent moon glows. Kian draws the curtain, hiding the starry sky. "Is chicken parmigiana okay?"

"It's one of my favorites." Like Pavlov's dogs, I salivate at its mention. "How can I help?"

"Just sit down and relax. I got this." Kian cracks two eggs into a mixing bowl.

Leaning against the counter, I notice a photograph pushed into the corner. I push aside a ceramic utensil holder, spatulas and wooden spoons peeking out, and grab the photograph.

I study the people in the photo. I recognize Kian's mom from the portrait on the wall. Instead of a black gown, she's dressed more casually in black leggings, black combat boots, and a red dragon on her black tunic. A man I presume to be

Kian's dad stands beside her, a burly arm around her tiny waist, looking like a lumberjack with a flannel shirt and an overgrown beard. A preteen girl, maybe eleven or twelve, stands in front of the man. She wears baggy jeans and an oversized t-shirt, a shaggy boyish haircut covering most of her eyes. Kian is the tallest of them all, standing at least a foot taller than his mother. His arm is slung over her shoulder, a carefree smile on his face. Based on his height, this picture couldn't have been taken too long ago, but the innocence of his expression makes him seem so much younger than the Kian I know.

I study him now, bathing a chicken breast in a bowl of whisked eggs. I hold up the picture. "Is this your family?"

He glances up for a split second before he turns away. "Yeah." He presses the chicken breast into a pile of breadcrumbs, then flips it over, coating it on both sides.

Of all the stupid questions I asked tonight, this one takes the cake. Of course it's his family. Based on his reaction, he clearly does not want to talk about them. Awkward.

For a few minutes, we're quiet as he works, dipping another piece of chicken first into flour, then eggs, and finally breadcrumbs. "Are you sure that I can't help with anything?" I ask, breaking the silence.

Kian pours oil into a frying pan and turns on the burner. "I'm okay."

I wring my hands in my lap. I'm dying to know more about him, but asking about his family is obviously off limits. "How old are you?" I ask. That seems safe enough.

"Eighteen." The chicken sizzles in the pan.

"Eighteen?" I repeat, disbelieving. "How is that possible? You're only a year older than me."

Kian chuckles. "Do I look old or something?"

"No, I just assumed since you're working full time…" My voice trails off. "Did you graduate early?" That would make sense. I think he might've memorized every history and science textbook at Enchantments Academy. Downstairs, I jokingly called him a nerd.

"I dropped out."

I bite my lip to hide my surprise. Kian's brilliant. Why would he drop out of high school? He should be graduating at the top of his class. "Oh," I say, at a loss for words. "Did you go to Enchantments Academy?"

"I did." Kian uses tongs to flip over the chicken breasts. Hot oil splatters on the stovetop.

"You went to school with Damian," I say, almost to myself.

"Damian?" Kian raises his brows. "Don't you mean his royal highness? Do you know him?"

"Not really. I've heard of him, of course. He's the prince." I tap my finger on the counter, punctuating the lie. "He's engaged to my cousin Caliah. Did you hang out with Damian? When you were in school?"

"Me?" Kian barks out a laugh. "I wasn't welcome in his circles. Nor did I want to be."

"What do you mean?" My brow furrows.

"To be blunt, the prince and his crew are a bunch of arrogant pricks." Kian pushes white-blonde hair out of his eyes. "If you're not rich, powerful or royal enough, they want nothing to do with you."

I think back to my time at Nightingale Palace. As a crow, I peered through the vents, spying on the lavish events in the royal ballroom: beautiful people dressed to the nines, gourmet delights served on golden platters. "Caliah isn't like that," I say, envisioning my cousin in her royal blue gown, twirling around the dance floor, strawberry-blonde curls cascading down her back.

"I used to think that Caliah was one of the good ones," Kian sighs. "But she's nothing but a snake in sheep's clothing."

"What makes you say that? Caliah advocates for equal rights—"

Kian cuts me off. "It's performative bullshit. Virtue signaling to score points with the public and bolster support for her future political career."

"Why do you think that?"

"Caliah used to be friends with my sister, Sam," Kian says. "When she found out that Sam's a dud, Caliah dropped her faster than a hot potato."

"She what?" I rub my brow. "But Caliah seemed so sincere. I believed…" My voice trails off.

Ding-dong! "Are you expecting someone?" My palms turn clammy. Ding-dong!

"No." Kian opens a broom closet. "Get in. Do not make a sound until I tell you it's safe. Do you understand me?"

I push past a mop and crouch beside a bucket, my heart rattling in my chest. The closet door clicks shut. Blackness engulfs me.

Ding-dong! Ding-dong! Kian's footfalls soften as he moves down the hallway. The front door squeals open. "Sergeant Sterling, what's up man?"

"Reynolds." An unfamiliar male voice replies. "I didn't know you lived out here, bro. There's been an, um, incident, nearby. We don't want to alarm anyone, but we're looking for a fugitive. Have you noticed anything or anyone unusual in your neighborhood today?"

"Nah, man. I've been inside all day. Cooking dinner now."

"Is anyone else home? Maybe they saw something."

"I live alone."

"All by yourself in this big ole house?"

"I inherited it."

"Oh." There's an uncomfortable pause. "I'm sorry, man. I forgot."

"Don't worry about it. Level with me. What's going on? Why are you here?"

Sterling lowers his voice, but every word is still clear to me. I've become an expert at using magic to hear from a distance. "It's that Crowe girl. The one who escaped from the dungeon. She was spotted, man, not too far from here. She's blonde now, but it's definitely her. Did the nimwit really think that a box of hair dye would fool us?" Sterling laughs like he said something funny.

"I haven't seen her," Kian says. "But I'll keep my eyes open."

"Watch out, man. I hear that she's strong for a nimwit. She has blue power and she's vicious with it, like an animal, man. It's the human blood in her. A creature so primitive can't be trusted with magic. I blame her mother more than her. She never should've bred with a vermin." I hold my breath tight in my chest. Tears burn in the corners of my eyes, but I won't let them fall. I tighten my fists, frustration and anger pumping hot through my veins. I want to punch him in the face. I remind myself that I shouldn't care what he thinks. It still stings, knowing that my own people regard me with such contempt and disgust.

"Everything's been quiet around here. If I see anything, I'll let you know," Kian says.

"Thanks, man. Do you mind if I take a look around your backyard?"

"No problem."

The door squeaks shut. I wipe my sweaty palms on my jeans, Sergeant Sterling's voice replaying in my mind. Aurelian forces are scouring Kian's neighborhood, hunting for me. I'm less than an animal to them, an abomination.

I rake my fingers through my long black hair. No one is mistaking me for a blonde.

But they saw someone.

Someone with my face and blonde hair.

My blood runs cold.

Saria.

CHAPTER 10

Saria

The wind whistles through the trees. I take another step forward, gingerly lowering Edith's clogs to the ground, careful not to make a sound. Edith's parting words echo in my head. "Be vigilant out there. The woods are alive tonight. It may seem quiet, but I can sense them, creeping between the shadows, lurking in the darkest crevices. Keep your wits about you, little bird."

Her warning sent shivers down my neck, but nothing could keep me from going to 13 Opal Moon Road. Branches rustle, but there's no way to tell if it's the wind, an animal or our enemies. An owl hoots. A twig snaps. Red grabs my wrist and pulls me behind a boulder. Keisha crouches beside me. Leaves crunch. A wolf howls. "What was that?" Keisha whispers.

"Shhh," Red warns. "They're close."

I can hear the footsteps now, boots hitting dirt, muffled voices drawing near. I'm frozen like a statue, pressed against the cold rock, muscles clenched. The footsteps march closer. I don't move. I don't even breathe.

The voices grow louder. Red pulls me to him, his arms wrapped around my waist, his body shielding mine. An acorn pops, crushed beneath combat boots. They're inches away. I can make out their breaths now, huffs of air escaping their throats. We're moments from being discovered. Depending on how many of them there are, Keisha and Red may have a fighting chance.

What can I do? I'm powerless. Red told me to stay out of the way and let them handle it. But that doesn't sit well with me.

A miracle happens. They keep on walking. The footsteps that had grown louder disappear into the distance, their voices drowned out by the wind's song.

Then, it's silent. My heart thuds in my ears. It's so loud that I pray no one can hear it. Red laces his fingers through mine. He leads me around the boulder, back on our path.

The white blur comes out of nowhere. It stops in front of us, and a wolf comes into focus. Its sleek white fur glistens in the moonlight. It snarls, baring its teeth. I stagger backwards. Another wolf leaps forward, smaller than the first, yellow eyes glowing like two full moons.

Moments later, we're surrounded. It seems like the entire pack wants a piece. They watch me: ears erect, snouts wrinkled, fangs exposed. Red pulls me close, his hand on my hip.

Silver flames erupt from the ground, obscuring the very first wolf. The fire dies out as abruptly as it appeared. The wolf is gone, a middle-aged man in his place.

Yellow rays encircle the second wolf. The wolf fades as a teenage boy materializes, probably a year or two younger than me.

The older man claps the teenager on his back. "Well, son, it looks like it's our lucky day. Don't you recognize her from the news?"

The boy shakes his head, blonde curls tumbling over his forehead.

"Asher, think." The father's silver eyes flash. "It's the Crowe nimwit. The one who escaped from the incompetent Nightingale's dungeon. There's a huge reward on her head."

Asher curls his lip, revealing an oversized incisor. "We're going to be rich."

The father extends his arm. "Hand over the girl and no one gets hurt."

Red tightens his grip on me. "Over my dead body."

Asher shrugs his shoulders. "Alright. He asked for it."

The pack closes in with a symphony of eager growls. Wolves pounce, claws extended, jaws snapping. Blue magic shoots from Red's palm, throwing several wolves back. But there are so many more.

A gigantic wolf launches into the air. Enormous paws strike Red's chest, knocking him to the ground. The force pulls us apart. Standing, I pummel the wolf's back, my fists hitting him over and over, barely noticing the pain radiating from my injured shoulder. Even with the adrenaline rush, I'm not strong enough. The wolf doesn't even flinch.

Someone grabs me from behind. Fingers dig into my upper arm, gripping tight enough to leave a bruise. I turn and swing, aiming to punch my attacker in the jaw. Asher ducks, a grin plastered on his face. "Feisty little nimwit, huh?"

He drags me like a ragdoll. I flail and thrash, but it's no use. I hate being so goddamn weak. Asher twists my arms behind my back. Crack! My shoulder pops back out of its socket. I yowl in agony. Asher chuckles. "I thought they said that you were strong."

It's futile. I give up fighting. All I can do is watch. Red is still on his back, wolves enveloping him. Red lifts his palm. A beam of blue magic hits one wolf in the head. The wolf crumples to the ground. But dozens more close in. Claws drag down his chest, slashing his jacket, ripping open his skin.

A wolf lurches at Keisha. She jump-kicks him in the muzzle. The wolf whimpers, tucking its tail between his legs. Another wolf swipes at Keisha, claws grazing her cheek. She grabs it by the neck, tossing it aside.

Keisha and Red are putting up a good fight, but they're outnumbered. It's only a matter of time before they're defeated. I stand by, helpless.

I notice the bat before anyone else does. It swoops down, surging towards the wolf pack, spinning, faster and faster, a blur of black and red. A man emerges from the whirlwind, brown oxfords hitting the ground, dark hair pulled back into a long ponytail.

He holds his hand out like it's a rifle, staring down the length of his fingers like it's the scope. Purple flares shoot from his fingers. They hurl through space, each one expertly fired, hitting a half dozen wolves in their backs. There's a few strangled howls before the wolves keel over, stiff, eyes rolled back, tongues hanging out of their mouths.

The man cocks his fingers back, aims and shoots again. The purple flares blast forward, taking out the rest of the wolves. Asher pushes me away, sprinting towards the still bodies.

I stumble forward, steadying myself against a tree. Asher drops to his knees beside a wolf. "Dad!" He shakes the wolf. "Dad!" A purple fireball hits him in the back of the head. He topples over, landing in a heap on top of his father.

Red wriggles out from beneath a wolf body. In a flash, he's by my side. "Sari, are you okay?" He examines my shoulder, his fingers circling the injury. "Those bastards."

Keisha shoves a limp wolf off of her. She stands and dusts off her corduroy bell bottoms, staring at the pile of bodies. "Are they dead?" She asks.

"They're asleep." The man with the dark ponytail emerges from the shadows. He looks like a college professor: khaki pants, V-neck sweater vest layered over a collared button-down shirt.

"Mo! Holy shit, man, am I glad to see you!" Red says. The men greet each other with a quick hug and a pat on the back. "I didn't think you were coming, man. I haven't seen you in years. I can't believe my eyes: Amos Hamilton in the flesh!"

"I wasn't going to," Amos responds. "I don't believe in war. But after we hung up the phone, I couldn't stop thinking about what you told me: the terrorist's plan to open the portal, Alaina and her daughters being in danger. I had to go to the portal to see for myself. After the DOX militants gained entry to Aurelia…" Amos' mouth is a hard line. "I had to follow. But I won't compromise my moral values. I won't kill anyone."

"Thank you, Amos," I say, finding my voice. "For saving our lives. My mom told me a lot about you."

"All good, I hope?" Amos's smile doesn't meet his eyes. My mom told me that she was madly in love with Amos. If he wasn't a vampire, their love might've lasted forever. Their relationship was forbidden, and they feared the consequences of discovery. Also, my mom wanted a family, something that Amos could never give her. When they parted ways, they were both brokenhearted.

"Not just good. Wonderful," I say. "She admired you very much." Sadness flashes in Amos's eyes. Is it possible that he still loves my mom, all these years later?

Red clears his throat. "In all the chaos, I forgot to do introductions. This is Sari, Lani's daughter, and her friend Keisha. She's a slayer. I haven't come up with a nickname for her yet. How do you like Keshi?"

Keisha puts her hands on her hips. "Absolutely not."

Amos laughs. "Pleasure to meet you both."

Red eyes the wolves. "How long until they wake up?"

"Half-hour, an hour tops."

"Then we better get out of here," Red says.

"Where are you headed?" Amos asks.

"13 Opal Moon Road," I say. "To find my sister."

CHAPTER 11

Zoeli

"I have to find her." I pace across the kitchen, my heart in my throat.

Kian peeks through the curtains. "Sterling and another guy are still searching the yard. We have to wait for them to leave."

"I'm not asking for permission. I'm not waiting another second."

Kian slips on a pair of black boots. "Okay, I'll go look for her. You stay here."

I raise my brows. "Do you actually think that I'm going to sit here by myself and wait?"

"No, but it was worth a shot." He bends over, tying his shoelaces.

"They won't recognize me as a crow. I'll search by air. You take the ground."

"Aye, Lieutenant." Kian performs a military salute. "But if they see a crow flying out my window, they'll put two and two together and we'll both be in big trouble. You need to go out the chimney. The side door is closest to the woods. I'll go out there. If anyone sees me, I'll say that I heard something and was checking it out."

I nod. "When I find her, I'll caw three times. Meet me at the side door."

"And if I find her first?" Kian asks. "I haven't perfected my caw."

"You won't," I say.

"Is that a challenge?"

"Depends how you want to take it." Ribbons of blue magic snake around my feet, slithering up my torso over my shoulders, winding through my hair. I transform into a crow. I sail up the chimney, soot and dust sticking to my wings. I perch on Kian's roof, scanning the ground below. "She's not here," Sergeant Sterling says to a soldier dressed in Aurelian royal blue. "Let's check the house across the street." As they walk along one side of the house, Kian leaves from the other side, a black hoodie pulled over his head. He glances both ways before disappearing into the forest.

I soar above the trees. Below me, the woods are a dense canopy of leaves and branches. Even though I can't see the ground, I don't dare get closer. Too many people are out looking for me. Someone might see me or if they're skilled enough, sense my presence.

Instead, I must rely on my other senses. I hone in on my blue magic, feeling it bubble in my core. I pump it out, guiding it through my veins and into my ears. Every sound is amplified, reverberating in my eardrums.

The woods at night are a noisy place. A coyote yips. Rodents scurry through the brush. A frog croaks. Cicadas sing. A creek gurgles.

I hear footfalls, boots hitting the dirt. Then, something more unusual: a chorus of heavy breathing, a gasp, and a snort. I glide into the trees and perch on the highest branch to get a better look. A trio of Aurelian soldiers stare at the ground, their mouths agape. At least twenty comatose wolves are sprawled across the forest floor. A groan-like snore escapes a wolf's open mouth.

"She put them all to sleep. The entire pack." One of the men says, something like awe in his voice.

"She wasn't alone," Another soldier chimes in. "It must've been one of her friends. A nimwit couldn't do that."

"They weren't prepared, but we are," the last soldier says, stroking his machine gun.

I've heard enough. Blue lightning explodes from my claws, catapulting the soldier into a massive tree. Crack! His skull slams into the trunk. He falls over, unconscious.

"Holy shit!" The soldiers point their guns, aiming left then right, trying to figure out where the attack came from.

I launch a grenade-like blast of blue magic at both of them. They go down, toppling over like dominos.

Did you think that a nimwit could do that? I chuckle to myself.

I resume my search, pleased that Saria is that much safer without those pursuers on her tail. A few minutes later, I hear more footsteps. Soles lightly graze the ground, the softest touch, almost inaudible. But I hear them.

I swoop down, searching for the source of the footfalls. Even from a distance, I recognize my sister: the nuance of her gait, the way her hair falls down her back. She's with three others, one woman and two men. I have no way of knowing if they're enemies or friends.

Caw! Caw! Caw! I speed up, shifting as I go, a blue streak whizzing toward the ground. I land hard, my feet slamming into the dirt.

My eyes meet hers, eyes that could be mistaken for my own. The eyes that studied my 'boo-boos' before kissing them and patting on a band-aid, the eyes that lit up with laughter as we danced around the living room, the eyes that welled with tears after waking from a nightmare, until she climbed into my bed and we held each other. My sister's eyes. My twin.

I don't remember reaching out but she's in my arms. We cling to each other. Her hair sticks to the tears sliding down my cheeks. A piece of my soul snaps back into place.

"Zoe, you're here. You're here. You're alive. You're really here." Saria jabbers in between sobs.

"Shhh," I cup her chin in my palm. "We have to be quiet." I look over Saria's shoulder, studying the people behind her. I blink fast, wondering if my eyes deceive me. It must be a trick of the moonlight. "Keisha?" My jaw falls open. I examine her familiar face: high cheekbones, full lips, brown skin, black curls tied back in a sleek ponytail. "What the hell are you doing here?"

"It's a long story," Keisha says.

"Tell me later." I release Saria and pull Keisha in for a big hug. "Who are the guys behind you?" I whisper in her ear.

"They're our friends," Keisha whispers back. "Red and Amos. They've been protecting us."

I'll take her word for it. For now. "Follow me." I link one arm through Saria's, the other through Keisha's, as I lead the group through the woods.

The guy who Keisha called Red stays annoyingly close, almost hovering over my sister. I really hope this guy isn't bad news.

We duck under trees and wriggle through brush. Thorns tangle in my hair and pull on my clothes. I miss traveling as a bird.

When we arrive at Kian's house, he's waiting at the side door. "It's all clear," he says. "I've been keeping a lookout."

I keep my arm around Saria until she's safely inside.

CHAPTER 12

Saria

"Make yourself at home." Kian leads us into an airy living room. Large brown couches with beige accent pillows face an enormous wall-mounted television. "Take a seat."

"Thank you." I sink into the leather couch. I feel like I'm dreaming. My sister is right in front of me. I watch her chest rise and fall. I study the twinkle in her aquamarine eyes. She's here. She's alive. After months of sleepless nights, hours of stress and worry, we've found each other again. And she missed me as much as I missed her.

Red sits right beside me, his leg brushing against mine. He immediately goes to work on my injuries, massaging my arm, blue magic wrapping around my dislodged shoulder. Within moments, my pain is gone. Red gently coaxes my bones back into place. "Are you okay?" Red asks softly.

I nod. "Yes, much better." His face is so close to mine. The hairs on my arms stand straight up. I stare at his lips, and bite my own. Chemistry crackles between us, like there's no one else in the room.

"Geez," Zoe notices herself in the farmhouse-style mirror. "I'm a mess." She touches her soot-streaked cheek. "That's what I get for flying up that thing." She barks out a laugh, gesturing to the fieldstone hearth. I pull away from Red, breaking the trance.

When I saw the crow swoop down from the sky, blue ribbons of magic transforming into my sister, I was certain that I'd finally lost my damn mind. It was impossible. And yet, it wasn't.

"How did you..." My voice trails off. "The curse." After my mother broke magical law by marrying a human, she was punished by the magical court. Her shapeshifting power was stolen from her and her future children. From birth, my sister and I have never been able to become crows.

"It's broken!" Zoe smiles cheek to cheek.

"How did you do it?" I ask. It's nothing short of a miracle.

"I can't take credit. I had help from a few friends. It's how I escaped. I became a crow and I just," Zoe wiggles her hips, "wriggled through the bars." Zoe beams at me. "You can fly, too, Saria."

"Really?" I suppress a squeal of excitement.

"I'm surprised that you didn't discover it on your own. I thought you were soaring all over the place with Mom. I felt a little left out," Zoe says.

"No, I had no idea" I perch on the edge of the couch. "How do I shift?"

"It comes so naturally to me now." Zoe strokes her chin, thinking. "The first time, I was in the dungeon. I wanted to get out so bad. I visualized it, my body transforming into a crow, and then it just kind of happened."

I've been dreaming of flying since I was a little girl, even before I knew that I was a crow. I used to climb trees, climbing from bough to bough until I reached the very top.

I'd stretch my arms out, feeling the wind flow through my fingertips, feeling more at home than I ever did on the ground.

I've been waiting for this moment my whole life. I close my eyes. I imagine myself soaring through the sky, black wings beating on the wind. I can't think of anything that I'd rather do.

But nothing happens. Eyes open, I examine my very human hand, disappointment washing over me. "I can't do it."

Zoe's brow furrows. "Maybe you just need some more practice. You'll get there."

"Or maybe it's because she's powerless," Red suggests.

Zoe drops her gaze. "Oh."

"Red," I say. "Don't make her feel bad."

"I'm not trying to shame her. I'm proposing a solution," Red says. "She needs to give your powers back to you."

"He's right," Zoe says. "I'll do a power transfer."

I bite my lip. I can't deny that magic is a useful tool, particularly now, while Aurelia is under attack and terrorists want me dead. Heck, if it means that I can fly as a crow, sign me up. Still, I hesitate, thinking of who I used to be: scared, insecure, dependent on magic. As strange as it seems, I'm stronger now, sans magic, than ever before. "How does a power transfer work? Can you only return what's mine?"

Zoe twists the ends of her hair. "'I'm not sure how precise I can be. I've never even done a transfer before. If you get a little extra, I don't mind."

"No." I shake my head vehemently. "I don't want anything extra."

"I have an idea," Kian says, raising a finger up. "You can reverse the spell that stole Saria's power. Everything will be as it was before."

Nothing will ever be as it was before, but Kian couldn't possibly understand that.

"Reverse the spell," Zoe repeats. "Of course!"

"You'll have to perform the spell backwards," Kian explains.

"Yes, I should be able to do that," Zoe nods. "The spell was simple. I'll just need three black candles, and samples of Saria's hair and blood."

"I've got plenty of candles," Kian says. "You can go through the cupboard and take your pick."

"The evulsion is my biggest regret," Zoe stares at the floor. "Now I finally have a chance to make things right."

CHAPTER 13

Zoeli

Moments after the idea was presented, I got to work. I needed a quiet space to complete the spell, so Kian offered his sister's bedroom.

It should only take fifteen minutes to complete the spell reversal. I sit on the carpet, black candles arranged in a triangle around me. I clench a clump of Saria's hair in one fist, a rag stained by her fresh blood in the other. As I recite the chant backwards, I flashback to when I originally cast the evulsion. I was angry and jealous enough to steal from my own twin.

I was a fool. I thought that being powerful would solve my problems. Looking back, I didn't even know what problems were. I thought that Saria was stronger than me. I had no idea that I already had blue magic, the most potent kind, and just needed to learn how to access it.

I could dwell on how stupid I was, but that won't help me grow. The truth is that we all make mistakes, and hindsight is always twenty-twenty. I promise myself to do better from now on.

My blood runs hot as Saria's magic leaves me. My face flushes, ears buzzing like bee hives. Flames shoot down my spine. Then, it all stops.

It worked. I stand up, releasing my breath. I roll my shoulders back and stretch my arms up to the ceiling. The power I harbor is only mine, the magic I was born with. Damn, it feels good.

I notice a framed photograph of Kian and his sister on her bedside table. I pick it up, the pad of my finger leaving a streak in the dust beneath it. My brow furrows. It doesn't seem like anyone has been in this bedroom for a very long time.

The picture appears to be a few years old. Red acne mars Kian's cheeks, his frame lankier than it is now. At first glance, his sister Sam looks like a boy. She's dressed in baggy jeans, an oversized hoodie and scuffed sneakers. Her light-brown hair is cropped shorter than her brother's. Behind them, firework-like lava shoots from the Aurelian volcano, Mount Zamus. Carefree smiles spread across both of their faces.

Sam's jovial expression doesn't match the morose aesthetic of her bedroom. A skeleton wearing a black top hat is the sole poster on her black walls. A collection of dragon figurines are lined up on top of an antique dresser.

On impulse, I slide open the top drawer. Inside, a journal rests on top of a folded t-shirt. I run my finger along the raised lines in the leather, the embossed dragon that decorates the journal's cover. I flip open to the first page.

I know who I am, and I don't belong here.

I close the book and shove the drawer shut. I shouldn't be snooping in the first place. Curiosity isn't an excuse for invading Sam's privacy.

I go back downstairs, taking the steps two at a time. In the living room, Saria, Keisha, Red and Amos stare at the big screen television. I can hear Kian shuffling around in the kitchen, a pot clanging on the stove.

On the television, Uncle Talon stands at a jewel-encrusted podium, King Keifer by his side. "We believe that working together, we can make Aurelia the magical place that our ancestors intended it to be. King Keifer and I will lead side by side, myself as the high ruler, King Keifer Nightingale as your beloved king.

"Inevitably, with new leadership, there will be some changes. Some outdated and frankly unjust practices will be eradicated, including the laws that enforce discrimination towards vampires. Ever since the Great Witch-Vampire war, hatred of vampires has been ingrained in our culture. This animosity has blinded many of us to the fact that the vast majority of vampires wish to live in peace with us. Under my rule, prejudice towards vampires will no longer be tolerated."

"Well, that's one positive," Red mutters under his breath. I tilt my head, noticing the corpse-like pallor of his face. He's unnaturally pale, almost like his skin hasn't seen the sun in a century.

On the screen, Talon continues. "By shunning vampires, we're not only missing out on opportunities for love or friendship, we're denying ourselves the unstoppable power that we could achieve together." He taps the podium. A skull ring glints on his middle finger.

"If you were fortunate enough to learn the unedited version of our history, you'll know that vampires are our cousins. Both of our races are direct descendants of the demon Xaphan. Going forward, we will welcome our cousins into the land of Aurelia." Talon steps aside.

Keifer steps in front of the microphone. "I just want to reiterate what our High Ruler, Talon Crowe, has said tonight. There will be no more fighting. Our military has been ordered to stand down. Anyone who tries to take matters into their own hands will be prosecuted to the fullest extent of the law.

"As our High Ruler Crowe said, there will be some changes in the upcoming days and months. I believe that these changes will be good ones, ones that will lead to the advancement of our people. Aurelia is on the brink of a new beginning, one that I'm excited to be a part of."

Elric Wolfe, the court magistrate who sent me to the dungeon to rot, steps onto the stage. His skeletal fingers lace around a ruby-adorned crown. Uncle Talon bows his head, and Elric fastens the crown in his thick gray hair.

The two leaders stand side by side, bejeweled crowns glistening atop their heads. Talon takes Keifer's hand in his powerful grip, his pearly white teeth shining as cameras flash like strobe lights.

The screen pans out, revealing the young prince standing beside his father. Damian's lips curve into his signature lopsided grin. He claps his father on the back and then extends his palm to Talon. As Damian and Talon shake hands, the audience explodes with applause.

A chill runs through me, like ice cubes slithering through my veins. Goosebumps rise on my skin. Aurelia is doomed.

"Dinner's ready." Kian appears beneath the archway that separates the dining and living rooms.

My belly grumbles as I stand up. I haven't had a real meal in months. In the dining room, the delectable smells of chicken parmigiana, pasta with marinara sauce, and garlic bread make my mouth water.

Somehow, Kian managed to whip up enough food for all of us on such short notice. As Kian spoons a portion of pasta onto a plate, I think of Damian, dining on gourmet dishes prepared by servants and private chefs. I don't think he could prepare a meal if his life depended on it.

"This looks amazing!" Keisha slides into a chair.

I don't waste any time. I fill up my plate and dig in. The dinner is phenomenal: juicy chicken, crisp herby bread crumbs, gooey cheese, on a bed of al dente pasta. "Give my compliments to the chef."

"I'll pass along the message." Kian's boyish grin reminds me of how young he is. Only eighteen and all on his own. What happened to his family?

Red and Amos stand beside the table, watching the rest of us eat. Red clears his throat. "Thank you, Kian. This looks delicious, but, um, Amos and I will have to decline."

"I figured as much. I'm sorry that I don't have anything that you can, um, drink. But you're welcome to join us at the table," Kian says.

Red nods. "I would like that." He pulls out a chair.

CHAPTER 14

Saria

Even though the meal was hours ago, I'm still so full that I might burst. I put my hand on my bulging stomach. "That was one of the best meals I've ever had."

I close my eyes, feeling the familiar thrum of magic beneath my skin. I imagine myself flying: black feathers spread wide, zooming past the stars, cawing at the moon. I never wanted anything more. I open my eyes. Nothing.

"It's not working." I snap my lips shut, embarrassed by the sound of my own whining. I didn't get much sleep last night, or for weeks before while I was enslaved at the farmhouse. I'm bone weary tired and cranky. It's not a good look.

"You'll get there, Sar." Keisha squeezes my shoulder. "You just need more practice."

"Zoe didn't need more practice," I mutter, aware of how petty I sound. Old habits die hard, I guess. I really need some sleep, but I won't give up.

I bow my head, honing in on the seat of my magic. I find it: simmering but solid, a dense orb of light. It's like turning up the fire under a burner. As the energy boils, it melts, scorching orange lava flowing through my veins.

I envision a crow, but not just any crow, *my* crow, the crow I feel inside me, wings flapping with every heartbeat. I see her shiny feathers, strong legs, sharp talons, and stout beak. I push all of my energy into her, willing her to come out.

And still nothing. I open my eyes and groan. "What am I doing wrong?" Sweat beads on my forehead. A wave of dizziness washes over me. Black spots dance in my vision. "Ugh, I don't feel so good."

"You need to take a break. You're going to give yourself MOSS," Zoe chides. Magic Overuse Shock Syndrome, also known as MOSS, is caused by magic overexertion and can lead to fatigue, shock, and in more severe cases, even death.

"I guess," I murmur, a yawn escaping my lips. "I'm exhausted." Sunk back in a leather recliner, Keisha is also bleary eyed. "We should go back to Edith's and get some sleep."

"I'll make sure you get there safely before I, you know, dig myself a hole to sleep in." Red chuckles.

"Edith?" Kian asks. "Edith Dubois?"

I shrug. "I don't know her last name. She lives in a little cottage in the woods, out in the middle of nowhere, really. She's a bit eccentric, but she's really nice. She offered Keisha and I a place to stay."

Kian nods. "I know Edith well. She was a good friend of my mother's. Her cabin's tiny, more of a hut, really. I'm not sure where she would even fit the both of you." Kian takes a breath, looks around. "Listen, I have more than enough space. You're all welcome to stay here as long as you'd like."

Zoe's eyes light up. "Really? All of us?"

"As long as you don't eat all of my donuts," Kian teases.

"No deal." Zoe grins. "I don't make promises when it comes to pastries." She tilts her head, stretching so her ear comes down by her shoulder. "I've been sleeping upright on tree branches for months. My neck is killing me. I can't wait to stretch out on a real bed."

"Two of you can share my parent's king bed, and one can sleep in my sister's bed."

"Thank you so much," Zoe says. "Are you sure? I don't want to impose."

"It's nothing." Kian waves a hand. "I'm by myself in this big house."

Zoe and Kian's eyes meet, lingering for a moment before he looks away. "I'll go make sure there's clean sheets on all the beds." His footsteps disappear up the stairs.

Red rests his palm on my forearm. "I should go feed before I find someplace to rest."

"Okay," I say. Last night, when Red left for his morning sleep, I was all alone with a strange woman I just met. Tonight, I have my twin sister and my childhood best friend. Still, it's hard to say goodbye.

"Walk me out," Red says, lacing his fingers through mine.

"Go out the side door," Zoe says. "The trees provide coverage."

We walk down the dark hallway, my palm tingling from his touch. At the side door, moonlight shines through the glass panel. Red and I face each other.

"We did it," I say. "We found Zoe."

"I gave you my word," Red says. His hand cups my cheek, his thumb running along my jaw. I lean into it, like a cat. "I know that we shouldn't…." Red's voice trails off.

"Shouldn't what?" I ask, my voice husky. His blue eyes blaze with desire. I bite my bottom lip. I step closer to him, my body brushing his.

I can see the turmoil in his eyes, and the moment when his resolve falters and passion wins. He pulls me in, his fingers trailing down my back.

His lips meet mine. Heat rushes through my veins. Our tongues intertwine. Electricity shoots down my spine. I press my body against his: wanting, yearning.

"Ahem." Someone clears their throat. Red and I spring apart. Amos stands a few feet away, disapproval etched into his features. I'd been so caught up in the moment that I didn't even hear him come down the hallway. "Redvers, it's time for us to be on our way."

"Alright," Red sighs. "Goodnight, Sari. I'll be back after sunset."

Red and Amos step outside, letting in a gust of cold wind before pushing the door shut. Then, they're gone.

I hold my palm to my tingling lips. Every part of me throbs as two bats disappear into the inky black sky.

CHAPTER 15

Zoeli

It feels so damn good to be in an actual bed, but for some reason, I can't sleep. A thread of sunlight streams in between the curtains, casting a golden glow across the king-sized bed. Beside me, Saria sleeps, her breaths deep and steady, blonde hair swept across the silk pillowcase.

I still have so many questions for her. What happened to Logan? And what's up with her and this guy Red? By the time the vampires left, Saria was too tired for girl talk. When she wakes up, she needs to spill the tea.

She's probably wondering the same about me. When we were cellmates in Nightingale Dungeon, Damian used to sneak downstairs to visit me. Saria doesn't know what happened after I escaped: how he lied, cheated and kept me hidden in his closet while he went to school.

I can't believe that I kissed him last night. What the hell was I thinking? The man who shook hands with my arch nemesis on stage, cementing the partnership between Talon Crowe and the royal Nightingale family, is the same man whose lips pressed against mine. Bile rises in my throat. I'm disgusted with myself.

Damian will say that he's just playing a role. I could accept that explanation if he made any effort, even covertly, to stand up for what's right. He didn't even have the balls to tell his father about our relationship, let alone defy his political decisions. If I confront Damian, he'll hem and haw, claiming that he'll "figure it out," all while doing nothing. While he dilly-dallies and says "it takes time," Uncle Talon and his DOX supporters will destroy Aurelia, enslave humans, and enact laws that make duds second-class citizens.

There's no time to waste. Two floors below me, Kian's basement holds years of hard work, carefully laid combat plans, and the construction of a magical bomb that may still be a work-in-progress, but has the potential to change warfare forever. If Damian showed a tenth of the initiative that Kian does, we'd still be together.

So why can't I resist him? Every time we're together, my brain turns to mush and this godforsaken force pushes me to him. When Damian and I swam under the Aurelian waterfall called Clarity, a magical landform known for clearing up uncertainties, the wind whispered, *He's made for you.* I snort. That's a load of bullshit. Whoever created him for me must've been sleeping on the job.

Speaking of sleep, I'm still not. At least I'm comfortable in Kian's sister's soft pajama pants and oversized t-shirt. Thinking of her journal entry, I can't help but wonder where Sam is. Did she run away? Or did something far worse happen to her?

I roll back and forth, finding it impossible to relax. My throat's dry. Maybe a drink will help.

I tip-toe out of bed, careful to close the bedroom door lightly on my way out. I take the stairs two at a time to the first floor. I feel my way down the dark hallway, and flick on the ceiling light in the kitchen. I'm pouring a glass of water when the front door opens and shuts. I freeze. My heart slams into my ribcage.

Footsteps hit the floor, moving closer and closer. I raise my fists, poised to fight. Who the hell is here? And how did they get in? My heart thumps against my rib cage.

Kian enters the room. When he sees me, his eyes narrow, his lips firm in a grim line. What the hell is going on? Before we went to bed, Kian told me that he didn't have work today, so he'd be sleeping in. I glance at the clock. It's five-fifty AM.

I lower my fists. "Good morning," I say.

Kian stares, not responding, black pupils floating in blank space. Tension rolls off him in waves. It's so thick I could cut it with a knife. "Where have you been?" I ask.

Kian snorts. "I should be asking you that."

My brow furrows. "I didn't go anywhere. I couldn't sleep, so I came downstairs for a drink." I lift my glass.

"Where were you yesterday?" Kian leans on the kitchen island, his arms folded across his black sweatshirt. "Before you came here."

"I already told you. I was by the palace, fighting from the rooftops. I took down some DOX soldiers."

"You left something out." Kian frowns. "Something very important."

I turn my palms up. "I did?"

"You did." Kian's tone is sharp.

"Why are you giving me the third degree?" I ask, moving my hands to my hips.

"I think you know why."

"I really don't." I throw my hands in the air. "Is this because I ate all of your donuts? Are you cranky in the morning without carbs?" My attempt at humor doesn't land. Kian's scowl deepens.

"We've spent years building up The Resistance," Kian's voice is low, dripping with hostility. "All of our members are carefully vetted before giving them any information at all." Kian runs his finger along the jagged scar that slashes through his eyebrow. "With you, I skipped over all of our regular protocols. I thought, since the Nightingales imprisoned you, you wouldn't be sleeping with one of them." Kian's upper lip curls. "I was wrong. Last night, I shared half of our secrets with our enemy's lover."

"Kian, it's not what you think. Damian and I…." My voice trails off as I struggle to explain.

"When you tell Damian about The Resistance, I'll be sentenced to life in prison or worse. Traitors aren't treated kindly in the dungeon. But I'm not worried about myself." Kian grabs a can of ground coffee from the cabinet and slams it down on the counter. "The Resistance was going to change Aurelia for the better. We were going to take over, put the power in the hands of the people, and make it a proper democracy."

"And that is still going to happen," I say. "I'm not going to tell Damian about The Resistance. Your secrets are safe with me."

"Why did you lie to me about knowing Damian?"

"I didn't think that I had to share my entire dating history with you. Damian and I are done. I ended our …" I hesitate to call it a relationship, "situation months ago."

"Months ago?" Kian raises his brows. "Really?" His voice rises, anger getting the better of him. "Are you sure about that?"

I tug on the ends of my hair. It's the truth. Until yesterday, I hadn't seen Damian in months. Then, between the war, gore and fear that I'd never see Damian again, my emotions were running high. I was vulnerable. Add in that goddamn magnetic pull and I made a mistake.

If I tell Kian, he'll kick me out of The Resistance. Besides, there's no reason for him to know. Kian can trust me. I'd never tell Damian about Kian's organization or any of their operations. "Yes, I'm sure," I say.

Kian leans over the countertop, his knuckles white. "So, you weren't kissing the prince yesterday, about fifteen minutes before you showed up here?"

I stagger backwards, almost tripping over my own feet. "W-w-what…" I sputter, shaking my head. It's impossible. Damian and I were alone. No one besides us could possibly know. "Who told you that?" I ask.

"I met with one of my advisors this morning. They filled me in."

It doesn't make sense. How could anyone know what happened in the privacy of Damian's bedroom? "Who's your advisor?"

"I have many. They're always watching. I know secrets that you'd never imagine. Secrets that may come in handy when I need a favor."

A chill runs down my spine. "Did you have someone follow me?" I ask.

"I don't need to," Kian retorts. "My advisors are everywhere, even when you think you're all alone."

I cringe. "I thought you were one of the good guys. Yet, you hire people to sneak around—"

Kian cuts me off. "I never said that anyone was sneaking around."

"You said that your advisors are always lurking—"

"I said that they're watching, not lurking. Most of the time, they're right there, in plain sight."

I rub my forehead. "Will you stop speaking in riddles? I didn't get enough sleep for this."

Kian presses buttons on the coffee machine. It whirs to life. "We seem to have veered off topic. The problem here isn't my advisors or their techniques. The problem is your involvement with the Prince of Aurelia."

"I'm not involved with him. I don't even talk to him," I mutter.

"You kissed him yesterday." Kian pours coffee into a mug.

"Kian, listen to me." I try to catch his eye, but he looks away. Kian circles a spoon inside his mug, a swirl of milk blending with his coffee. "I know that it looks bad, but I promise you that I won't say a word to Damian. Yesterday was nothing but a temporary lapse of judgement."

"Maybe the next time you have a lapse of judgement you'll give up confidential information."

"I'm not going to keep repeating myself." I stuff my hands inside the pockets of Sam's flannel pajamas. "I want to help The Resistance, but I'll understand if you can't allow me to be a part of it anymore."

"It's more than that, Zoe." Kian takes a long sip of coffee. "If I tell the other faction leaders that a spy has classified information, they'll want you killed. The sooner, the better."

I narrow my eyes. "Is that a threat?"

"I'm just letting you know the magnitude of the situation." Kian inches closer, his eyes meeting mine. "It may seem harsh, but it's necessary. This is war, Zoeli." I stare right back at him. I should be terrified. This man has an arsenal of weapons, both magical and mechanical. If he wanted to kill me, he could blow my head off with one of many assault rifles.

But he won't. Studying the pale blue rings in his eyes, I'm sure of it. Kian isn't a cold-blooded killer. He may create bombs, even detonate them. He may direct armies in battle, and even scope out a few enemies himself, but he won't wrap his fingers around my neck and squeeze. Not without hard evidence that I betrayed him, at least.

Besides, if he really wanted to kill me, he wouldn't warn me first. He would just shoot me in the back of the head when I least expect it.

"Against my better judgment, I'm not going to tell the other faction leaders about this." Kian pours another cup of coffee. He adds cream and sugar, and then hands it to me. "If you ever see Damian again, I will find out, and there will be consequences. Do I make myself clear?"

"Is everything okay?" Saria's voice rings out from behind me.

I spin around. Saria stands in the doorway, her gaze shifting from me to Kian, her brow furrowed in concern.

"Yes," I say, taking a sip of my coffee. Kian made it just the way I like. I turn back to him. "We have an understanding."

CHAPTER 16

Saria

I take another bite of chocolate chip pancakes. "Mmm, these are delicious, Kian," I say.

"It's my mom's secret recipe." Across from me, Kian dips a forkful of pancake into the puddle of maple syrup pooling along the edge of his plate. "Growing up, these were my favorite. My mom used to make them every Sunday."

"Your mom's a hell of a cook," Keisha says, stuffing a hunk of pancakes into her mouth. She washes it down with a swig of coffee.

Kian's eyes turn glassy. "Yeah, she was."

"Oh, I, um, I'm so sorry." Keisha says. "I didn't realize."

"It's okay," Kian says. A heavy silence follows. Forks clink against plates. Coffee glugs down my throat. I'm curious what happened to Kian's mom, but it feels rude to ask.

"So, um, Saria." I startle at Zoe's voice. "How are you feeling?"

"Well, I definitely have my power back." I can feel it burning beneath the surface, sparks crackling under my skin. "But I still can't shift." I've been trying all morning, since the moment I woke up, but no dice.

Zoe props her chin on her fist, elbow on the dining room table. "I don't get it. The curse was broken."

I purse my lips, thinking. "Mom never mentioned it, either. Don't you think she would've noticed if her shape-shifting power was returned to her? She would have felt it, right? Like how I can feel my power is back inside me now."

"I've studied the textbooks from Enchantment's Academy. From what I understand, once the curse was broken, we'd all be able to fly. It doesn't make sense that the shape-shifting power would only return to me." Zoe turns to Kian. "Can you think of another explanation for this?"

"Who? Me? The high school dropout?"

"If it wasn't for your circumstances, you would've been valedictorian," Zoe says. "You know more than Google."

Kian's goofy grin is at odds with his unusual, almost uncanny features. "When it comes to certain topics, perhaps, but I'm not well studied in curses."

I shrug. "Maybe I'm just not doing it right."

"Maybe we should ask Edith," Keisha suggests. "She's a little wacky, but she knows her stuff. She led us here, after all."

"You know what." Zoe brushes an errant strand of glossy hair out of her eyes. "I thought she was out of her mind when she told me that my sister fell for a vampire, but it turns out she was right!"

My cheeks burn. "I'm not exactly known for my great taste in men. Chad, anyone?" I throw up my hands. "But just because Red's a vampire doesn't mean that he's a bloodthirsty killer. He's actually really gentle and caring." I pause, remembering the night his fangs sunk into my neck. "Well, most of the time." I giggle. "And did you see his eyes? They're literally neon blue."

"He does have nice eyes." Keisha nods her approval. "And for a dead guy, he's got a banging body."

"Wait until you see him dance," I say. "It's impossible not to swoon."

"And that's my cue to do the dishes," Kian quips. He piles used plates and utensils on an empty platter smeared with remnants of chocolate chips. A few moments later, we hear dishes clatter in the sink.

"I'm so behind. Fill me in. What happened to Logan?" Zoe asks.

I drop my gaze, hands wringing in my lap. I think of Logan: hazel eyes shining behind his thick glasses, skinny legs swinging beside mine on the tallest tree branch, sandy hair blowing in the breeze. Even though he was terrified, he always climbed to the top with me. Then, when we became more than just friends, wrapped up in his arms like a cocoon, shrouding me with peace and love. The way he'd stare at me with unbridled awe, like he couldn't believe his luck. Then, at the very end: Logan standing in the doorway, tears sliding down his face, the bouquet of autumn flowers strewn across my bedroom floor.

"I'm sorry," Zoe says. "I shouldn't have brought it up."

I look up, wiping the dampness beneath my eyes. "I loved Logan. I really did. But then, I don't know what happened. We drifted apart while Red and I were getting closer. Then, I, I, um, I screwed up."

"Oh, Saria, don't beat yourself up. We all make mistakes. I've made more than my share. You're human." Zoe rests her hand on my shoulder.

"Half human." Keisha points out with a chuckle.

"Logan's loved you since preschool. I'm sure he'll forgive you. Do you want him back?" Zoe asks.

There's not a simple answer. "Logan was my best friend. I miss him so much. I wish that things hadn't ended the ugly way they did. But," I swallow hard, a knot in my throat. "Time apart has given me clarity. Logan is a wonderful guy. What we had was really special, and exactly what I needed at the time. But he's not my forever person." Part of me still wishes that it wasn't true. If Logan and I had never grown apart, if I'd never known the electricity of Red's touch, I might be waking up in Logan's bed, content in his arms.

But there's no use dwelling on what-ifs and might-have-beens. We can't change what it is. One day he's going to make a woman very happy. It's just not going to be me.

Kian re-enters the room. "Everyone ready to go visit Edith?" He rests his forearms on the back of a dining chair. "I owe the crazy old hag a visit."

"Crazy old hag?" Zoe raises her brows. "I thought she was a family friend."

"In his defense, it's a pretty accurate description," Keisha says.

"It's a term of endearment. She likes it." Kian grins. "Come on. Get your shoes and coats on. Edith will have Saria flying like a pro in no time."

"Hell yes!" I slip on Edith's brown suede moccasins. They're two sizes too big, but a hell of improvement from the stilettos Talon forced me to wear. Once I'm a bird, I won't need shoes at all. I'll be sailing through the clouds, wind whooshing through my feathers. I puff out my chest and open my arms, a smile spread across my cheeks. "I can't wait."

A crease materializes between Zoe's brows. "I don't want to be a downer, but I think we should manage our expectations. Edith's only right about half the time."

"What do you mean?" I drop my arms, hope deflating like a popped balloon.

"She's on point, Zoe. She gave us Kian's exact address," Keisha says.

"And she was right about Saria falling for a vampire," Zoe agrees. "But there was something else she said." Zoe taps her chin. "Something about Aurelia's demise. A fox-vampire and magic coming undone. It didn't make any sense."

A fox, a vampire, and magic coming undone. Three puzzle pieces that I know connect somehow. The answer niggles in the back of my mind. I squeeze my eyes shut, trying to remember.

The pieces click together. My hand comes down on the table, slapping it harder than intended. "Eleanor Fox!" I shout.

Everyone turns. "Who?" Zoe asks.

"When I was Talon's personal slave, I overheard everything: their strategies, their philosophies, even some secrets," I say.

Kian leans in, brushing snow-white hair out of his eyes.

I suck in a deep breath, gathering my thoughts. For everyone to understand Eleanor's integral role in the DOX invasion, the story must be told from the beginning. "Over a hundred years ago, the Aurelian government developed a spell to secure the portal. Seven talented witches, one from each royal family, were selected to perform the spell. It was a very elaborate spell, designed by scholars to last for an eternity. Eleanor Fox, a young woman at the time, was one of the seven spellcasters. Once the spell was complete, all records were deliberately destroyed, so that no one could attempt to reverse it.

"Eleanor never told anyone about her strange fascination with vampires. She sought them out in the human realm, and asked to be changed. She knew her chances of survival were slim, but she was willing to make that bet. Anything for power and eternal life. When she woke up craving blood, Nellie knew that she could never go back home. If she returned, she'd be killed or imprisoned. For many years, she went by Nellie Baker, her nickname and mother's maiden name. Her mysterious disappearance baffled the Aurelian authorities. As years passed, she was presumed dead, although her body was never found.

"Fast forward to a hundred years later, when Talon and Licinia discover Nellie's true identity. They hatch a plan to reverse the spell that secures the portal. Nellie isn't hard to convince; she's been missing her homeland for years. They conduct a series of memory spells to recover every detail of the spell, because, well, it's been over a hundred years so she couldn't possibly remember it all. Once that's done, they acquire seven royals willing to participate, all descendants of the original spellcasters with their own reasons for wanting DOX to control Aurelia.

"So, there you go," I say. "Eleanor Fox is a vampire," I put my pointer finger up. "And a fox." I raise my middle finger. "When they undid the security spell, that's called magic coming undone." I put up a third finger. "A vampire, a fox, and magic coming undone. Edith was spot on."

"Well, shit," Zoe said. "I never would've guessed."

"I never doubted the crazy old hag." Kian shrugs on a black leather jacket. "Are you all ready?"

I lift my chin high, hope restored. "Let's go."

It's time to fly, baby.

CHAPTER 17

Zoeli

A twig snaps beneath my boots. Saria jolts, hands flailing out. She grasps onto my jacket, clutching the fabric in her fist. "It's okay," I whisper. "It's just me." I take her hand, squeezing it in mine.

"Yesterday, we were attacked by a pack of wolves right around here," Saria's voice trembles. "We should've waited for Red to wake. Between the wolves and DOX and—"

"I'm not waiting around for anyone," I say, my tone harsher than I intended. "For months, I've been on my own. I don't need your vampire boyfriend or anyone else to protect me."

On her other side, Kian pats Saria on the shoulder. "It's not too far now. In a quarter mile, we'll take a right. About another fifty yards, and we're there."

Saria releases a shaky breath. She trudges forward, arms rigid by her sides. "Everything is going to be okay, Sar."

I spoke too soon. A bush quivers. Leaves shake as its branches spread apart. A white furry creature bursts from the foliage. Saria jumps, moccasins flying off the ground, hand clasped over her mouth.

A fluffy rabbit stands stock still, its ears upright. It looks more startled than us.

"Oh, Jesus." Saria says, hand on her heart. "I thought it was a wolf."

"Deep breaths, Sar," Keisha says. "You're going to give yourself a heart attack."

"Hey, little guy." Kian crouches on his heels and taps the ground. "Come here, little bunny." To my surprise, the bunny hops his way, dirt spraying from beneath its paws. Kian scoops the rabbit in his palms. He lifts him to his face, and they stare at one another, nose to nose. It makes sounds, almost like a cluck, cluck, cluck, its nose wiggling away. A few moments later, Kian puts the bunny back down. "Thanks, little guy." Kian pats its head. As Kian stands up, the bunny darts back into the brush.

"What was that all about?" I ask, my brow furrowed.

"What's wrong? You don't like animals?" Kian asks.

"I love animals," I say. "But I don't usually pick up random rabbits in the woods."

"Well, maybe you should start." Kian shrugs, slipping his phone out of his pocket. He stares at the screen, apparently reading a text message, worry lines etched across his forehead.

"Everything okay?" I ask.

"Yeah, sure." Kian slides his phone back into his jean's pocket. He points to a shrub a few feet ahead. "Make a left by the deerberry."

Keisha tilts her head, a crease between her brows. "You just told us to stay on this path for a quarter mile."

"Did I?" Kian looks left then right, as though he just realized where he is. "I must've misspoken." Bullshit. Kian isn't fooling me. He's too smart to forget something he said five seconds ago. "This way." He turns left at the deerberry.

As Keisha and Saria forge ahead, I grab Kian's wrist, holding him back. "What the hell is going on?" I haven't forgotten Kian's earlier threat. What if this is some kind of trap? Maybe we aren't headed to Edith's house at all.

"What do you mean?" Kian feigns confusion.

"You're a bad actor," I say. "And you forget that I know these woods as well as you do. We're going the long way. Why?"

A guilty expression sweeps over his features. My chest tightens. What if assassins from The Resistance are waiting just around the bend, ready to put a bullet between my eyes?

Kian speaks softly. "I got word from my advisors that DOX is hiding out in the other direction, but I didn't want to alarm anyone. Your sister looks one scare short of a nervous breakdown."

"She's tougher than she seems." Defending my sister is a knee-jerk reaction. Then, Saria glances over her shoulder: bloodshot eyes, green-tinged skin, trembling lips. Maybe lying to her wasn't the worst idea. "Okay, we don't need to tell her about that. Are you sure that this way is safe?"

"As sure as I can be." Kian checks his phone again. "I told you that I have eyes and ears everywhere. You can trust me."

I'm not sure about that. At any moment, either a DOX militant or a Resistance assassin might pop out and try to slit my throat. They won't catch me off guard. I ramp up my hearing, ensuring I have the upper hand. A branch creaks. An insect buzzes. A woodpecker hammers a tree, its tiny beak like a drumroll. My fingers twitch, ready to blast an enemy with an onslaught of deadly blue magic.

My chest doesn't fall until I see Edith's cottage: beige stucco walls and brown trim around the windows. "We made it," Saria says, a big breath escaping from her lungs.

Edith waits outside, bare feet in the cold grass, a thin nightgown swirling around her despite the lack of wind. "Ah, the twin flames! Together again! What a marvelous sight!" Her smile spreads ear to ear, crow's feet forming around her eyes. Stained teeth hang over her thin lips.

"Twin flames?" Saria whispers to me. "Does she mean us?"

I shrug. "I guess so. We're the only twins here."

"Oh, Kian." The woman reaches up and pinches Kian's cheek like a grandmother would. "When did you get so big? Just yesterday you were a tiny baby cooing in my lap."

Kian leans down and kisses the old lady on top of her head. "I'm a man now. Eighteen-years-old and six-foot-three."

"And so handsome, too," Edith cups his face in her hands.

Kian grins. "I fear your eyesight is failing in your old age." Splotches of pink appear on Kian's white cheeks.

"Nonsense." Edith stares up at Kian. "Who made up the beauty standards anyways? Most men that society deems handsome are boring to look at. I'd choose asymmetrical and scarred over straight teeth and thick dark hair every time."

"Asymmetrical and scarred?" Kian chuckles. "I guess your vision isn't so bad after all. You're just crazier than I thought."

"Crazy people are the most fun." Edith winks. "Come in, come in. It's cold outside." She leads us to her cottage, muddy heels marking her front steps. She unhooks the iron latch, pulls open the door, and steps inside. "I'll make some tea."

Inside, the four of us squeeze onto Edith's blue polka dot loveseat, Kian's thigh pressed against mine. I stare down at his jeans, remembering the moment I showed up unannounced in his window. My cheeks heat as I picture him in nothing but a t-shirt and underwear, thigh muscles bulging beneath his pale skin, intricate designs coloring his arms.

Edith's right about Kian's looks. The first, even second and third times I saw him, I barely registered anything aside from his eerie eyes and jagged scar. Unlike men with so-called perfect features, Kian's handsomeness takes time to notice. It isn't because I've learned to see past his weird eyes, prominent scar, slightly crooked nose and gap between his teeth. I'd say that the opposite is true. It takes a fourth or fifth glance to notice that those imperfections are sexy as hell.

Dishes clatter in the kitchen. Edgar, Edith's black Persian cat, stretches out on the wood floor, sunbathing in a square of sunlight reflecting through the window. I'd try to pet him, but the temperamental cat would probably bite my hand off. I think of Batman, my cat back home. I yearn to hold him and stroke his smooth black fur. I wonder if I'll ever see him again.

A few minutes later, Edith reappears, holding a silver serving tray. Tiny blue flowers are painted on the white porcelain tea set. Edith sets the tray on the coffee table and hands each of us a cup of tea.

Warm mug clamped in my fist, spicy steam soothing my sinuses, a pang hits me in the heart. The sweet scent of chamomile brings me back home, late nights sitting at the kitchen table with my mom, sipping tea, laughing and chatting long after the clock struck midnight. Tears well in my eyes. I can't imagine that she's doing well, given that both of her daughters are missing. Clink, clink, clink. My teacup shakes in my hand, clicking against the saucer. I put them both down on the table.

Edith settles in the rocking chair across from us. With her unkempt gray hair, wrinkled nightgown, wild green eyes, and mud-caked feet, she looks like she escaped from an insane asylum. "To what do I owe the pleasure of this visit?"

"I have a problem," Saria says. "That I'm hoping you can help with."

"What is it, dear?"

"I can't figure out how to fly."

Edith takes a sip of tea. "Of course not. There's a curse that prevents you from doing that."

"The curse was reversed," I say.

Edith tilts her head to the side. "Are you sure about that, dear?"

"Well, yes," I say. "A few friends of mine got together to perform the spell reversal—"

Edith bursts into laughter. "Yes, I know. They weren't too far from here. I know everything that happens in these woods."

I turn my palms up, confused. "Okay, so then you know that they broke the curse."

Edith cackles again: a manic, deranged sound. "Oh dear, did you really think that Damian and a few of his minions were any match for the originators of that curse?"

My brow furrows. "I mean, it worked. You've seen me. You know that I can become a crow."

"I know that he's your soulmate, but you shouldn't give Damian credit that he doesn't deserve. That boy has a big enough head as it is. It wasn't Damian or Caliah or any of the others who freed your crow, Zoeli. It was you."

"Me?" I shake my head. "I don't understand. That's impossible."

"It's certainly possible," Edith says. "Think back to that night when they were doing the spell. Where were you?"

"In the dungeon."

"And what were you doing?"

I close my eyes, thinking back. It was so cold, breath white, my back against the frosty stone wall. Back then, my telepathic connection with Damian was wide open. Night after night, I heard him practicing in his head, reciting the chant over and over again. He was as prepared as a person could be. Still, we knew it was a shot in the dark.

I could feel Damian's nervous energy, like an electric current buzzing in our telepathic chain. When he told me that they were starting the reversal, I never wanted anything more. I was ready to get out of that godforsaken hell hole, morph into my God-given crow and soar across the Aurelian sky, free.

I had the entire spell memorized. My lips began to move. "I said the chant backwards," I say aloud.

"There you go!" Edith snaps her fingers. "That's what did it."

"But what about the rest of the spell? There was so much more to it: crystals, herbs and oils, mixing together, boiling in the cauldron."

"Well, perhaps that helped a bit. At least it opened up the process," Edith relents. "But in the end, it was all you, Zoeli.

You're the one who broke the curse, through your own sheer will and power. That's why you can shapeshift, but your mother and sister cannot."

"So, the curse is still intact for me," Saria says, disappointment evident in her tone. "Or maybe I could break it, like Zoe did?"

"Well, I suppose that you could try, dear," Edith says. "But it takes incredible power to accomplish something like that."

"And I'm not strong enough," Saria grumbles. "I get it." She folds her arms across her chest.

"Don't worry, Sar." I place my hand on her shoulder. "We'll find a way." I bite the inside of my cheek, still unconvinced. "I read all of Damian's textbooks," I say. "There was nothing about this."

"That's because the Aurelian leadership doesn't want the people to know how much power they have. It makes them easier to control," Saria says. "When I was Talon's slave I heard a lot of things. There was a witch named Vaeda who used love spells, a crime that is taken very seriously in Aurelia."

Edith shrieks with laughter. "It's only a crime when women do it. Men get away with it all the time. It may be looked down upon, but I've never seen a man brought up on charges. When it's a woman, she's prosecuted to the fullest extent of the law. I remember Vaeda. She was just a kid, only eighteen years old. The little vixen was bewitching all of the most affluent boys and stealing their money. It was quite the scandal. The families were outraged. As a punishment, the Nightingales cursed her with a hideous appearance for twenty years. Poor girl. Whatever became of her?"

"She managed to get a hold of the curse," Saria says. "She performed it in reverse and freed herself, just like Zoeli."

Edith's lips curve into a mischievous grin. "I'm not surprised."

I shake my head. "So, I did it myself?" I say, still not quite believing. "And all this time, Damian made me feel like I owe him something."

Edith guffaws. "Well, that's what narcissists do, my dear. But rest assured, you are not indebted to him in any way. Tied to him in an unbreakable way, yes, just the same as with your twin flame."

"I don't want that," I mutter under my breath. "I don't want to be tied to someone like him." Beside me, Kian studies my face, his eyes wide. Great. Now that he knows that Damian's my soulmate, he'll never trust me. He'll probably kick me out of The Resistance for good.

"Why do you keep calling us twin flames?" Saria asks.

"Because you are, my dear. Two halves of the same flame. You're the orange and gold, the outer part of the flame. With your magic so close to the surface, your greatest talent is your ability to influence others, almost effortlessly."

"I don't want that talent," Saria says. "I want people to like me for me."

"My dear, as you grow older, you'll understand that you have a gift," Edith says. "You'll learn to control it, to turn it on and off at will. You won't use it for personal gain or to make others admire you. You'll subtly nudge people in the right direction when they're unsure of where to go. People will flock to you: moths drawn to a flame. I see you rising into a leadership role, inspiring and helping others who need it the most." Edith takes a sip of tea. "But you must realize that the future is malleable, and no one can truly predict it, not even me. I've seen snippets of all the good you could do, but only if you choose the right paths. Do you understand me?"

"I understand, and I have to thank you, Edith." Saria's voice drops an octave. "Over the years, I've had a difficult relationship with my magic. You've given me hope that I can rectify that, that I can find a way to use my magic and still be genuine."

"Oh dear, don't you ever think that your sparkle makes you any less genuine. My girl, you were born to shine. There's nothing that's more authentically you. Just don't overdo it the way you used to, if you know what I mean."

"I do." Saria smiles, and for the first time in a long time, I get a glimpse of that sparkle that I miss so much. I lace my fingers through hers and squeeze.

"And you." Edith's green eyes meet mine. "You're the blue part of the flame. As you've learned, blue power is harder to access, but the strongest of all. You have power that our greatest leaders of all time have only dreamed of. You're destined for greatness, my dear, but you also must make wise choices."

"I will," I promise. "I'll be very careful in the choices I make." It's a shame that I couldn't pick my own soulmate. Whoever did made a piss poor decision.

I'll fight the pull that Damian has on me as much as I can. For myself. For Aurelia.

CHAPTER 18

Saria

"Thanks for having us," I say. "For all of your wise words and the delicious mac and cheese." I rub my full tummy.

"It was nothing dear." Edith smiles, the crepey skin on her cheeks bunching up like an accordion. "You all be careful now. Get back to Kian's safe."

"We'll be fine, but I worry about you. It isn't safe out here, all alone," Kian says.

"Nonsense." Edith waves a wrinkled hand. "Now get out of here before I smack you."

"Take care of yourself. If you need anything at all, you know my number." Kian kisses the old lady on the top of her head.

The sun is an orange orb in the sky. It won't be long before Red wakes. I can't wait to tell him everything that Edith said. While I'm bummed that I can't shapeshift, I'm super excited about the possibilities for my future.

The four of us trudge through the forest, following Kian's lead. We walk in silence. I stare at the ground, taking care with every step. I avoid branches and pebbles, anything I could accidentally kick or crack. Even the smallest noise could expose us.

The footfalls come out of nowhere. Boots hit the dirt, shaking the ground like a stampede. At least a dozen soldiers race through the trees, machine guns pointed at us. My heart rate jumps to one million beats per minute.

This is it. This is the end. I suck in my last breath. I wish I had more time. I'd hug my mom extra tight. I'd tell Logan how much I miss him. I'd tell Giselle that my life wouldn't have been the same without her. And I'd thank Red, for saving my life in more ways than one. For showing me a passion that I never knew existed. For pouring moonlight on my darkest days.

Bang! Boom! Blam! Blaow! The crack of gunshots sears my eardrums. Kian waves his hand, golden mist escaping his fingertips. The glittering mist acts like a cement wall. The bullets get stuck, screeching to a halt mid-air, inches from penetrating our skin. "How did you do that?" I ask, my mouth falling open.

"A defensive spell." Kian grits his teeth, a vein bulging in his neck. "But those three are trying their best to disarm it."

I follow his gaze. Three Aurelian soldiers are huddled together, each holding a chunk of crystal in their fists. Heads bowed, they chant under their breaths.

Blue comet-like missiles shoot from my sister's palm. She hits four soldiers in the chest, knocking them over. As their bodies thud to the ground, their fingers go slack, loosening their grip on their machine guns. Weapons skitter across the forest floor. One skids to a stop right in front of me. "Get it." Kian points to the gun. "I would, but I can't break my concentration." He talks through clenched teeth, his hair slick with sweat. The golden mist swirls around us, capturing bullets, keeping us safe, but not without immense effort from Kian.

I bend down and pick up the machine gun. It's heavier than I expected. My hands shake as I try to figure out how to hold the damn thing. My lower lip trembles. It's a lot harder than it looks in the movies. I have no idea what I'm doing. I'll probably end up blowing my own foot off. I can't do this.

Keisha takes the gun from my hands. Stance wide, she aims masterfully, shooting three soldiers in the head. I feel useless, unsure of how I can help. More soldiers appear, weaving through the trees. Magic wands are clasped between their fingers, crystal shards pointed our way.

Blue fireballs blast from Zoe's palms, hurling more soldiers to the ground. A few manage to thwart her attacks, waving their magic wands until the blue projectiles change course. Focused ahead, Zoe doesn't notice the soldier sneaking up behind her, machete clamped in his fist. "Zoe!" I scream. I didn't find my sister just to lose her, to stand by and watch her get gutted like a pig. I have to do something. "Zoe!" I scream, but I can't tell if I made a sound over the buzzing in my ears.

Kian turns towards Zoe, eyes widening when he notices the soldier creeping up behind her. The soldier holds up his machete, mere inches from tearing open her flesh.

Kian leaps into the air, launching through space like a superhero. He collides with the soldier, tackling him to the ground. They tumble over and under each other, each fighting for control. The soldier wins, rolling on top of Kian and pinning him down. He plunges his machete into Kian's guts. "No!" My shriek is lost in the cacophony: the boom of gunfire, the whoosh of magical energy, combat boots banging into the dirt.

The magical mist dissipates, our protection gone. I drop to the ground, my belly pressed against the dirt. Bullets whiz inches above me.

This is it. For the briefest moment, Edith had me believing that I could actually do some good in this world. Now we'll never know.

Suddenly, the gunshots stop. All is silent, like I lost my sense of hearing. Maybe I did.

A white spotlight shines down from above. Wow, that was fast. I guess I'm already dead. I imagine it sucking me up like an alien spaceship, transporting me to the afterlife.

"Saria!" My sister's voice interrupts the quiet. Footsteps pound on the dirt. "Saria, are you okay?"

I raise my head, squinting in the bright light. Zoeli stands over me, her aquamarine eyes wide with worry. "Oh, thank God, you're alright." I take her hand, and she pulls me to my feet.

"Saria! Zoeli!" Keisha runs to us, arms open wide, and pulls us into a hug. I hold tight to both of them, my trembling legs threatening to collapse beneath me. "Are we dead?" I ask.

"No, but I think that they are," Zoe says.

The light is blinding. I survey the scene, hands cupped over my eyes like a visor, trying to make out shapes in the white blur. At least twenty Aurelian shoulders are sprawled on the ground: motionless, eyes closed.

Kian staggers towards us. He's hunched over, hands pressed into his stomach. His sweatshirt and jeans are soaked with bright-red blood. Blood drips from his wrist and fingertips, a trail of red droplets following in the dirt behind him.

"Kian, are you okay?" Zoe crouches to examine his wound.

Kian winces. "Eh, it's just a scratch. I'll be fine."

"A scratch?" Keisha raises her brows. "You were butchered by a whole-ass machete."

"We have to get you to a hospital," I say.

"And tell them what?" Kian asks. "That I was traipsing through the forest with Aurelia's most wanted fugitives? That I fought with them against the Aurelian army? I'll be charged with treason and sentenced to death."

"Right," I murmur, feeling stupid. "But you need medical attention."

"I'll put a bandage on when I get home," Kian says. "I'll be alright."

A glowing white orb hovers over us, glittering rays extending from its center like a starburst. "What is that?" Zoe breathes.

Kian stares, open-mouthed. "I have no idea."

"It's a woman," I say. "I saw her in Edith's bathroom." I know it sounds ridiculous. The three of them look at me like I lost my mind.

The orb descends, changing shape as it lowers to the ground. The sphere lengthens, bending and morphing into a woman's curves. Rays of light meld together, forming into arms and legs.

Her gown flutters in the wind, ripples of golden waves cascading down her voluptuous frame. Her skin sparkles when the sunlight hits, like it's embedded with diamonds. Her eyes are like purple gemstones.

She doesn't seem real. Her flesh is like white smoke, as if I reached out to touch her, my hand would glide right through. "Come with me, my children," she says. "I will guide you home."

I guess this is it. We're dead after all. This angel is bringing us to the afterlife. Kian steps forward. "Who are you?" He asks.

"I am the goddess Astrid," the angel says. "I mean you no harm. I only wish to keep you safe."

"Astrid?" Kian's jaw falls open.

"The grandmother of witches," Zoe breathes. I've never heard of Astrid, but my twin's done her homework. While she was hiding in Damian's room, she read all of his history textbooks. Based on her awed expression, Astrid is someone very important.

"Follow me," Astrid says. Cloaked in her light, she leads us through the woods. We trek through the forest, squeezing through bushes and climbing over boulders until Kian's house comes into view.

Kian opens the side door. "So, we're alive then?" I ask. "We're not going to the afterlife?" As we step inside, there's a low chorus of laughter. We're alive. I suck in a greedy breath, grateful for the oxygen pumping in my veins.

"Will you come in for a cup of tea?" Kian asks Astrid. "Or do goddesses not drink?"

Astrid's laughter is the tinkle of wind chimes. "Goddesses do not need food or drink for nourishment, but I certainly can enjoy a bit of flavor on my tongue."

"Come in, then," Kian says. "It would be an honor."

Astrid's bare feet glide across Kian's oak wood floors. "I'm breaking all of the rules today." The goddess sighs.

After showing us to the dining room, Kian and Zoe disappear into the kitchen. At the table, Keisha and I gawk at Astrid's unearthly beauty. She seems more solid now, her skin smooth and glossy like glazed pottery. Her violet eyes are framed by jet black lashes.

Kian and Zoe return. While Kian places a cookie platter and a steaming teapot down, Zoe gives each of us a teacup and saucer. Kian pours Astrid a cup of tea. She raises it to her cherry lips and takes a sip. "It's delicious," Astrid says. "Thank you."

Kian slides into the seat beside her. "Thank you for saving our lives." Astrid stares down at her tea. "Did you, um, kill them?" Kian asks.

Astrid gasps. "No, I would never! I only put them to sleep and erased their memory of the last twenty-four hours. When they wake, they'll have no recollection of what happened. They won't remember seeing any of you." She looks pointedly at Kian.

"Thank you." Kian releases a long breath.

"It's the least I can do, really. After all, I'm the cause of this whole mess."

My brow furrows. "You? I don't understand. Are you involved with DOX?"

"What? No, of course not. Well, not directly." She looks up at the lantern-style chandelier, light from the flame-shaped bulbs reflecting in her glassy eyes.

"Then how are you at fault?" I ask.

"I fell in love with the wrong man." Her shoulders hunch in, like she's ashamed. "When I was a young goddess, I thought that I knew everything. As it turns out, I knew nothing at all. I should've listened to the elders."

Keisha folds her arms across her chest. "I'm lost. I'm going to need you to map this out for me. Like, break it all the way down, because I don't have a clue what you're talking about."

Astrid takes a sip of tea. "I'll start from the very beginning. While gods and goddesses have a separate realm where we spend most of our time, we're also tasked with overseeing the human realm. Mostly, we're restricted from meddling in everyday human affairs, but every so often, we develop an affinity for a particular human. We'll watch over that human, leading to said human referring to us as their 'guardian angel.' But I digress." Astrid squeezes a dollop of honey into her tea. "While fraternizing with humans is discouraged, any type of contact with demons is strictly forbidden. As gods and goddesses, we uphold virtue and integrity, while demons are hedonistic, the antithesis of everything that we stand for. Demons also have their own realm, but they also tend to meander about the human realm, leaving havoc and corruption in their wake." Astrid stirs her tea, swirls of honey and sugar spinning in her cup. "Xaphan was a ladies' man: handsome, charming, charismatic, and a full-blooded demon. He was known for loving and leaving. Over the thousands of years of his existence, it's estimated that he's fathered over a million children with human women."

Keisha raises her hand. "Excuse me? Are you saying that there's humans walking around earth with varying degrees of demon blood?"

Astrid nods. "Many of them. These men and women who have uncanny charisma often rise to positions of power and influence. They're political leaders, CEOs, entrepreneurs, and some of the wealthiest people in the human world. They attribute their success to hard work and intelligence, unaware of the presence of the demon blood in their veins."

"Damn." Keisha shakes her head. "That explains a lot."

"They're one of the main reasons why gods and goddesses must watch over the earth. Although we do our best to stay out of human business, we've thwarted plans that threatened to end mankind more than once." Astrid tucks her hair behind her ears. "There's very specific circumstances where we're permitted to intervene. A certain apocalypse is one of those times.

"I knew all about Xaphan. Unlike the human women, I can't use ignorance as my excuse. I was young and foolish. When he told me that I reformed him, I believed him. As naive as I was, I thought that our love would unite our kinds, that gods and demons would all come together and sing kumbaya." Pain flashes in Astrid's eyes. "But once I fell pregnant, he left me just like all of the others. I was just another conquest, another notch in his belt.

"When I birthed my son, Zamus, he wasn't allowed in my homeland. The Council of Gods determined that he couldn't live in the human realm either. They feared that the melding of goddess and demon blood would produce a creature deeply brutal and immensely powerful, a combination that they deemed dangerous to humans. Instead, the council created a world just for him, a place where he was sentenced to isolation for all of eternity. But even that wasn't enough for the council. To be even more safe, they removed all of the power from his soul, confining it to the volcano later called Mount Zamus.

"And so, I was left to raise my son alone in this new world. I feared that the council was right, that he would grow to be evil and cruel like his father. But as he grew older, I became sure that that wasn't the case. Zamus was smart and creative. Wild at times, but kind and compassionate. He wasn't a danger to others, and he didn't deserve to spend the rest of his existence alone."

Astrid sighs. "A mother's love is unlike any other. And so, I did many things I shouldn't have, and I have since paid the price for my actions. My first offense was bringing animals over from the human realm. The first was a cat we named Pandora, and since she needed something to eat, I brought over birds, mice and squirrels, too. Pandora was Zamus's first companion. When they cuddled, Zamus gently stroking her head, Pandora purring on his chest, I knew that my son was capable of love.

"I taught Zamus to read, write and do math, but I was overcome by guilt. And so, I kept bringing over more playmates: deer, snakes and lizards. The list went on and on. Pandora developed an unlikely friendship with a Komodo dragon we called Puff. One day, the three of them were playing too close to the volcano. Pandora fell in, and Puff jumped in after her, presumably to save her. They were swallowed alive by the lava. Zamus was inconsolable, that is, until a few minutes later, they re-emerged, no longer two creatures, but one. That was the birth of the very first dragoni."

A crease materializes between Zoe's brows. "I didn't see that in the history books."

"And I'd like to keep it that way," Astrid says. "I'm rambling and giving away secrets that I shouldn't. I suppose

I'm just excited to have someone to talk to. It's been years since…" Astrid's voice trails off. "Never mind. But please, understand that most animals who fall in the volcano will simply die a painful horrid death. What happened that day was nothing short of a miracle. Magic I believe was born from the love of those two creatures.

"This information cannot leave this room. If the true origin of the dragoni became widely known, sick minds would conduct experiments on animals, driven by the desire to create a powerful beast. How many innocent animals would boil to death in the lava as a result? And what if they were successful? An animal used as a lethal weapon is not only inhumane, but likely to turn on its creators." Astrid shakes her head, brown waves swaying with the movement. "No, nothing good could come from this secret coming to light. Does everyone understand?"

The four of us nod. "We'll never tell," Zoe says.

Astrid swallows. "As Zamus grew into a young man, his animal companions were no longer enough. I scoured the globe for the perfect woman for Zamus. After years of searching, I found Aurelia, and almost instantly knew that she was the one. She, like Zamus, loved and cared for animals. She, like Zamus, had a sharp mind and a sarcastic sense of humor.

"I broke every rule in the book when I created a portal between the human realm and Zamus's home. I showed him around earth, warning him to keep a low profile. If the gods discovered that he'd left his realm, we'd both pay the price.

"Zamus never knew that I orchestrated his first encounter with Aurelia. As my son was walking down the city street, I hovered overhead, invisible. As we watch over the human realm, we prefer to remain unseen. An observant human may notice us from time to time: a glimmer in the air as they narrowly miss being hit by a bus, an uncanny beam of light illuminating the gangster crouched in the dark alleyway.

"Aurelia walked in the opposite direction, inches from my son, her head down in a book. She was moments from passing him by, unnoticed. I gave her a little shove. She fell at his feet. As he helped her up, she made a self-deprecating joke about her clumsiness, how she must've tripped over her own two feet. Then, their eyes met, and that's how their love story began.

"I told Zamus not to, but after a few months of dating in the human realm, he brought her through the portal. He wanted her to know every part of who he was. The volcano erupted, dousing her in hot lava made from demon's and god's magic. Any other human would've died instantly. Zamus held her in his arms, enveloping her with his love, and miraculously, she kept breathing. The lava soaked into her skin, forever changing her. While she maintained some characteristics of a human, she acquired powers. She lived for centuries, birthing thousands of children before she died of old age. Her children created their own customs and rituals. They learned to use crystals, herbs and chants to access their magic. So, you see, Aurelia created the race known in modern times as witches, and thus, the realm was named after her.

"Now you understand, I created this whole mess. If it wasn't for my foolish liaison, Talon's heart wouldn't be poisoned by demon blood. It was my rebellion and scheming that led all of us here."

"That's nonsense," Kian declares. "You're not culpable for the actions of others. All it takes is one quick look at my eyes to know that I'm chock-full of demon blood, but I still choose to do the right thing. A blood type doesn't make someone evil. It's our actions and our decisions that define who we are."

Astrid snorts. "Tell that to the Council of Gods. According to them, all of the world's most heinous events: wars, genocides, massacres, can be linked back to my decision to sleep with Xaphan. By introducing Aurelia to Zamus, I multiplied Xaphan's bloodline by the thousands."

"It sounds like Xaphan was doing a fine job of spreading his seed around long before you came around," Kian says. "What happened when the council found out? Did they punish you?"

"It was years before they discovered what I'd done. They were furious, of course, but it was too late. They couldn't undo what had been done, and the gods don't believe in violence. They let us be." Astrid rakes her fingers through her glossy brown waves. "I was lucky that they let me off with a warning. In no uncertain terms, they told me that next time, they would take away my powers, contain them like they did to Zamus." Astrid pauses, white knuckles gripping her China teacup. "For thousands of years, I kept to myself. After the way they treated my son, I wanted nothing to do with the gods. I divided my time between here and the human realm, watching and not intervening. Until today. By saving the four of you, I've once again broken the law."

"Didn't you say that you're permitted to intervene in certain circumstances?" Keisha asks.

"This wasn't one of them," Astrid replies.

"But you said that gods can help when a world is in catastrophic danger." Keisha says. "I think the situation in Aurelia would apply."

"They don't care what happens to Aurelia," Astrid says softly. "As far as they're concerned, the rest of the realms would be better off if everyone with even a drop of demon blood was dead. They'll sit back and watch you all kill each other." Astrid taps her fingernails on the table. "My actions today were illegal. If the gods find out what I did, I'll pay the consequences."

"So then why did you?" Kian asks. "Why did you save us?"

"As a goddess, I can see the possibilities for the future. While the future is never predetermined, I'm able to see a version of what could be, depending on how the cards line up. In these glimpses, I've seen the mark that each of you could make on the realms. And even though nothing is certain, after watching you for so long, I have faith that you will play the cards correctly. If I stood by and let them kill you, your decks would be thrown away, along with any chance for you to make the impact that I know you can." Astrid's gaze drifts from Kian to me to Keisha before her purple stare lands on Zoeli. "You, in particular, Zoeli. I've seen what you and Damian—"

"Ugh!" Zoe's hands ball into fists. "Why does his name always come up alongside mine?"

"You already know. Clarity didn't mislead you," Astrid says. "He's your soulmate."

Zoe frowns. "I don't want a soulmate. Especially not him. I want the freedom to choose who I love."

"Not everything is a choice," Astrid says. "Some things are beyond our control."

"Not this," Zoe mutters. I pass her a chocolate chip cookie, but she pushes it away. When my sister declines sweets, something is really wrong. "I'll stay miles away from him if I have to. I won't ever see him again."

Astrid arches a brow. "Most women would be thrilled to have Damian as their soulmate."

"I'm not most women," Zoe responds.

Astrid gives her a patronizing look, like she's an ungrateful child. "He's handsome, wealthy and a prince."

"And a lying, arrogant cheater," Zoe finishes the sentence for her.

"Oh, I see. You're angry at him. You'll forgive him in time. I've seen glimpses of your future together. The two of you will create the most amazing child, destined to achieve magic that we never imagined possible."

Zoe narrows her eyes. "I'm not an incubator for some kind of eugenics project."

Astrid sighs. "That's a vast mischaracterization of what I said, but I can tell that today is not the best time to broach this subject. You'll come around."

"I have free will."

"Of course you do."

"I do," Zoe insists. But her voice rises in inflection, like it's more question than conviction. "I do." Zoe says again, stronger this time.

Astrid's lips curve into a knowing smile.

CHAPTER 19

Zoeli

After Astrid leaves, I need a moment to collect my thoughts. I slip inside Kian's parent's bedroom and sit on the edge of the king-sized bed that Saria and I slept on last night, head in my hands. Ever since Clarity said that Damian and I were made for each other, I've clung to a shred of hope that the waterfall was wrong. But now that Astrid and Edith have both confirmed it, there's no denying it. Damian is my soulmate.

Not only that, it's been predetermined that we're going to have a child together. I'm only seventeen. I haven't put much thought into my future children, but I do know that I want them to have a father who exemplifies courage, compassion and selflessness. I doubt that Damian will ever be that man. Tears prick in the corners of my eyes.

Knock, knock, knock. There's someone at the bedroom door. I wipe my eyes and lift my head. "Come in."

The door cracks open. Kian's white-blonde hair is wet against his skull, the clean scent of a sandalwood soap wafting into the room. "Hey, I hope I'm not bothering you." He clears his throat. "Can we talk?"

I swallow hard. I knew this was coming. I lift my chin, relaxing my features into my best unbothered expression. I'm not mad at Kian. Heck, I can't even blame him. If I was in his position, I'd kick me out too. The enemy is my goddamn soulmate.

Kian hands me a shopping bag. "I found more clothes in Sam's drawers that I think will fit you." He sits beside me on the mattress, bedsprings creaking beneath his weight.

I peek inside the bag. It's full of his sister's clothing: oversized hoodies, baggy jeans, cargo sweatpants. Most of the clothes look like she found them in the men's department. While they aren't quite my style, I'm not in any position to complain. All of my clothes are back in the human realm. My arrival in Aurelia was unplanned: wrists in cuffs behind my back. I arrived at Kian's house with only the clothes on my back.

It's nice of him to send me off with a parting gift. I clutch the bag, plastic crinkling in my fists. "Thanks," I murmur. "And thank you for earlier. For saving my life." I cringe remembering the man behind me, his machete inches from plunging into my back. When Kian intervened, it ended up gashing him instead.

"It's no big deal." Kian shrugs, his lips curving into that boyish grin that once again reminds me of how young he is. He shouldn't be living all alone in this big empty house. What happened to his parents? Where did his little sister go?

"I'm pretty sure saving someone else's life is the definition of a big deal," I say.

Kian's pale skin turns pink and splotchy, his bashful smile twitching at the corners. "I'm not looking for accolades," Kian says. "I came in here to say..." While Kian takes a long breath, I brace myself for what I know comes next. I won't cry or beg. I won't make Kian feel bad. I'll take the news gracefully. "That I'm sorry," Kian finishes his sentence.

"You're sorry?" I repeat, astounded. "What for?"

"For giving you a hard time about Damian." Kian rubs the back of his neck. "I couldn't have been more wrong about you. When I heard about you and Damian, I thought you were just another dumb girl fooled by his looks and charm. But it turns out that the opposite is true. You've managed to defy a soulmate connection, a near impossible feat." Kian's eyes meet mine. At first glance, there's nothing but black dots floating in the white space. I study them until I find the faintest blue ring around his pupils. "So yeah, I misjudged you and I'm sorry about that."

"You're forgiven," I say. "But only because you saved my life." My lips curve into a teasing smile. "So, that's all you have to say? Here I am, worrying that you're going to kick me out of The Resistance."

"Are you kidding me?" Kian brushes silky white strands out of his eyes. "After everything I found out today, I'm even more excited to have you on our team. You single-handedly reversed a decades old curse, proving that you're stronger than seven royals—"

"Edith said that the others might've helped," I cut in.

"She said that if they did, it was marginal," Kian says. "You're a powerhouse, Zoeli. I'm impressed. Impressed isn't even the right word. I'm blown away."

My cheeks are hot. "So, you're not worried that Damian's my soulmate?"

Kian presses his lips together, a crease appearing between his brows. "No. I probably should be, but I'm not. I can tell that your heart is in the right place. You're real tough, too. I don't think anyone, not even a soulmate, could influence you to betray our team. You're your own person. The fact that you're able to resist the pull of your soulmate says it all. You have tremendous strength and character."

"Thank you for saying that," I say. "And for giving me this chance, and for trusting me."

"I still don't trust you around my donuts." Kian jokes.

"And you shouldn't."

"Well, I won't bother you anymore." As Kian stands up, he winces, face contorted in pain, palm pressed against his stomach.

"Oh, Kian," I say. "Let me look at your wound. I can heal, you know? It runs in my family."

"I'm alright," Kian grunts. "It's just a scratch."

"Bullshit." I point to the bed. "Take off your shirt and lay down."

"I'm fine, really," Kian says.

I stand up, hands on my hips. "I said to lay down."

"Healing is hard work. You really don't have to—"

"Shut your mouth and lay your ass down before I blast you with a blue fireball that will make that machete look like child's play."

Kian holds up his palms like he's under arrest. "Alright. Don't shoot." He pulls his hoodie over his head. As he gets comfortable on the bed, adjusting his neck on a fluffy pillow, I study his pale skin. His arms are covered in tattoos, art wrapping around his toned biceps and forearms. While his stomach and chest are untouched by ink, they're disfigured by scars. Raised lines stretch from his abs to his chest bone. I gasp. It looks like he was mauled by a bear. "What happened to you?"

Kian shrugs. "Got in a fight with a lion."

"How did that happen?" I sit beside him, surveying the maze of thickened pink skin. It's a wonder that he survived.

"It's a long story," Kian replies in a clipped tone that tells me that he doesn't want to talk about it.

A white cotton bandage is anchored just above his belly button. "I'm going to have to take this off." As I peel the gauze away, Kian tenses up, white fists gripping the sheets. Underneath, a red, angry wound gapes open, exposing inflamed tissue and a shiny pink membrane that may be part of his intestines. I shake my head. "You call this a scratch? If you bend over, your organs might fall out."

"Is that a problem?"

"Okay, Mr. Tough Guy." I roll my eyes. "I'm going to get started. It might sting at first. If you're really uncomfortable, let me know and I'll tone it down." I summon the healing magic into my hands. I trace the wound, making circles with my fingertips.

Kian sucks in a hard breath.

"Are you okay?" I ask.

Kian nods, his face squished up, eyes squeezed shut. I keep working, knitting the skin together, one cell at a time. A few minutes later, Kian's eyes open. His face relaxes, his breaths slow and steady. "Feeling better?" I ask.

"Yes." His voice is thick. "So much better."

Sweat drips down my back, my muscles aching from the effort. Glittering blue strands lace around my fingertips. I massage the site, relieving the last of the inflammation. "All done," I say, breathless.

I lift my hand. The wound is gone. There's no scar, no redness. It's like nothing ever happened. "Wow." Kian's eyes grow wide, amazed. "That's incredible. Thank you."

I shrug like it was easy even though my head and hands sear with agony, like I took his pain as my own. My gaze drifts past the scars that he clearly does not want to talk about to the tattoos that meld together to cover both of his arms. "I like your tattoos."

Up close, I can make out the individual pictures. I recognize his mother's face from the photos around the house, her blonde hair blowing back beneath a full moon. I study the rest of the designs. A red-and-yellow striped snake coiling around his bicep. A man's big burly hand clasped around the tiny hand of a child. The elliptical eyes, triangular snout, and jagged teeth of a dragoni. A little girl with beige-blonde hair and wide green eyes riding a dragon. A soldier with a wand in one hand, a shotgun in the other. Words in all capitals: **THE RESISTANCE**. And so many more animals: a sparrow, a turtle, a moth, and a duck. It's an eclectic arrangement to say the least.

"They aren't tattoos."

"They aren't?" I raise my brows. "Then what are they?"

"They're soul marks on my skin," Kian says.

"I've never heard of soul marks." I admire the art on his skin, noting the vibrant colors and intricate detail. "What are they?"

"My mom believed that all of the important things are sketched on our souls: every pivotal moment, each meaningful relationship. We remember the big things, but there are so many small things that we may not even realize left their mark, a tiny ripple effect that changes our lives forever." Kian takes a deep breath, his gaze glued to the portrait of his parents on the wall. Embroidered black roses cascade down his mother's wedding dress all the way to the hemline. The strapless sweetheart neckline exposes the colorful designs that cover her arms and shoulders. "My mom decided to take the marks from the inside and wear them on the outside. She created a spell that did just that, and then she encouraged others to do the same. She said that it helped her get to know herself better. She dreamed of a world where everyone was vulnerable and open.

"Her spells even caught the attention of the royal families, but when they tried to replicate them, they failed. Rather than admit their inadequacy, they said it was all a hoax. It was all over the newspapers: Soul marks are a scam. Kinley Reynolds is a fraud who tattooed herself for personal monetary gain." Kian's voice trembles with anger. "It was total bullshit. Before they destroyed her reputation, visitors would stop by asking for customized spells, recipes and advice. She helped a lot of people, and she never charged anyone a dime. And she should have. She didn't make a lot of money working as a store manager at a clothing boutique."

"But you were able to get it done," I say. "Did they call you a fraud, too?"

"It wasn't until after she died," Kian says. "And I never told anyone. I figured they would just call me a liar, too." He stares at his mother's portrait, his eyes glassy.

"How did she die?" I ask. "If you don't mind my asking." There's a long pause where I wonder if he does mind. I can hear my saliva slosh down my throat, breath swishing through my lungs.

Kian never takes his eyes off the portrait on the wall. "Two years ago, my mom was driving home from work. A few drunk teenagers decided to go for a joy ride. They hit her head on."

I put my hand to my lips. "I'm so sorry."

"She should've survived." A vein bulges in Kian's forehead. "Everyone involved in the crash was rushed to the hospital, but the most talented healers were reserved for the arrogant pricks in the other car. While they tended to the prince's superficial scratches, my mother bled to death."

"What?" My jaw falls open. "Are you saying that Damian..." I can't even get the words out. It's too horrible.

"His cousin Colson was driving," Kian says. "Damian in the passenger seat, Austin in the back."

I shake my head. "He never told me..."

"Well, it wasn't his finest moment," Kian says. "He had a concussion and fifteen percent blood alcohol content. I doubt that he remembers much of that night, but I remember every last detail. I remember the fear in my mom's eyes when she coughed and blood spurted from her throat. I'll never forget how helpless I felt as I watched her skin turn gray and the light fade from her eyes. How I screamed for help, but they said that no one was available. How cold and stiff her hands were when she was gone, but I wouldn't let them go. How the hospital staff tried to placate me with their patronizing platitudes, then gaslit me and called me crazy when I called them out for their unlawful practices."

"I am so sorry." The words are thick in my throat. "Did the hospital get in trouble? Did Colson?" I ask, even though I think I already know the answer.

Kian huffs. "Of course not. The king wasn't going to let his son or nephew take the fall. They denied that anyone was under the influence. According to official reports, it was just a tragic accident, and very unfortunate that the hospital was short staffed that evening. They failed to mention that the king ordered three healers to sit by the prince's bedside, monitoring his symptoms as he slept off his hangover. Other healers were occupied by Colson's bruises and Austin's cuts. None of them had life threatening injuries like my mom."

I shake my head in disgust. "There has to be something that you can do."

"There's no proof," Kian says. "Only the nurses who were in their hospital rooms know the truth, and they're too afraid to speak out."

My brow furrows. "But you know," I say. How did Kian uncover details about Damian's health condition, including details like his blood alcohol content? "How did you find out?"

Kian looks away. "I told you I have sources."

"Your advisors?"

Kian reaches for his sweatshirt, but I place a hand on his arm, stopping him. I'm not ready for him to leave, not yet. I point to the little girl riding the dragon on his forearm. She's a lot younger and has much longer hair, but I recognize her eyes. "That's your sister," I say. "Sam."

Kian looks down. "It is. She loves dragons."

"I saw the collection in her bedroom."

Kian's Adam's apple bobs in his throat. "When Sam was thirteen years old, she cut her hair short and would only wear boy clothes. She refused to answer to Samantha. She only wanted to be called Sam." Kian clasps his hands together.

"And on top of that, she was failing school. Her middle school teacher said that she didn't have a magical bone in her body, and she was denied admission to Enchantments Academy. Not long after that, we lost our mom. My sister said that Mom was the only person who truly understood her. She felt like the person who loved her the most was gone."

"She must've been devastated," I say.

"She slipped into a depression. We all did, but Sam took it the hardest. My dad saw his daughter falling apart. Sam was losing weight and could barely get out of bed most mornings. My dad wanted to give her hope for a world where she could be accepted, a purpose for her to keep going, so he threw himself into activism. Together, my dad and Sam organized marches and rallies. At first, their protests focused on demanding equal rights for duds. At that time, Sam wasn't comfortable talking about her sexuality. As word spread about their protests, Sam became more well known and people began questioning her sexual orientation. Some of them were outraged, calling her disgusting or rebuking her as a sinner. But many other people reached out in support, others who were also experiencing same sex attraction and the emotional turmoil that comes along with it."

I nod. "In the US, gay people began to fight for their rights in the 60s. It took a long time and a lot of protesting, but today gay marriage is legal and there are laws that protect LGBTQ people from discrimination. Still, there are plenty of homophobic people who treat LGBTQ people badly."

"Aurelia is way behind the US. Our leaders regard gay people with disdain and revulsion. Transgenderism is a crime. Sam was still exploring her own identity, unsure if she was gay, bisexual, or transgender.

"When people started reaching out in solidarity, sharing their own struggles, Sam was inspired to stand up for them. My dad and Sam coordinated more demonstrations, publicly celebrating gay and transgender people. I went to all of them. It was beautiful to see. People paraded through the streets, signs raised high, chanting love is love.

"Since Sam believed that ignorance was the root of hate, she was passionate about educating others. She created a website. She handed out pamphlets at the protests. Sam envisioned a world where gay people could kiss in public, and where transgender people could get the medical treatment they need. She did everything she could to spread her message far and wide."

"Wow. That's incredible. She's so brave."

"Too brave," Kian says, his lips settling into a firm line. "As the protests became larger and more popular, we started getting death threats. People sent emails and letters. They drove by, screaming obscenities." Kian clenches his jaw. "Sam was so excited when King Keifer Nightingale showed up at our front door. She thought that he'd heard about our efforts and was ready to enact laws to protect marginalized people." Kian shakes his head. "She was so naive."

"What did Keifer do?" I ask.

"He sat on our couch. We made him tea. And then he admonished us. He said that he would not allow the normalization of filthy, deviant behavior. He said that if we didn't stop the protests, we would be sorry."

"That bigoted piece of shit."

"I heard Keifer's warning loud and clear. I wanted them to stop. I knew that Keifer meant business, but my dad wouldn't back down. The movement got bigger and bigger, and then one day, my dad didn't come home from work."

My heart drops into my stomach. I reach out to take Kian's hand. My fingers interlace with his. "Kian, no."

"He just disappeared into thin air." Kian's voice is strangely calm, like he's a reporter reading from a teleprompter. "We searched everywhere. My sister was hopeful, but I already knew what happened. A few days later, they found his body floating in the Nightingale River, a gunshot wound in his head." I gasp, my fingers tightening around his. "It was officially ruled a suicide. Said he couldn't deal with the grief of losing his wife coupled with having a lesbian dud for a daughter." Kian shakes his head, his lip curled in disgust. "My dad never would've killed himself. He was too strong, and he wouldn't have left me and Sam." Kian's voice cracks at the end, his facade crumbling.

"I'm so so sorry," I say. "I don't even have the words…" My voice trails off. "I just want you to know that I care. I do. And I'm going to do everything I can to help you avenge your family."

Kian swallows hard. "Thank you." He stares at the wall, a faraway look in his misty eyes. "Sam and I were orphans. We were also kids going to school full time. My parents made ends meet, but they weren't well off. I had access to their bank accounts, but in a matter of months, we were going to run out of money. We wouldn't be able to afford groceries or property taxes. If I didn't figure something out, we were going to be homeless. Without a high school diploma, my job options were limited. I was terrified, but I couldn't let Sam know that. She already had enough to worry about.

"On top of everything, Sam was being bullied at school. When Sam was friends with Caliah, the bullies showed some restraint. Once Caliah dropped her, they were merciless."

I bite the inside of my cheek. "Caliah's not who I thought she was."

"Sam would walk through the woods to get home from school. One day, she came home crying. Her t-shirt was ripped and—" Kian's nostrils flare. "She told me that scumbag Weston Lyon was waiting for her in the forest. He pushed her against a tree and told her that he was going to show her a good time. He said that when he was done with her, she would turn straight. She tried to get away, but he was older, bigger and stronger."

"Did he—?"

"He tried," Kian cut me off. He touches the dragoni's face on his arm. "But my buddy Orion stopped him. He's the brother of your dragoni friend, the one I saw you petting in the woods."

"Moz," I smile, thinking of the dragoni I named after Mozart because of his beautiful music.

"His name is Zuma, but Moz works, too."

"Oh, I'm sorry. I didn't know he already had a name. I didn't even know that he has a brother."

"Oh yeah, he has three brothers and two sisters," Kian says. "Growing up, Sam and I spent most of our time in the woods. We got to know the whole dragoni family. Zuma is the friendliest, but if you're around long enough, the others will warm up to you." Kian pats the dragoni on his arm again. "Orion can be vicious when he needs to be. When he saw Weston attacking my sister, he crawled right out of the river and took a big ole bite of Weston's leg." Kian chuckles.

"While Weston howled in pain, Sam ran away and Orion slipped back into the river. I wish the bastard would've bled to death." A vein bulges in Kian's neck. I stroke his palm with my thumb. His skin is clammy against mine. "I was so pissed off. I wasn't thinking clearly. I went out looking for Weston. I didn't stand a chance. I only got one hit in before he shifted into a lion and—" Kian looks down at his scars. "And that's that."

I stare at the gnarled skin, the red, jagged cuts, and imagine lion claws digging into his flesh. "It must've been excruciating," I say.

Kian shrugs. "It wasn't too bad."

I meet his gaze. "Liar. You don't have to be a tough guy around me."

Kian's cheeks redden. "I couldn't afford medical care, so they assigned me a low budget healer. Even with the discount, her services drained my bank account. She saved my life, but she couldn't get rid of the scars. You did a much better job."

I admire my own handiwork, running my finger along the unmarred skin where the machete cut open his flesh. "My mom would be proud," I say, and instantly regret it. Because Kian's mom is dead. Even though we're worlds apart, my mom is alive.

In less than a year's time, Kian lost both of his parents. I can't even begin to imagine the magnitude of his grief. It isn't fair.

Damian, my so-called soulmate, never had to worry about paying bills or being homeless. Until I came around, I don't think he ever lost a damn thing in his whole life. And still, they say that we'll end up together, so maybe he'll never really lose anything at all.

If Damian had to face the kind of loss that Kian has, I have a feeling that he'd crumble. But Kian isn't moping around or feeling sorry for himself. He's planning a revolution.

"Queen Taya came to visit me in the hospital," Kian says. "She'd heard about my parents, and she wanted to express her condolences." Kian takes a deep breath. "When I told her about King Keifer's visit and his threats, she was appalled. It was clear that she had no idea what her husband was up to. I could see the disgust on her face as she connected the dots, the pieces clicking together in her mind. She was thinking what I was thinking: that Keifer arranged my father's death." An artery pulsates in Kian's neck. "I told her that my sister and I were going to be homeless, that I had no money and no job. She offered me the prison guard position on the spot, with a starting salary double what senior guards make. It was an offer I couldn't pass up. Taya's even called me a few times since then, just to check in and ask if I'm okay."

"Taya tries, but nothing will ever make up for what her husband did."

Kian snorts. "If she really wanted to do the right thing, she'd kill him in his sleep."

"She's not a killer."

"I wasn't either, until they made me one," Kian says. I look down at his fingers, still interlaced with mine, and wonder what they're capable of. "When I was released from the hospital, I was excited to go home and tell Sam about my new job, but she was gone."

"Gone?"

"She took her duffel bag and some clothes. Border patrol has a record of her crossing the portal that morning."

"She ran away," I say.

"I have no idea where she went. We don't have any family or friends who live in the human realm. I don't even know where to search." Kian looks down. "I'm sorry. I've been going on and on rambling about myself. You must think I'm so rude."

I shake my head. "Not at all. I like learning about you. I can't believe everything you've been through, how much you've overcome, how strong you are."

"I want to learn about you too. I want to hear about your life and where you're from. I've never been to the human realm," Kian says.

I raise my brows in surprise. "Really? Why not?"

"My eyes," Kian says. "I don't exactly blend in with these hideous things."

"I like your eyes," I say.

Kian's cheeks turn pink. "Tell me about you," he says.

So, I do. I tell him about how my sister and I grew up playing in the woods, much like him and Sam. Even from a young age, Saria and I were competitive with each other. We'd race each other up the tallest trees. I describe the feel of bark beneath my palms, the smell of fresh rain mixed with dirt. And how every time I tried to beat Saria at anything, I'd fail, over and over and over again.

Saria was the beautiful twin, the talented twin, the athletic twin, and I was the big ole loser. I admit to being jealous and resentful. I allowed my own insecurities to drive a wedge between myself and my twin sister. I tell him about Chad, the pretty-boy prick who pretended to be interested in me, only to stand me up and post it for all of the internet to see. Later on, when Saria started dating Chad, I couldn't look at her in the same way.

I tell him about all of the people who are most important to me. I talk about my mom, her job at the hospital and how she risked her own ass to save patients with her healing magic. I tell him about my dad, his tech skills and wild inventions. I go on and on about Yaz, my best friend and the lead singer of our band, The Exiled Crows. I tell him about the rest of the band: our drummer, Scott, and bass guitarist, Justin. I tell him all about my guitar, how I'd spend hours locked in my room practicing chords and finger techniques.

And then, as I get closer to the present, I tell him about Damian, how he pulled to the side of the road in his SUV when I was walking home from school. Even as I was turned off by his arrogance, I felt an inexplicable pull towards him, something I'd never felt before.

I tell him how Damian brought me to Enchantments Academy, and the body scan that revealed my store of blue magic. I tell him about Uncle Talon's threats, how they ultimately culminated in a battle at the portal. After I fought for Aurelia, the king clasped handcuffs behind my back and dragged me, my mom and my sister to the dungeon.

I go on and on and on, but Kian doesn't seem to mind. He nods at the right times, asks questions that show he's really listening, and seems genuinely interested in everything I have to say. It's like the floodgates opened, and there's no stopping me now. It's been so long since I've had someone to talk to. I didn't even realize how badly I needed this.

I tell him about where I've been since I escaped from the dungeon: how Damian lied to me about the nature of his relationship with Caliah, how I left him and lived in the trees amongst the birds.

"And now you know more about me than most of my best friends," I say.

"So do you," Kian says. "But that's because I don't have any friends."

CHAPTER 20

Saria

As I tell Red about our day, the worry lines seep into his skin: wrinkles etched into his forehead, creases between his brows. "You could've been killed."

"I had Zoe, Keisha and Kian to protect me."

"But they failed." Red's blue eyes blaze. "If Astrid hadn't shown up—"

"But she did," I cut him off. "And I'm fine."

"I wish I was there. The worst part about being a vampire is being dead all day. For years, I've yearned for the daylight, the warmth of the sun on my skin. But now, there's so much more. There's you. I want to be with you to protect you. But I can't, and that kills me."

"Besides missing the sun, do you like being a vampire?" I ask.

"I love it," Red says. "There's so many benefits: never aging or getting sick, rarely feeling pain, gaining immense power and strength overnight, and each year, getting even stronger. I have the privilege of limitless time: years upon years to travel the world, acquire endless knowledge, and accrue exponential wealth. I live a great life. I know how lucky I am."

"So, you wouldn't change it?" I ask. "If you could go back in time and do it over, would you still become a vampire?"

"Well, I wasn't given a choice," Red says. "But if I could go back, knowing what I know now, I wouldn't change a thing." Red raises his brows. "Why do you ask? Are you thinking of changing over?"

"Maybe," I admit. "It would make me a lot stronger. You say that you're worried about my safety." More than that, it would mean that Red and I could be together, but I don't say that part out loud.

Red shakes his head, his lips a grim line. "You know, Amos gave me hell about our kiss when we left last night. And maybe he was right, with you getting crazy ideas in your head about becoming a vampire."

I fold my arms across my chest. "What's the problem? You admit that you like being a vampire. That you prefer it."

"The problem is that you would be giving up having children, having your own family one day."

"You had to give that up, too."

"The tradeoff ended up being worth it for me."

"Maybe it would be worth it for me, too!" Yet, deep down, I know that he's right. I do want to be a mom one day. I just can't imagine doing that with anyone but him.

"You're too young to make that decision," Red says, running his fingers through his thick black hair.

"You were the same age as me when you changed over," I say, but the determination is gone from my voice.

"Sari, I didn't choose this life."

"What happened?" I ask. "You never told me the story."

Red sucks in a deep breath. "It was the middle of the night and we were all asleep: my mom and dad, me and my older brother." Red swallows. "It was summertime. Air conditioning didn't exist back then. It was hot and sticky outside. The windows were wide open. They climbed right inside. They killed all of us. Drained us dry."

I feel the blood drain from my face. "Red, oh my God."

"It seems that one of the vampires had a moment of moral quandary, because he turned back as the others left. He stood over me, and I heard him say, 'He's just a kid.' As I took my last real breath, the vampire took a knife from his own pocket and sliced his own wrist. I was flying down a tunnel, heading for the light, when suddenly I was jerked back into my own body. When I came to, the vampire had his wrist to my mouth, his blood dripping down my tongue and into my throat. He told me to drink. I was inexplicably thirsty, my mouth dry like the desert, so I drank and drank and drank until everything started to ache. My muscles were sore. My head hurt. As I lost consciousness, the vampire told me that the pain would only last a few hours, and that I needed to hide in a totally enclosed shelter before the sun came up. I never saw him again. I woke up in a puddle of blood, my dead family members lying next to me."

"I'm so sorry." I slide closer to him on the brown leather couch. I wrap my arms around him, and rest my head on his shoulder.

"I struggled with PTSD for years. I wished that I had died along with them. There were so many times that I almost walked out into the sun. I still don't understand why they did it. Was it just a random attack?" Red wrings his hands together. "Was there a reason that they targeted my family?"

"I can't imagine that your family did something to piss off a group of vampires."

"Me either." Red shrugs. "But I guess I'll never know."

I lift my chin, my mouth inches from his. It was only last night, but it feels so long ago since his lips touched mine, since electricity raced through my veins.

Red turns away. "I'm hungry. I have to go feed."

I don't let him go, my arms tightening around his waist. "Drink me," I say. I tilt my neck, my jugular just below his mouth. He licks his lips. His breath is hot on my neck.

He pulls away. "Sari, I can't." He wriggles out of my embrace. "There's plenty of animals in the forest. I won't kill them. I'll just take a little."

I pull my knees to my chest, my face hot with humiliation. Rejection stings.

"You don't want to be a slave to this blood lust, Sari. You don't want this life."

"Don't tell me what I want." His footsteps click down the hallway. The front door squeals open and clicks shut.

I put my head between my legs, panting. I'm already a slave, just not to blood lust. I'm a slave to my desire for Red.

CHAPTER 21

Zoeli

Two months later

I shuffle down the hallway, stretching my arms overhead. As I enter the kitchen, the aroma of sizzling grease and meat makes me salivate. Kian uses a spatula to push eggs and bacon around the griddle. The toaster pops. The coffee machine whirs as my favorite caffeinated beverage trickles into the carafe. "Kian, I told you that I was going to cook breakfast this morning." I put my hands on my hips in mock anger.

Kian shrugs, a sheepish grin on his face. "You were sleeping, so I decided to get started."

"Get started? It looks finished to me." I point to the dining room. "Go sit down and relax. I'll plate our breakfast."

"I can help."

"Get out of here," I demand.

"Alright, alright." As Kian leaves the room, I take four dishes out of the cupboard. I spoon a hearty portion of eggs and bacon, and a slice of toast onto each plate.

I'm mad at myself for sleeping in. Since Saria, Keisha, and I moved in, I worry that we're not pulling our weight. Since we're in hiding, we can't exactly get jobs and contribute financially. Every time I try to cook or clean, Kian seems to beat me to it. Even though he never complains, I can't help but feel guilty that I'm not chipping in.

As I place their plates on the table, Saria strolls into the dining room, rubbing her eyes. Keisha is not far behind her, yawning as she grabs a cup of coffee. "It smells delicious in here."

The doorbell rings. I skip down the hallway, peer through the peephole, and crack open the front door. "Hi, Garth. Come on in. You're just in time for breakfast. I'll make you a plate." Garth, a master sorcerer and expert physicist, spends almost all of his free time in Kian's basement, working on the bomb that combines both magic and science, a weapon that can crush buildings while sparing innocents.

"Thanks, Zoe." Garth follows me to the dining room, pushing his glasses up the bridge of his nose. Even though he's around my parents age, he has no wife or kids, having dedicated his life to science.

We gather around the dining room table. Over the past couple of months, we've become like a family, settling into predictable routines. Today begins just like any other of Kian's days off: with a hearty breakfast.

Afterwards, Garth will disappear downstairs, where he'll spend hours focused on building the bomb that could end this war. While Garth scribbles quantum physics equations and spell ingredients on a white board, Keisha, Saria and I will work out together: alternating between squats and deadlifts on leg days, and barbell curls and tricep extensions on arm days. Even as we grow our supernatural abilities, it's still important that we maintain peak physical condition.

After a quick shower, I'll spend the rest of the day with Kian: strategizing military tactics, planning missions, and honing our defensive and offensive spell skills. Lately, we've also been learning how to pick locks, practicing both magical and non-magical methods. Sometimes, Saria will join us, but often, she naps. Most of the time, she stays up all night with Red, so she's exhausted during the day. She tells me that they're working through the night, practicing their battle skills, but I'm not so sure. When I woke up in the middle of the night to use the bathroom, I caught them dancing around the living room, heads thrown back in laughter.

Keisha has taken a special interest in Garth's project. She's become his self-appointed assistant. After a hard day's work, she'll run upstairs, excited to describe the intricacies of creating an explosion that can supersede the protective spells surrounding Hadrien's sleeping quarters. I'll smile and nod, impressed by her enthusiasm. If I'm being honest, I don't have a clue what she's talking about. Science was never my strong suit.

Zoe!

Ugh, for the past few days, Damian won't stop bothering me. I keep erecting my shields, and then he finds new ways to blast through them.

Leave me alone.

Zoe, I need to talk to you. It's important.

I've heard that before. I'm not coming back to you, Damian. Give it up.

This isn't about that. Zoe, please, listen to me. The desperation in his voice makes me take a pause.

Alright. What is it?

Remember how I told you that Talon didn't want to do anything drastic early on? He worried that making changes before gaining the trust of the populace could trigger rebellions.

Yes. I was relieved that we had a little time.

Time's up. Something very bad is going to happen. I want you to know that I did everything I could to stop it. I tried.

What's going to happen?

Promise me that you won't do anything stupid.

Tell me what's going on, Damian.

I don't want to tell you like this. Come over so we can talk in person.

Nice try.

You don't miss this? An image appears in my mind: Damian and I laying in his bed, arms wrapped around each other, legs twisted in his silk sheets.

I groan. Goodbye, Damian.

Zoe, wait!

I put up steel walls, coating them with a rock-like substance, thicker and thicker, drowning him out until he's gone.

CHAPTER 22

Saria

Ever since my wrongful imprisonment and subsequent kidnapping, I have good days and bad days. On good days, I feel almost normal: grateful to have a warm place to sleep, thankful for my sister's safety, hopeful for the future. My mind is quiet, my thoughts coherent.

Difficult days range in intensity: bad, worse or worst. In the first kind, my heart and mind race faster than a runaway train. I feel short of breath, my palms clammy. I worry about everything and everyone: my parents, if I left the coffee pot on, my friends back home, the end of the world.

On worse days, I have a hard time getting out of bed. I force myself to go through the motions, a fake smile plastered on my face. The worst moments replay in my brain like a carousel: guards spitting at me, teeth chattering on the dungeon floor, Gio slamming my head into the living room wall, Talon whipping me to a bloody pulp because his dinner was five minutes late.

The third type is a living nightmare. I slip in and out of reality, unsure what's real and what's imagined. Sometimes, I believe that I was never released from Nightingale Dungeon, that everything that's happened since then was invented by my mind, that I've actually been withering away in a cold cell all this time. My flashbacks are so vivid that it's impossible to tell what's real. One minute, I'm laughing in Kian's living room, the next minute, I'm in a dark forest tied to a tree, ropes burning my wrists, Licinia cackling as I struggle to break free.

Today is one of the worst days yet. Zoe watches me, a worry line between her brows. She asks me if I'm okay. I force a smile and say I'm fine. Her eyes narrow as if she doesn't believe me, but she lets it go.

Even though it's mid-afternoon, I crawl back into bed. Sleep is my only escape from the chaos in my mind.

"Sari?" I open my eyes, just a crack. Moonlight streams in through the window. Red stands over the bed, a fitted black t-shirt stretched across his muscular chest. He runs a finger along my cheek. My skin tingles from his touch. "Wake up, sleepyhead."

My lips curve into a smile. "Is it nighttime already?" I stretch my arms overhead and sit up in bed.

His eyes meet mine, glistening like blue topaz. "Sari, is everything okay? Zoe said you seemed off today."

I don't have the energy to lie. Red will see right through me anyway. "It was a rough day," I admit. "Lots of flashbacks. My heart was racing so fast I thought it might explode."

Red runs his fingers through my hair. "How are you feeling now?"

"Better," I say. "My body feels calm, but…" I take a long breath. "I'm sad, you know? I'm homesick. I miss my parents, my friends, my bedroom, and going to school. Heck, I even miss doing homework. Just the normalcy of life back home." I move closer to Red, my shoulder brushing against his. "I'm sorry that I got you caught up in this whole mess."

"Are you kidding me?" Red puts his arm around my shoulders. "The day you walked into my office was one of the best of my whole life."

I laugh. "Yeah, I'm sure the day I showed up out of nowhere asking you, a perfect stranger, to rescue my prisoner sister from an Aurelian prison, thereby pulling you into an inter-realm war between a corrupt government and a brutal terrorist organization beats watching the northern lights from an igloo in Finland or climbing to the peak of Mount Everest," I say, citing examples from Red's travel stories.

"It was." There's no sign of sarcasm in his tone, but I still laugh. "I'm serious," Red says. "Because you weren't there."

"Stop it," I say, even though the last thing I want him to do is stop. If I wanted to be honest, I would say, 'Tell me more,' but the last thing I want is to be rejected. Again.

"What can I do to cheer you up?" Red asks.

"I can think of a few things." It slips out before I can help myself.

"Sari." Red sighs. "You know that I can't do that."

"Can't? Or don't want to?" I fold my arms across my chest, my cheeks burning red with embarrassment. I should've just kept my damn mouth shut.

"You think that I don't *want* to?" Red's brows shoot up. "Are you out of your damn mind? You're the most beautiful woman I've ever seen. There's nothing I want more." Red stands up, pacing back and forth across the room. "We can't do this. I'm a vampire. You're not. There's no future for us together."

"I might not have a future at all! There's a price on my head. The High Ruler of Aurelia wants me dead. If I'm killed tomorrow, I'll never know what it feels like to have the one thing that I want more than anything."

"What do you want?" Red asks.

I groan. "Do I really have to spell it out for you? I want you. Y- O- U."

Red walks towards the door. Great. He's leaving. I scared him away. Again.

He puts his hand on the doorknob. And then he twists the lock.

Red turns back around. His blue eyes blaze with desire. "I can't resist anymore."

I bite my upper lip. "Blame your underdeveloped brain."

In a flash, he's on the bed. When his mouth touches mine, it's electric.

CHAPTER 23

Zoeli

I can't sleep. Part of the reason could be that I'm stuck on the couch since Red and Saria locked me out of the bedroom.

But it's more than that. Damian's words keep echoing in my mind, twisting my gut. *Something very bad is going to happen.* What could it be? Was it a ploy to get me to come over? With Damian, I never know.

Leather cushions squeal as I roll back and forth. The clock on the wall tells me that it's 2 AM. Keisha and Kian went to bed hours ago. Red and Saria are probably still awake, but I'm not going to interrupt them.

I need some fresh air to help clear my head. In a flash of blue, I become a crow. I squeeze inside the fireplace, climb up the chimney, and soar into the night sky. Above the trees, wind whipping through my feathers, I soar through the stars.

It can't be more than twenty degrees, but I barely feel the cold. This is the only time I get to be free.

I fly to the Azula Sea, home of the merkind, and one of my favorite places in Aurelia. The surface is like glass, glossy and smooth. A pink frog jumps from one lily pad to the next: sploosh, splosh, splish. A dragonfly whizzes past.

I wait ten minutes, perched on a bough, but there's no sign of her. I spend another five minutes gliding in circles, hoping she appears. I'm just about to leave when I see her. She shimmies up onto her favorite boulder, her white hair slick against her back. She's absolutely exquisite: purple eyes framed by long white lashes, clear copper skin, a long green tail that covers her bottom half, shining like emeralds.

She sprawls out on the rock, basking in the moonlight. A few minutes later, another merkind, the boy who looks so similar to her, pops his head out of the water. I don't understand their language, but I can tell from his tone that he's angry. After a few back and forths, she slides off the rock and slips into the water.

I've been out for over an hour. I guess it's time to go home, well, Kian's house. I should try to get some sleep. I fly over the trees, heading back to Kian's, when something peculiar catches my eye.

On the ground, someone with snow-white hair weaves through the trees, their boots crunching the leaves on the ground. I alit on an old oak tree, hidden by the mass of tangled branches. I lean forward, peering at the familiar person down below.

My eyes confirm what I already suspected. It's Kian. Why is he wandering through the woods in the middle of the night?

A bunny hops towards Kian, dried leaves scattering in its wake. Kian reaches down, his palms cupped together. The bunny climbs into his hands, ears upright. Kian lifts him to his face, nose-to-nose with the bunny. Kian makes a sound with his throat. The bunny clucks and grunts.

A crow swoops down, circling Kian's head before landing on his shoulder. Kian turns to the crow, whistling under his breath. The crow makes a coo-like noise. The bunny responds with a clicking sound, like the three of them are having a conversation.

What the heck is going on here? The crow is an ordinary crow, not a shapeshifter, not that that would explain what's happening here anyway.

My mind stirs into overdrive. That night at Nightingale Palace, the night I kissed Damian, I saw a crow in the ducts. Is it possible that the crow stuck around, peering through the vents into Damian's bedroom?

I remember that day in the forest when Kian scooped up that white rabbit. The rabbit wiggled its nose and made clicking sounds, just like tonight. Shortly thereafter, Kian decided to change course.

I connect the dots. It seems impossible, but the evidence is right in front of me. I think I know who Kian's advisors are.

* * *

I pace back and forth in Kian's living room, watching the clock. It's almost 4 AM, and he's still not home. How long can he chat with a bunny and a crow?

The glare of headlights slice through the living room window. A heavy vehicle rumbles by. Moments later, more headlights shine through the glass. I peer through the blinds, curious who's driving around at this hour.

At least a dozen oversized vans drive in procession: tinted windshields, no windows, dark gray exteriors blending into the night. The ground shakes, like a mini earthquake. My heart drops into my stomach. I'm not sure what's inside those vans, but my gut tells me that it's not anything good.

I collapse onto the couch, sinking into the leather cushions. The reckless part of me wants to get up, follow those vans, and find out what's going on. Damian's voice echoes my mind, *Promise me you won't do anything stupid.* "I will make no such promises," I say aloud to myself. But I'll admit that going out tonight probably isn't the best idea. I'm alone, tired, and unprepared.

When Kian gets home, I'll talk to him and we'll figure out a plan. Together. It seems like Kian and I do almost everything together lately. Not that I'm complaining. He's quickly becoming one of my favorite people.

The side door squeals open and clicks shuts. I can hear Kian's boots: clank, clank, clank down the hallway. He appears in the archway between the hallway and the living room. His eyes widen when he sees me. "What are you doing up?" Kian holds a dragoni against him, the creature's head resting on his shoulder.

I ignore his question, my jaw falling open. "Moz?" The dragoni twists his head around, his triangular-shaped eyes meeting mine. He wriggles out of Kian's arms, dropping to the floor. He scurries to me, wagging his tail. "Hey, buddy." I stroke his head, my fingers buried in his black fur. I rub behind his elf-like ears. He sings: the rich tones of a piano merged with a heart-piercing violin. I look up at Kian. "Why is he here?"

"It isn't safe for him out there. His brothers and sisters were taken by men in royal blue uniforms. Aurelian soldiers. Men who answer to Talon and Keifer." Kian's eyes are misty.

I gasp. "Why would they do that?"

"Ignorance, I imagine," Keifer grumbles. "There are myths about dragonis: that they can spit fire, that you can train them to fight your enemies, that their blood contains a magical elixir that you can drink to become more powerful. These falsehoods make dragonis appealing to our power-hungry leadership. They'll find out the truth soon enough, but not before they capture, cage and abuse every last living dragoni." His fists clench at his sides.

Moz rolls onto his back, showing off the yellow scales on his belly. I caress his stomach, the dragoni purring with pleasure. "How did you know?" I ask.

"Know what?" Kian asks.

"That Moz's brothers and sisters were taken by Aurelian soldiers."

"Well, they're gone," Kian says. "I looked, but I couldn't find them anywhere."

"You said that they were taken by men in royal blue uniforms," I say. "You were very specific about it."

Panic flashes in Kian's eyes as he realizes his mistake. "I was just assuming." He looks away, his gaze fixed on the wall. "What are you doing awake?"

"I couldn't sleep," I say. "I went out for a while, just flying around to clear my head. I saw you, Kian."

"You saw me," he repeats, tapping his fingers on his jeans. "I couldn't sleep either. I went for a walk."

"I saw you with the bunny and the crow," I say.

Kian shrugs, then looks down at his hands. "I like animals. What can I say?"

"You were communicating with them."

Kian barks out a laugh. "That's ridiculous."

"I know what I saw, Kian."

Kian picks at his fingers, his gaze fixed on a hangnail.

"I want you to know that I didn't go out looking for you. I thought you were in bed. I'm sorry if I invaded your privacy. To be fair, your animal friends have been following me around and reporting back to you, so I think we're even."

"I didn't tell Shadow to follow you," Kian retorts. "I only told him to check on what's happening in the palace. I had no idea that you were even there."

"Shadow?" I raise my brows. "Is that the crow?"

Kian's pupils meet mine. "Zoe, promise me that you'll never tell anyone about this."

"I promise." I say, zipping my thumb and pointer across my lips and then twisting them, miming the turn of a key. "But I don't understand why it's such a big secret."

"I have a very rare ability," Kian says. "When I was a kid, my mom asked Edith to consult her crystal about it. Edith warned us to never tell a soul. There are many people who would view my gift as a threat."

I wrinkle my brow. "Why's that?"

"I have access to all of their secrets. There's always an animal around: a mouse lurking behind the walls, a turtle camouflaged between mud and rocks, a tiny white moth lingering on the ceiling of a private hospital room, a moth that can report the prince's condition, blood alcohol content, and the number of talented healers idling by his side while my mom bleeds to death a few doors down."

"Oh my gosh." I take a step closer to Kian. His arms are covered up now, but I remember the moth on his arm.

"They say ignorance is bliss," Kian says. "There are things I wish I never knew. Things that keep me up at night."

"Maybe, but not knowing the truth doesn't change the truth."

"Yeah, but it would hurt less."

"If you weren't strong enough to handle it, you wouldn't have been given this gift," I say. "If you didn't know what you know, you never would've started The Resistance. You're going to save the world, Kian Reynolds."

Kian's lips curve into that sheepish smile. "Save the world? I don't know about that. I'm not as tough or strong as you seem to think. Ask Weston Lyon."

"A non-shifter fighting a lion isn't exactly fair," I retort. "And don't you tell me you're not tough. I saw that stab wound you were walking around with, acting like it's no big deal. I'm sure that Weston would be crying like a baby."

Kian shrugs, his cheeks blotchy with pink spots. "I guess." He's as modest as Damian is arrogant.

I just want to be closer to him. I take another step forward, and then another. Moz rubs his cheek against my leg. "Look, you already saved this guy. Next, you're going to save the whole damn world. Mark my words."

Kian looks at the dragoni. "I was too late to rescue Orion and the others," he says wistfully. "But I'm glad I got Zuma. I know he's your buddy, too."

"Zuma," I repeat. "I'm going to have a hard time getting used to that."

"You don't have to," Kian says. "He likes that you call him Moz. He said it's your special nickname for him. He's quite fond of you."

I take another step closer. "He said that?" I ask.

Kian nods. "Sure did."

I take one more step. "I think that it's really cool that you can talk to animals." He's so much taller than me. I crane my neck to look up at him. His breath is hot on my face. He dips his chin, his mouth mere centimeters from mine. I close my eyes, my lips tingling in anticipation.

As Kian pulls away, he mumbles something under his breath. His warmth is replaced by an icy draft that chills me to the bone.

I open my eyes. Kian is already halfway down the hallway. "What did you say?" I ask.

"I can't compete with Damian, even if he wasn't your soulmate." Kian yanks open his bedroom door. "Goodnight, Zoeli."

I have so much to say, but the words are stuck in my throat. I want to tell him that when it comes to integrity and character, he's got Damian beat by miles. If he's looking for an objective measure, Kian would demolish Damian on any IQ test. Besides Kian's intelligence and work ethic, he gets sexier to me every day.

I'm not sure if I should say it or not. After all, he isn't wrong about the soulmate thing. I don't know what the future holds, but Astrid says that I'm to be the mother of Damian's child. How long can I fight a destiny that was predetermined by the gods?

Before I can decide, Kian closes the door.

It's probably better this way. We have a mission to focus on. According to Damian, something very bad is about to happen. Romance would be an unnecessary distraction.

I lay back down on the couch, pulling a chenille blanket to my chin. Moz curls up next to me. He sings a soft, relaxing melody. His song lulls me to sleep, his fur like a silk scarf against my neck.

CHAPTER 24

Saria

One Week Later

Beep. Beep. Beep. I peer inside the oven. The roast is browning nicely, a delicious aroma wafting into the kitchen. "The meat is almost done," I say. "Just a few more minutes." I reset the timer for five minutes.

At the stovetop, Zoe stirs milk and butter into a pot of mashed potatoes. She spoons a mouthful of potatoes into her mouth. "It needs a little more salt." She sprinkles in some salt, and then takes another spoonful. "Mmmm. That's yummy."

"Hey!" Keisha grabs a stack of plates from the cupboard. "I see what you're doing. Don't act like you're doing a taste test and then hog the mashed potatoes." Keisha teases.

Zoe drops her spoon. "Guilty."

As Keisha and Zoe set the dining room table, I wipe down the countertops. Layal leans against the kitchen island, her fire-engine red hair tied up in a messy bun. An original member of The Resistance, Layal seems to feel comfortable popping up at Kian's house unannounced. When she dropped by and smelled something cooking, she invited herself to dinner. "It's been awhile since I've had a sit-down dinner," Layal says. "Usually, I just grab a snack from the fridge and eat in my bedroom."

I raise my brows, surprised. "Don't you live with your parents?"

"Unfortunately," Layal drawls. "For another two hundred eighty-five days. Then, I'm outta there."

"Two hundred eighty-five days?" I ask.

"Until my eighteenth birthday," Layal explains. "And then I'll move out and hopefully never see those shitheads again."

"I'm sorry to hear that." I can't imagine a world where I could eat dinner with my family every night, but would choose not to. I'd give anything to take a bite of my mom's homemade lasagna, to hear her soft voice, to laugh at one of my dad's corny jokes. My eyes brim with tears, blurring my vision.

Layal shrugs. "So, how's it going with you and Red?" She wiggles her brows. "I swear, I have never seen two people look more pathetically in love." She says it like she's vomiting. Layal once told me that her humor is an acquired taste. I don't think I've gotten there yet.

"It better be good," Zoe says. "I haven't been sleeping on the couch for nothing."

I laugh. "It's not good. It's phenomenal." Even phenomenal doesn't cut it. It's mind blowing. Out of this world. I try not to think about the future, and just enjoy what we have in the now.

As Zoe puts down the last glass, her brow wrinkles. "Kian should've been home by now."

The timer dings. When I open the oven, heat warms my face. I stab the roast with a meat thermometer, red juices streaming from the place it was pierced. The digital screen reads 145 degrees. "The roast is done," I announce.

Zoe paces back and forth across the kitchen. "Where is he? He's never this late."

Layal cocks one eyebrow, her foxlike eyes lighting up with amusement. "Saria's not the only twin who's in love," Layal drawls, stretching out the word love.

Zoe's cheeks redden. "It's not like that. Kian's my friend. I'm just worried because he's late. That's all."

Layal smirks. "You're not fooling anyone, but you are wasting your time. Kian's not interested."

Zoe purses her lips. "How do you know? Did he say something to you?"

"You seem awfully concerned for someone who's just a friend." Layal cackles.

Annoyance flashes in Zoe's eyes. "What's your problem, Layal?"

Layal shrugs. "Just calling a spade a spade. You're into him, but Kian doesn't even care that girls exist. Lord knows, I've tried a few times. He's completely oblivious."

"You think he's not into girls?" Keisha asks.

"I don't think he's into anyone," Layal says. "Even back in school, he was a loner. He didn't really have any friends, and didn't seem to want any either. He prefers to keep to himself." Layal clasps her hands together. "What about you, Keisha? Has anyone caught your eye?"

Keisha and I exchange a look. As far as I know, Keisha isn't crushing on anyone, but if she was, Layal would be the last to know.

"No, but I do miss my book boyfriends," Keisha says. I smile, remembering long summer days down the Jersey Shore: Keisha lounging on a beach chair, her brown skin glistening in the sun, her nose in a book. Every so often, she'd lift her head to gush about Xaden or Mr. Darcy or whichever leading man she was swooning over at that moment.

Layal bursts into laughter. "Book boyfriends? You've got to be joking. Do people actually develop emotional attachments to fictional characters?

"You obviously haven't been reading the right books," Keisha retorts. "Your loss."

The front door squeals open. Zoe darts out of the room, and I follow. Kian shuffles inside, a ginormous pine tree hoisted over his shoulder. He drops the tree in the middle of the living room.

"What's that?" Layal asks.

"A Christmas tree," Kian says.

"Christmas?" Layal wrinkles her nose. "We don't celebrate Christmas in Aurelia."

"We don't, but the girls do." Kian tilts his head towards me, Zoe and Keisha. "And maybe I'll start. I'm excited to learn more about it."

A huge smile on her face, Keisha helps Kian lift the tree into its stand. Crouching down, Keisha tightens the bolts until the tree stands up straight. The scent of fresh pine triggers a montage of memories: Dad lifting me up to put the gold star at top of our tree, Zoe and I singing Christmas songs as we wove strings of lights through the branches, on Christmas Eve, Mom and I mixing up the dough and spooning the batter onto a cookie tray, baking delicious homemade cookies for Santa, and Christmas Day, sprinting downstairs at the crack of dawn, finding presents piled up around the tree.

Zoe holds her hand by her heart. "Kian, you didn't have to do this."

His eyes meet hers. "You said that you're sad about missing Christmas. I know this doesn't make up for not being home, being trapped here and everything else, but I hope it makes your season a little more jolly holly."

Zoe laughs, her eyes never leaving his. "It's holly jolly, but good effort." For a few moments, they just stare at each other. They smile at each other like fools. The way that Kian's gazing at Zoe right now, I think that Layal's dead wrong. Kian's attracted to Zoe, he just doesn't know what to do about it.

I run my fingers along a branch, pine needles raking against my palm. "Do we have any decorations?"

Kian's lips curve into a playful grin. "That's my next surprise. I'll be right back." His footsteps disappear down the hall. The front door opens and shuts. Kian reappears holding a big cardboard box. On the side of the box, Crowe is scrawled in black permanent marker.

My jaw falls open. "Is that what I think it is?" Kian slides the box onto the floor. Zoe and I kneel beside it. We sift through the ornaments, most of them personalized or homemade. My fingertips trace a cardboard snowflake, hand-decorated by blue glitter and silver rhinestones. On one of its ribs, I signed my name, *Saria, Age 8.*

Zoe holds up a ball-shaped ornament, another arts-and-crafts project that left a mess on our dining room table. We peer through the see-through plastic into the scene inside.

White cotton is spread out along the bottom like snow. White poms-poms form a snowman, and green construction paper is cut into a tiny Christmas tree. Zoe looks up at Kian, her eyes wet. "How did you get this?"

"I made a pit stop at your parent's house."

Zoe gasps. "But we talked about that. We said it wasn't safe, that Talon's men could be watching, waiting for me or Saria to come home. If anyone saw you…" Zoe's voice trails off.

"Don't worry," Kian says. "I asked around before I got too close. I found out that there were a few men monitoring the property, but they packed up and left weeks ago. It was all clear."

"Who did you ask?" I ask, my brow wrinkling.

"Oh, um, I have a few sources," Kian responds. "Anyway, I met your mom and dad. They were thrilled to hear that you're safe. They've been worried sick. They said it was the best Christmas gift ever, just knowing that you're both alive."

Zoe throws her arms around Kian. She cranes her neck to look up at him, tears streaming down her face. "Thank you, Kian."

"No problem." He wraps his arms around her, holding her close.

I spread my arms wide enough to encompass them both. "Thank you," I say.

"Group hug!" Keisha joins the embrace, her arms stretching around the three of us.

Layal snickers, her eyes rolling up in her head. "Enough with the sentimental melodrama. I'm hungry. Can we eat now?"

"We made a roast," Zoe says to Kian. "And we cleaned the house. We wanted to thank you for everything you've done for us. But it's not nearly enough."

"You've already done more than enough for me," Kian says. "More than you even know."

CHAPTER 25

Zoe

Christmas Morning

I open my eyes to the smell of waffles and sausage. I stretch out, the leather cushions of the couch squealing beneath me. "Merry Christmas." Kian stands over me, holding a steaming cup of coffee in each hand. He holds one out towards me.

I sit up, accept the coffee, and take a sip. "Merry Christmas."

Keisha bounds into the room, her black curls bouncing on her shoulders. "Merry Christmas! What's this? Presents?"

I turn, following Keisha's gaze to the gifts under the tree. Kian's lips curve into a boyish grin. "It looks like Santa came down the chimney last night."

Keisha picks up a rectangular box wrapped in shiny green paper, adorned with a red velvet bow. She reads the label, "Dear Keisha, From Santa."

Saria enters the room, her mouth open mid-yawn. "What's going on?"

Keisha holds up a silver bag. "Come get your present."

"Present?" Saria takes the gift. "Dear Saria, From Santa." She reads the label, smiling, and turns to Kian. "Thank you, Kian. You've outdone yourself."

"It wasn't me." Kian turns his palms up. "Are you telling me you don't believe in Santa?"

Keisha giggles. "Shall we?"

"You first," Saria says. Keisha rips green wrapping paper, revealing a cardboard box underneath. She flips open the box. Inside, at least a dozen books are lined up, spines facing up. Keisha's eyes light up as she plucks a book from the stack. She holds it up, displaying the muscular man and voluptuous woman embracing on the cover. "I've been waiting so long for this one. It's the third book of a trilogy, and the last book ended on a cliffhanger. Don't you hate when authors do that?"

"It's the worst." Saria agrees. "My turn." She tosses tissue paper aside, digging inside her gift bag. She pulls out a miniature house: slanted roof, raw wood sides, a circular cut-out for a window. "It's a bird feeder," Saria says.

"It has a camera right there." Kian points out a black lens affixed just above the seed port. "Since you can't really wander the woods around here, this gives you the opportunity to bird watch from home. We'll set it up so the camera is synced to my TV."

"Oh, Kian, I love it," Saria says. "This is so thoughtful."

Keisha points to the last gift. "Your turn, Zoe."

The large rectangular-shaped gift is covered with red-and-white striped wrapping paper. Standing up, it's taller than my waist. I tear the wrapping paper, exposing a black case underneath. I lay it on the floor, unclasp the silver latches, and open it. The shiny black electric guitar is decorated with bright blue lightning bolts, like my blue magic. My mouth opens and shuts. "Kian, this must've been really expensive."

"Do you like it?" He asks.

"Are you crazy? I love it, but—"

"That's all that matters." His lips curve into that boyish grin.

I pluck one of the strings. "I wish I could show it to Yaz. She would love it." When I look up, the smile's gone from Kian's face. He stares at his phone, ridges etched into his forehead. "What's wrong?" I ask.

"I got a text from Layal," Kian says, his mouth a grim line. "Turn on the news."

I grab the remote and flip to the local news network. A stage is set up on the lawn outside Nightingale Palace. A bald-headed man is bound to a wooden post, arms behind his back, thick ropes wrapped around his white polo shirt. "Mr. Fawley," Keisha says, her gaze glued to the screen.

Talon stands on stage, a few feet away from the prisoner. He wears a black tuxedo, thick gray hair slicked back, a ruby crown glistening on his head. He taps a crystal-tipped wand against his palm. "Dustin Fawley and his family have made our lives miserable for generations. For hundreds of years, they've dedicated their lives to hunting and killing witches. We've been forced to hide in the shadows, fearful of discovery. Not anymore. It's time for Fawley to pay for his crimes. Today, we'll do to him what his family has done to us for centuries." The crystal tip of Talon's wand turns to flames. The crowd bursts into applause.

"Light him up! Light him up! Light him up!" The audience chants.

"Please! I have a family! I have a wife and kids!" Mr. Fawley begs, tears streaming down his red face. Talon touches his torch to the wood stacked beneath Fawley's loafers. "Please! Please don't!" His eyes widen with fear. The flames encircle his feet, lick his ankles and climb up his jeans. He screams in anguish. The crowd goes wild. Moments later, fire engulfs him, black smoke rising, swirling into the brightly colored sky.

Keisha hangs her head. "Fawley isn't a bad man," she says, her voice hoarse. "He did some questionable things, but he meant well. He believed that everyone supernatural was evil. He didn't understand."

Even if Fawley didn't know better, that doesn't absolve him of his crimes. It was his responsibility to educate himself. Ignorance is never an excuse for senseless violence.

Still, I can't say that he deserves this. I stare at the barbaric scene, my heart hammering in my chest. Audience members share hugs and high-fives as a man dies in front of them. Talon raises his wand like a trophy. The crowd hollers. "Talon! Talon! Talon!"

As a group of soldiers dressed in royal blue remove the charred body from the stage, Talon clears his throat into the microphone. "Now it's time for the next event that we've all been waiting for: the auction."

"Auction?" Saria asks, hugging her knees to her chest. "What are they auctioning?"

"Today is a very special day," Talon says. "Today we change the law of the land. King Keifer and Prince Damian, please join me on stage. Unfortunately, Queen Taya is feeling a bit under the weather this morning, and so Damian has offered to take her place. There is a provision in the

Aurelian constitution that allows a prince to stand in for the queen once he turns eighteen."

Eighteen. Until this moment, I forgot all about Damian's birthday. A few weeks ago, the palace must've been a madhouse. Judging by Caliah's birthday shindig, they probably had caviar, filet mignon, live musicians, and hordes of beautiful women dressed in ball gowns swooning over the handsome prince.

He's an adult now. Damian climbs the steps, looking eerily like a younger version of his father. They're both dressed in royal garb: blue velvet capes with golden nightingales embroidered on the backs, bejeweled crowns holding down their jet black hair. Talon holds out his palm to shake Keifer's hand, claps him on the back, and then offers his hand to Damian. For a moment, Damian stands stock still, his hands at his sides. Maybe this is it. This is the moment where Damian stands up for what's right. The moment where my so-called soulmate finds his balls. I hold my breath. Damian shakes Talon's hand. I curl my lip in disgust. The crowd whistles.

"For many years now, we've been forced to follow laws that require us to treat humans as equals. Although it may seem like a nice sentiment, it's inherently false and disturbs the natural order of the universe. The truth is that humans are our inferiors, and treating them otherwise is detrimental to all of us.

"All beings, supernaturals and humans alike, have a limited amount of energy, supernatural or otherwise. When supernaturals use their energy on menial tasks that could be accomplished by humans, we sacrifice the betterment of our species. Imagine if all of the energy we utilized for such tasks was preserved for honing our magical abilities and crafting spells. Think of how much farther along our species would've progressed.

"The same holds true for humans. As an inherently inferior species, the human is constantly searching for a higher species to guide them. The feeble-minded human finds the expectations of autonomy overwhelming. They lack the capacity for intelligent decision-making, and often find themselves in dangerous and difficult circumstances. By taking them under our wing, we're doing them a favor, freeing them from the burden of responsibilities that are beyond their capabilities. Once they get used to the idea, humans will find that they are much happier under our care, finding both purpose and reward in serving us." Talon pauses, nodding at a lanky man in the front row.

Elric Hawke rises, his gray ponytail tied tightly at the nape of his neck. He walks onto the stage, long skinny legs that seem to glide along the floor, slithering like a snake. He displays a piece of paper like a grade schooler showing off his artwork. "The amendment has been written, High Ruler Crowe. We redact any mention of the equality of human beings from our constitution. From here on out, supernaturals, including but not limited to witches, vampires, gods and demons, are deemed superior beings. As such, any supernatural wishing to buy, sell, or enslave a human, has the legal right to do so." The audience cheers.

Elric slides the paper onto a podium, and hands Talon a pen. The High Ruler of Aurelia scrawls his signature. Next, King Keifer steps up. He takes the pen and signs the paper. Keifer hands the pen to his son. Damian stands at the podium, studying the document in front of him. I swallow hard.

Come on, Damian. Don't do this.

Zoe, I'm sorry, but please don't make this any harder on me than it already is. I don't have a choice.

Damian drags his pen across the paper. I grimace. The goddamn coward. The crowd erupts with cheers.

Talon's lips curve into a sinister smile. "It's official, then. Shall we begin the auction?" The audience howls. "Bring out lot number one."

A soldier dressed in royal blue leads a boy wearing an orange jumpsuit onto the stage. The boy is tall and thin, almost gawky. There's a piss stain on his crotch. His sandy-blonde hair is mussed-up, falling over his forehead. The camera zooms in on his face. Oh my God—-

Saria screams, an ear-splitting sound. I rush to her side. She collapses in my arms, bawling into my shoulder. "Logan, no, no, no. Logan, no, no. They can't do this. They can't. They can't."

But they can. And they are. Bidders shout numbers, higher and higher, eager to enslave the boy. I suck in a deep breath, trying to hold it together. I have to be the strong one. I have to tell Saria that everything is going to be okay.

"Five-hundred thousand dollars. Going once. Going twice. Sold to Demetrius Lyon for five-hundred thousand dollars."

"Demetrius Lyon?" I ask.

"Weston's father," Kian grumbles.

"Bring out lot number two," Talon orders. An Aurelian soldier escorts a teenage girl with long curly hair. Saria isn't watching; she's still sobbing into my shoulder.

"Oh my God! No! Get your hands off of her!" Keisha yells at the television, her hands waving wildly, like she might try to jump into the screen.

Talon shoves the brunette to the front of the stage, facing the audience. Giselle is as beautiful as I remember. Tears stream from her big brown doe eyes. Her full lips tremble.

The bidding war begins. Men shout back and forth, numbers doubled and then tripled. "Three million dollars," Talon says. "Going once. Going twice. Sold to Weston Lyon."

In the front row, Weston grins, his gaze running up and down Giselle's body. "The Lyons aren't doing too bad this morning," Talon remarks. Weston and his father exchange high-fives. Fire shoots through my veins. I'm going to murder someone.

Zoe, don't do anything stupid.
Stop spying on my thoughts.
I'm warning you. They're baiting you. If you try to rescue them, you'll get caught.
I'll never forgive you for this, Damian.

"Bring up lot number three," Talon says. A petite girl with purple streaks in her hair is pushed onto the stage. It feels like someone punched me in the chest.

Yaz kicks, flails and fights the whole way across the stage. "Ah, a feisty one." Talon chuckles. "Someone needs to beat this one into submission. Any takers?"

The bidding begins, but I can barely hear over my heart drumming in my ears. "One million dollars. Sold to Melvin Fox."

To hell with Damian's warning. I'm going to kill these fuckers.

CHAPTER 26

Saria

Minutes after my ex-boyfriend and best friend were sold like pieces of meat, Kian was on the phone assembling a team. I can only recall pieces of what's happened in the hours since then. The world seems to come in and out of focus. One moment, I'm curled up on the couch in the fetal position, quivering like a leaf. The next moment, I'm pacing across the room, my hands clenched in fists. Ding-dong. The doorbell rings. People enter. There's chatter, but I can't understand any of it. It sounds garbled, like they're talking underwater.

I'm weightless, like I'm floating through a dream. Maybe none of this is real. I'm trapped in a nightmare, and Logan and Giselle are back home, tucked safely in their beds. Ding-dong. Ding-dong. More people enter, blurs of color and shapes, but I can't make out their faces.

I'm shaking so hard I drop my cup of tea. Ceramic shatters, jagged pieces scattering across the kitchen tile. I hear the whispers, "Is she okay?" I'm not okay. If anything happens to Logan or Giselle, I'll never be okay again. I would tell them if I could find my voice. Any attempt to speak comes out as a strangled whimper.

"Saria." A young woman with golden brown hair comes into focus. "I'm Blossom, and I want to help you." She holds up a vial of honey-colored liquid. "I mixed up a potion for you. It should help calm your nerves." I swig it down like a shot. The elixir burns the back of my throat.

I don't remember walking downstairs, but eleven of us sit around a table in the basement. Zoe is beside me, her fingers laced through mine. As grateful as I am for my sister, I want Red. When I'm like this, he's the one who can make my bones stop rattling. For now, I'll have to do without him. He's dead until sundown.

On the television, the auction continues. "Lot number two hundred twenty," Elric announces. Rubi Wolfe stares at the screen, her skin a greenish pallor. "How many more? They're mostly teenagers. Children stolen from their beds at night." She reaches over and slides her arm around her daughter Jasleidy. A tear slides down Rubi's cheek. Jasleidy rests her head on her mother's shoulder.

On Rubi's other side, her husband Chester Wolfe, squeezes her hand. "We'll do everything we can to save these kids." He wipes a bead of sweat from his receding hairline.

I can feel the elixir setting in: my muscles relaxing, my brain fog lifting. I can feel the soft cotton of my t-shirt, the tag itching the back of my neck. The floor is hard beneath my feet. My heart drums in my chest. I'm real again.

"We need to organize a protest." Blossom sits up straight, jotting notes in a leather bound journal. With her other hand, she rubs her enlarged belly, manicured fingers stroking her silk maternity dress.

"A group of protestors were just killed at Nightingale Square. A sniper shot them down from a nearby rooftop," Garth says. His glasses slide down the bridge of his nose, revealing watery brown eyes. "One of them was an old classmate of mine. We used to be buddies back in school."

"I'm sorry for your loss." Stellan, Blossom's husband, pats Garth's back. "Hang in there, man." The rest of us echo Stellan's sentiment: a chorus of sorry, thoughts and prayers, knowing none of our words can bring back a friend.

Blossom toys with the delicate heart locket hanging from a thin gold chain around her neck. Her lower lip trembles. "I never thought I'd see the day that peaceful protestors can be shot in broad daylight, right in center city. We've lost our morality and our freedom of speech. We have to get out of here, Stellan."

"And go where?" Stellan asks. "Aurelia is our home." He rakes a hand through his dark brown hair.

"I'm not raising my daughter here. We'll move to the human realm. We'll make a new home." Blossom rests her hands on her baby bump.

"I'll do whatever is best for you and baby Rose." Stellan caresses his wife's belly, then interlaces his fingers through hers. Four loving hands cradle the baby inside.

"This is beyond protesting," Kian says. "We're going to have to move up our timeline and take action. Garth, how's it going with the bomb?"

"Um," Garth pushes his black-rimmed glasses up his nose. "I'm pretty sure that the spells embedded in the explosive crystals will circumvent any and all protective spells surrounding and within the palace."

"How confident are you?" Kian asks

"Let's see," Garth taps on the salt-and-pepper stubble covering his chin. "If I had to quantify it, I'd say I'm ninety-percent positive that my bomb will turn the palace into a pile of ash."

Kian makes a single clap with his hands. "We'll drop the bomb tomorrow. We'll strike during the day when Hadrien's asleep. Once the palace is demolished, our troops can hit the ground and take out whoever's left."

"Kian, the bomb isn't ready yet," Garth says. "I'm still working on the mechanism intended to salvage the innocent. If we drop the bomb tomorrow, hundreds of bystanders, servants, and visitors will be killed."

"Don't forget the prisoners in Nightingale Dungeon, many of whom are wrongfully imprisoned," Zoe chimes in. "Rosa, my old cellmate, is still down there. She has a sick husband and a toddler daughter at home, waiting for her return."

"Zoe, in every war, there's what we call collateral damage," Chester says. "Not every innocent life can be spared."

Zoe lifts her chin. "I won't co-sign a plan that knowingly murders people I know and love."

"I'm with my sister." My voice stammers, but I need to speak up. "Killing innocents makes us as bad as them."

"You're being unreasonable," Chester argues. "We have to weigh the harm versus the good. If we do nothing, thousands more young women and men will be enslaved, abused, possibly tortured."

"You think I don't know that?" Zoe slams her fist on the table. "My best friend was just bought and sold at an auction. I'm not suggesting that we do nothing. I'm suggesting that we find another way."

"There has to be another way," I echo. In my mind's eye, I see Logan: his sandy-blonde hair and goofy grin. My heart clenches up, an ache that radiates from my chest to my gut.

"There isn't another way! Do you understand how powerful Hadrien is? We can't fight him—"

"Chester, calm down," Kian interrupts. "Let's take a moment and think this over. I may have been a bit overzealous."

"Just give me a few weeks," Garth says. "I'm almost there. I just need to work out a couple of kinks. When I get this done, we'll be able to drop a bomb, obliterate the castle and all of the evildoers within, and save every innocent life. I just need a little more time."

"That's too long," Zoe says. "I won't sit around and wait while my best friend withstands weeks of mistreatment."

"When she's with Melvin Fox, she'll have to endure a lot more than poor treatment," Layal drawls from the end of the table. Her hair is like a cloud of flames framing her foxlike features.

"What does that mean?" Zoe asks.

"Melvin Fox is my uncle. My very rich, very powerful uncle. His company mines for katium, crystals and other precious minerals." Layal tucks a wispy red strand behind her ear. "From the time I was four years old, Melvin took a special interest in me. He complimented me, called me his princess and bought me expensive gifts." Anger flashes in Layal's green eyes. "I was too young to understand that he was grooming me for what came next. The abuse went on for years before I found the courage to tell my parents." Layal looks down at the tabletop. "Then, they called me a liar."

I gasp. "Layal—"

"They said I was a troubled child looking for attention. I should've known they would side with him. My dad works for my uncle, and my brother wants to go into the business one day. They care more about money than they ever cared about me."

"I'm so sorry," Zoe says.

"I don't want your pity," Layal snaps.

Jasleidy's pretty features twist into a scowl. "I wish there was something we could do."

"I'd like to kill that POS." Keisha twists her hands like she's wringing out a towel.

"Believe me, I've tried," Layal drawls. "His security is top notch. He's got it all: intricate protection spells surrounding every square inch of his property, a team of talented bodyguards, surveillance cameras, and a high-tech security alarm system."

"We'll find a way in and get Yaz out of there," Zoe says. "I won't leave Yaz in the hands of a sexual predator. Or Giselle, for that matter. Weston Lyon chose her with a specific purpose in mind. He has a history of sexual assault."

My chair seems to wobble beneath me. I grip the sides of the seat as the whole world tips off its axis. "Breathe," Zoe says. Her arm is heavy on my shoulder, the anchor that prevents me from being swept away. "Inhale, and then exhale."

I suck in a deep breath. I hold it for a moment, then push it all the way out. The world is steady again. "Are you okay?" Zoe asks.

"I'll be okay," I say, "when Giselle is out of there." My voice rises with determination.

"Understood," Kian says. "We need a plan. If we fight on the ground, we'll lose. I won't put my people at risk if we don't stand a chance of winning."

"If we attack during the day, Hadrien will be asleep," Chester argues.

"They'll wake him up," Kian says. "He doesn't require sleep."

"Exposure to the sun and a lack of sleep will weaken him significantly," Chester says.

"Maybe," Kian taps a pen on the table. "But even if he loses fifty percent of his power, he's still a force to be reckoned with. I have to protect the people who are trusting me to make the right calls."

"Just give me a few weeks," Garth says. "I'll finish the bomb, and then we can drop it on the palace. We'll take out most of the big players, and then we'll fight any remaining enemy troops on the ground, just like we planned."

"I'm not waiting a few weeks," Zoe said. "I'm going to rescue our friends, even if I have to go alone."

"You won't be alone," I say. "I'm going with you."

"Don't be stupid," Keisha says. "You're playing right into Talon's hands. You're going to walk right into his trap and get yourself killed."

"Not if we do it right," Zoe says, her arms folded across her chest.

"You said you won't wait a few weeks. What about a few days?" Layal says, looking up from her phone.

"A few days?" Zoe asks.

"I just got a text from Weston. He'll release Giselle and Logan on the evening of December 31 while his parents are at Melvin Fox's New Year's Eve party. And he promised not to lay one finger on Giselle during the time that she's there."

"He said that he'll release them," I repeat in disbelief. It seems too easy.

"Why would he do that?" Zoe's brows draw together.

Layal lips curve into a mischievous grin. "Because there was a little birdie who wanted her wings. I convinced Weston that helping free the birdie would be in his best interest, even though he knew that it was a highly illegal and treasonous act. What he didn't know was that I hid a camera in a bush and recorded his every move. Now I have him by the balls." Layal cackles.

"Nice work." Keisha looks impressed.

"What about Yaz?" Zoe asks.

"That's going to be trickier," Layal says. "I already told you: my uncle's security is no joke. But I think our best bet is during the New Year's Eve party. If it's anything like previous years, there'll be hundreds of guests, a live band, and lots of drunk, loud people dancing and milling about. In the midst of all the chaos, we'll find a way to get Yazmin out of there."

"My husband and I were invited to his New Year's Eve bash," Blossom says. "Stellan used to work for Melvin." She lowers her gaze, like she's ashamed.

"I worked in katium sales," Stellan explains. "I left the company three years ago. I couldn't keep working for that bastard. We still get the New Year's party invitation in the mail, but we've declined ever since I quit."

Layal's green eyes flicker with excitement. "Change your RSVP. I have an idea. You're both going to the party."

Stellan protectively rubs Blossom's baby bump. "I won't do anything that puts my wife or daughter in jeopardy."

Layal waves her palm. "I would never ask you to do anything that risks your safety. What? You don't trust me?" Her face is pure calculated innocence.

CHAPTER 27

Saria

New Year's Eve

Hunkered down in the backseat of Layal's Jeep, I check the time. "Where is he? Isn't he supposed to be here by now?"

"He just texted me. He's almost here," Layal says from the front seat. "He had to wait for his parents to leave, and then disconnect the security system and cameras. He can't exactly walk them out with the video running. He has to set it up to look like Giselle and Logan dismantled the security system and escaped on their own. When his parents get home, he'll say he was out all night. Right after he drops them off, he's going to a party."

"I wish he would hurry up," Zoe says. "We have a lot to do."

Two headlights slice through the darkness. "He's here," Layal says.

I peek out the back window. We're parked on a deserted, dead end road shrouded by trees. The white SUV seems to move in slow motion. My heart pounds against my rib cage. The SUV parks next to us.

Weston hops out of the driver's seat, a mop of bronze curls tumbling over his forehead. He opens the back door. "Get out," he says.

Giselle steps out, her gaze darting side to side, chin trembling. Logan is close behind her. He walks on stiff legs, his shoulders hunched.

I burst out the back door, my heart in my throat. "Giselle! Logan!" I throw my arms around them, sobbing. Logan feels thinner than I remember, his bones sharp beneath his t-shirt.

"Will you keep it down?" Layal scolds. "If someone hears you, we'll all be in deep shit. Now get in the car and stay down." She hisses.

Giselle and I tumble onto the car floor, still clinging to each other. I take Logan's hand and pull him inside, his hazel eyes foggy. "Where are we going?" He asks.

"You're going to stay with Rubi and Chester Wolfe for a little while until we can figure out a way to get you home," I say. "They'll treat you well. They have two daughters. Jasleidy is our age, and her younger sister Marlena is seven."

"I want to go home." Tears pour down Giselle's cheeks.

"I know, but it's not that easy. Border patrol covers the portal, monitoring everyone who comes and goes," I explain. "The Wolfes are kind people. They'll take good care of you."

Layal slides into the driver's seat and turns the ignition. Wes leans against her car, peering through the open window. "I held up my end of the bargain." Weston says. "Are you going to delete the video?"

Layal shrugs. "I'll think about it." She slams the gas pedal to the floor. We peel out of there, leaving Weston in a cloud of dust.

We hunch down in the back as Layal merges onto the highway. "We'll be there in five minutes," she says.

I keep one hand around Giselle's shoulders, the other on Logan's wrist. I stare at him: messy hair, gawky arms, chest moving up and down with every breath. Tears of relief spill down my cheeks. I lean over to kiss him on the cheek. He may hate me, but I still love him. I always will.

We exit the highway, turn left, then right. We veer around curves, climbing up a winding hill. Finally, Layal comes to a stop. "We're here."

I duck behind bushes, keeping low as we follow Layal up the stone walkway. A large colonial home looms above us, lights glowing from inside several rectangular windows. The front door swings open. Chester and Rubi wait inside. "Come in." Rubi waves her hand. "Quickly, come in." As soon as we're inside the foyer, Chester closes the door and twists the lock.

Rubi steps forwards, her hands in her jean's pockets. "Welcome to our home, I'm Rubi, and this is my husband, Chester," Rubi says, putting a hand on her husband's arm. "There's nothing we can do to make up for what our country's leaders have done to you, but while you're here, we promise to try." Rubi smiles serenely,

High heels clink on the tile floor as Jasleidy enters the room. A tight blue minidress hugs her curves. White leather boots compliment her tanned, toned legs. "Goddamn!" Layal says. "You're so hot you might set this place on fire!"

Jasleidy giggles, blue eyes twinkling. "Thanks, Lay! I can't believe you're going to miss Austin's New Years Eve Party."

"I have a prior commitment," Layal responds. "But if anyone asks, I was there all night."

"You got it." Jasleidy winks, then turns to Giselle, her hand extended. "Hi, I'm Jasleidy, but my friends call me Jas, so you can call me Jas."

Giselle steps backwards like Jasleidy's hand might bite her. "It's okay," I say, squeezing Giselle's shoulder. "Jas is our friend."

Giselle sucks in a shaky breath. "I'm Giselle." The girls shake hands.

Jasleidy turns to Logan next, her hand out. "Hi, Jas. I'm Logan." He wipes his palm on his jeans before taking her hand.

"I'm so sorry, but I have to run to a party. My parents will help you settle in, but we'll have plenty of time to get to know each other while you're staying here."

"Have fun and be safe," Rubi says. There's a chorus of goodbyes as Jasleidy slips out the front door.

A moment later, a smaller version of Jasleidy bounds into the room, dressed in an oversized tracksuit. "Hey! Why didn't anyone tell me they were here?"

"If you lowered the volume on your video games, you would've heard them," Chester says. "You're going to go deaf with all that noise."

"This is Hazel, our other daughter," Rubi says. Hazel still looks annoyed, hands on her hips. "Relax. You didn't miss anything."

"Can I show them upstairs?" Hazel asks, her eyes lighting up.

"Go right ahead," Rubi says.

"Follow me!" Hazel skips up the stairs, the rest of us in tow. Her ponytail, affixed by a big pink bow, swings behind her. We climb the stairs, carpet soft beneath my feet. At the top of the staircase, we turn down a long hallway. At the end of the corridor, a thin rope dangles from the ceiling. Hazel jumps, reaching for the rope. It slips through her fingertips.

"I'll get that." Chester wedges his way through the group. He pulls the rope, an overhead hatch opens, and a wooden ladder unfolds onto the floor.

Hazel nudges her dad out of the way. She glances back, her eyes twinkling. "Come on. I'll show you your rooms." she says, leading the way up the ladder.

The top opens into a large room with raw wood floors and a vaulted ceiling. In the center of the room, a big fluffy couch faces a wall-mounted television. Hazel gallops over to the childish artwork hanging on the wall opposite the TV. "When I heard you were coming, I painted this for you. I thought it would cheer you up." I study the painting: a sloppy green hump decorated by red smudges. "It's a grassy hill full of roses," Hazel explains.

"It's beautiful," Logan says. "Thank you for painting it for us." Even in the worst of times, Logan is kind and appreciative. I didn't deserve him. I hope he finds someone who treats him much better than I did.

Giselle mumbles something under her breath that sounds like it might've been thank you. Hazel grins ear to ear. "Look over here." Hazel points to the bookshelf next to her artwork. "I brought up my favorite books, coloring sheets, crayons, and a few board games in case you get bored." She taps on one of the board game boxes. "This one is my favorite. I'll show you how to play."

Logan smiles back at her. "I'd like that."

Hazel's blue eyes twinkle. "Come this way. I'll show you your room." Hazel leads us past bamboo room dividers into a smaller space with a twin bed and wood dresser. "Do you like it? I didn't know what to paint for a boy, so I hope you like dragons." Above the bed, red fire spews from the mouth of a blue dragon with pointy ears and triangular wings.

"I love dragons," Logan says. "You're quite the artist."

"I worked so hard on it." Hazel practically jumps into the air. "Giselle, I painted something for you too."

We follow Hazel back into the main room, past the couch, television, and another set of bamboo dividers. Fluffy purple pillows and a velour comforter sit on top of Giselle's twin bed. Another painting by Hazel is affixed above the dresser, a purple butterfly with pink hearts at the ends of its antennae.

"We wish we could invite you to stay in the main part of our home." Rubi brushes a strand of brown hair out of her eyes. "But you're safer in the attic. If any of our nosy neighbors saw you in a window, I'd be willing to bet that they'd turn us all in, especially if there was a reward involved."

"I just want to go home," Giselle mumbles. I take her hand and squeeze it.

"As soon as we can get you home safely," Rubi says. "Until then, we'll try our best to make you as comfortable as possible."

"Thank you," Logan says.

"It's the least we could do. You must be starving. I'm going to run downstairs and get some snacks," Rubi says.

"Make yourselves at home," Chester adds. "If there's anything you need, anything at all, let us know."

"Thank you," Giselle mumbles. As soon as Rubi and Chester leave the room, Giselle collapses on the bed, tears brimming in her eyes. "When can I go home?"

I sit beside her. "As soon as we find a way to get you home safely. I promise." I massage her shoulders, my fingers entangled in her long wavy hair. "While you're here, I'll come visit you all the time. Keisha, too."

"Keisha?" Giselle's eyes widen. "I've been so worried about her. Is she here in Aurelia?"

"Yes. She wanted to come tonight, but she had to work on something," I say. Ever since our last meeting, Garth and Keisha have been working on the bomb around the clock. When Garth asked her to stay behind tonight, we assured her that we understood. After all, the bomb is the key to saving the rest of the kidnapped slaves and overthrowing Talon's regime.

"Don't be sad," Hazel says. "We're going to have lots of fun! I have games and movies and lots of stuffies. I'll even let you borrow my unicorn to sleep with. She's my favorite stuffie."

Giselle stares straight ahead. "I can't believe that this is my life."

"Whenever I'm upset, my teacher tells me to turn my frown upside down." Hazel takes Logan's hand. "Do you want to play me in checkers?"

"That's a two player game. Is there a game that we can all play?" Logan asks.

"Oh yes, I have lots of games! I have Candyland and Pictionary and—"

"Oh, I have to go," Zoe says, checking her watch. "I have to get Yaz." She turns to me. "You can stay here and hang out. Help them settle in."

I stand up. "Not a chance. You came with me to get Logan and Giselle. I'm going with you to get Yazmin."

"It's going to be very simple, really," Zoe says. "If all goes well, Melvin won't even notice that Yaz is gone until long after we're gone."

"*If* all goes well. What if it doesn't? Don't underestimate me, Zoe. I saved Red from the witch hunters. I escaped from Talon. I snuck into Aurelia and I found you. I've been practicing offensive magic." I hone in on my magic, pulling it from my core and guiding it through my veins. My brow creases in concentration. My hands burn like they're on fire. Orange flames burst from my fingertips.

Layal lets out a low whistle. "Not bad for a half-breed."

My eyes narrow. "Say it again, Layal. I dare you."

Layal rolls her eyes. "Can't anyone take a joke anymore?" She slings her purse over her shoulder. "Come on. Let's get out of here."

CHAPTER 28

Saria

"Good luck," Rubi whispers, sliding open the back door. "We'll take good care of them."

"Thank you." On impulse, I throw my arms around the woman. "I don't know how I'll ever repay you."

"Don't even waste one moment worrying about that. Just keep yourself safe," Rubi whispers into my ear.

"Will do." I step outside, a cold gust hitting me in the face. My breath is puffs of white in the darkness. Layal and Zoe are close behind me.

It's a dead quiet, moonless night; even the stars seem dull. Next door, the neighbor's house is a dark outline in the pitch black. The only sounds are our sneakers padding along the driveway.

A black sedan is parked next to Layal's Jeep. Above the driver's seat, I can barely make out Kian's hair, a white blur in the blackness. The passenger door pops open, and Red steps out.

"Is everyone okay?" Red asks.

"They're doing alright," I say. "All things considered."

Red nods. "We were tailing you the whole time, making sure that everything went okay."

"I know." It was agreed that the boys would stay close but out of sight. Weston and Kian don't have the greatest history, nor do Logan and Red. Logan blames Red for ruining our relationship. In a way, he's right. If it wasn't for Red, I might've stayed with Logan forever. Happy, secure and comfortable, never knowing the ferocity of passion I feel for Red was possible.

"Can you two stop talking?" Layal hisses. "Rubi said her neighbors are nosy."

"They aren't home," Red says. Every window next door is as black as the night sky.

"Just keep it down, please." Layal grumbles.

Red takes my hand and leads me behind a large oak tree. His back against the tree trunk, he pulls me to him. "How did it go?" His breath is hot on my neck, sending tingles down my spine.

"It went well," I say. "Exactly as planned."

"That's not what I mean," Red says. "How was it seeing him?"

"Is this about Logan?" I ask, quirking one eyebrow. "Are you, dare I say, jealous?"

"I, um," Red stutters. I can't see his face in the blackness, but I can imagine his cheeks reddening. Red doesn't blush often, but when he does, it's the cutest thing in the world. "I, mean, I guess I am. You used to date him."

"I've known Logan since we were kids," I say. "He's a wonderful person and I'll always care for him, but it doesn't compare to how I feel about you." I'm in love with Red, but I'm careful not to use the "L" word. I don't want to trigger another diatribe about how we can't have a future together. Even worse, I don't want him to disappear, claiming that it's for my own good before I get too attached. It's too late for that. The heartbreak coming is inevitable, but every kiss reminds me that it's worth it. I'll hold onto him for as long as I can.

I lift my chin and Red's lips brush against mine. Electricity shoots through my veins. He groans, pulling me even closer. Our bodies fit together like a glove. Our tongues intertwine. Fire burns in my core. "You, Redvers Castigan, have no reason to be jealous. No one can make me feel the way that you do." He kisses me again, deeper and harder this time.

"Ahem." Layal's head peeks out from behind the tree. "I hate to break up your little make-out sesh, but we have to go."

A light flicks on in the house next door. My heart surges into my throat. "Oh shit," Layal mumbles. "Let's get out of here."

Red laces his fingers through mine. "I'm coming with you."

Layal shoves Red towards Kian's sedan. "Not a chance. You two can't keep your hands off of each other. I need you both focused, and I don't want bodily fluids in my backseat."

"We'll be right behind you," Red says, opening Kian's passenger door. He leans in for one more kiss. My lips tingle from his touch.

As he slides into Kian's car, I duck into Layal's backseat next to Zoe. My sister taps her feet on the ground, looking annoyed. "Took you long enough."

Layal turns the ignition, her Jeep purring to life. "I got a text message update from Blossom," Layal says. "It's a good thing that she's pregnant. She was able to hide a gown and a blonde wig underneath her flowy maternity dress. She walked right into Melvin's party without anyone noticing a thing."

"Her baby is already a little hero," Zoe says. As Layal backs out of the Wolfe's driveway, Zoe slouches, careful to keep her head below the window.

"Yazmin is serving appetizers at the cocktail hour. As Blossom grabbed a few hors d'oeuvres from Yazmin's tray, she leaned in and whispered that she's going to help her escape. Yazmin seemed skeptical at first, but after Blossom mentioned Zoe's name, she agreed to meet her in the bathroom at midnight.

"While everyone at the party is kissing, cheering, throwing confetti or whatever other dopey things they do to ring in the New Year, Yazmin will quietly disappear into the bathroom. She'll change into the gown and wig that is currently taped to Blossom's baby bump. Then, as hordes of disorderly drunk party goers head out the front door, Yazmin will slip into the crowd, unrecognizable in her disguise."

"As much as I hate to say it, you're a genius, Layal," Zoe says.

"Save it for after we've completed the mission."

"The first one went off without a hitch," Zoe says.

"Thank God." Ever since we brought Logan and Giselle to safety, it's like a weight has been lifted off my chest. I can breathe again.

"Uncle Melvin has a long driveway, but it's not big enough to accommodate all of his guests tonight. Many cars will be parked on the street. We'll park at the end of the line of cars, far enough to be unseen by Melvin's surveillance cameras and security guards. Blossom will tell Yazmin to walk down the line of cars until she sees my red Jeep. She'll get in and we'll drive right out of here. Easy peasy."

An ominous feeling descends on me, stirring in my gut. *Something bad is going to happen.* The world spins around me. I press my hand over my mouth, afraid that I might throw up. *Turn around before it's too late.* I shake my head, warding off the intrusive thoughts. The plan is simple. Easy as pie, right?

But the feeling doesn't go away. Sweat pools along my hairline. The hair on the back of my neck stands on end. The closer we get to Melvin's house, the stronger the feeling gets. "We should turn around," I blurt out.

"What?" Zoe spits out the word.

"I have a bad feeling." I know I sound crazy and stupid, but I have to say it.

Zoe narrows her eyes. "We're going to get Yazmin. If you want to stay behind, get out now. Otherwise, keep your negative energy to yourself."

I suck in a deep, shaky breath. Zoe's right. She helped me rescue my best friends. Now it's my turn to help her rescue hers. I can't let my paranoia take control. "Okay, let's go," I say.

Layal turns onto the main road, Kian's headlights shining behind us. I try to ignore the knots twisting in my stomach.

We pull into a wealthy neighborhood: enormous houses, crystal sidewalks, manicured lawns, close enough to the palace to see all the vivid ribbons of color in the sky.

My jaw drops when I see Melvin Fox's mansion. A triangular gable is supported by Corinthian columns. The arched doorway is framed by glossy ivory stones. "It isn't fair," Zoe murmurs. "Why are men like him rewarded with power and riches, while my friend Rosa rots in a dungeon because she was desperate for medical care?"

"Karma will come for Melvin," Layal says. The edge in her tone tells me that if karma waits too long, Layal will take care of him herself. We pass a dozen luxury vehicles, parking at the end of the line. "We're out of range of Melvin's security cameras." Layal checks her watch. "Only a few minutes until midnight."

Dread seeps into my skin and burrows inside my bones. *Something terrible is going to happen.* I swallow the words before they fly out of my mouth. They stick in my throat, constricting my windpipe. I gasp for air.

Even from this distance, we can hear the countdown to midnight. "Five, four, three, two, one! Happy New Year!" Music blasts. People hoot and holler. My heart slams into my chest walls.

A few minutes later, partiers begin to trickle out, waving goodbye in their gowns and suits. Engines revs up. Headlights shine. Car doors open and shut.

As time passes, the crowd thickens. A woman in sparkly red cocktail dress stumbles forward, tripping over her own three-inch heels. She laughs at herself as a tuxedoed man catches her, kissing her cheek as he guides her towards a souped-up SUV. Right now, I'd give anything to trade places with them, just for a moment to be so happy and carefree.

"There she is." Zoe points. I almost don't recognize Yazmin in her long blonde wig. She skirts through the crowd, her emerald gown billowing in the breeze. She steps onto the sidewalk, looking left then right, studying the lines of cars.

"This way, Yaz. This way," Zoe murmurs under her breath, even though there's no way that Yazmin could possibly hear her.

Yazmin turns in our direction. As she walks down the sidewalk, one foot in front of the other, my chest tightens. She moves closer and closer, green satin swaying with every move of her hips. Then, she's at the door, peering through the back window. As soon as she sees Zoe, she flings open the back door. "Zoe! It's you. It's really you."

"Get in," Layal hisses, shifting the Jeep into drive. She hits the gas as the door closes.

Zoe wraps her arms around Yazmin, rocking back and forth in their embrace. "You found me," Yazmin cries. "You really found me. I thought I was going to be trapped there forever." Her wig goes askew, purple tendrils peeking out from underneath.

We roll out of Melvin's neighborhood, leaving the boisterous crowd and the affluent neighborhood behind us. "We did it," I say, but the foreboding feeling only grows stronger. *Something terrible is going to happen.*

As we drive on, the landscape becomes more rural. The distance between residences grows greater and greater, until I don't see any houses at all. The woods is a canopy above us. Tree trunks and brush make thick walls on either side of us. "We really did it," I say, if only to convince myself.

Layal's Jeep screeches to a sudden halt. "What the hell?" Layal studies the blinking lights on her dashboard. "Check engine? I just had a tune up."

Someone materializes in the middle of the road, the Jeep's headlights shining on the figure like a spotlight. At first glance, the man is absolutely ordinary: plain face, dad bod, basic brown hair, checkered shirt. Hadrien smirks. "Shit!" Layal shouts.

"Get out of the car," Hadrien says. We all stay put, frozen in place. I feel safer in here, surrounded by glass and steel. It's just an illusion. With a flick of his pinky, Hadrien could tear this vehicle in two.

"This can be easy, or this can be hard," Hadrien says. "And by hard, I mean hard for you." He chuckles. "Talon asked me to bring his nieces to him alive, but he gave me permission to take more drastic measures if necessary." He leans on the hood of Layal's car. "Get out of the car. Now."

My heart hammers into my throat, stealing my breath. I blink away black spots, willing myself not to pass out. But does it even matter? We're all dead anyway.

The bat swoops down at lightning speed, shifting into a man as he hits the land. Amos' ponytail blows back behind him. "Get away from them."

"Who the hell are you?" Hadrien's voice conveys annoyance, not fear.

"Your worst nightmare," Amos replies, his tone vicious, eyes dark and narrowed. My jaw falls open. I haven't seen this side of Amos before. When Amos fought the wolves, it was different: mechanical, controlled, almost emotionless. Tonight, fury radiates from him.

Hadrien barks out a laugh. "You seem to greatly overestimate yourself." He flicks wrist. "Goodbye and good riddance." Hadrien's tone reeks of condescension. His eyes blaze red like burning hot coals. Amos doesn't even flinch.

A crease forms between Hadrien's eyes. He flicks his wrist again.

Amos stands tall, his chin held high. "What now, big guy?" Amos asks.

Hadrien stares at his own hand. His expression contorts rapidly, shifting from confusion to disbelief to anger.

Purple lasers shoot from Amos' fingertips, blasting Hadrien in the chest. Hadrien staggers backwards, howling in pain. It only takes him a moment to collect himself. Hadrien's lips twist into a disturbed grin. "You want a duel, buddy, you got it. I've been waiting for a challenge. Not that you'll be much of one." Hadrien launches into the air, fists extended. When their bodies collide, there's a clap like thunder.

"Damn car won't start," Layal says, unbuckling her seatbelt. "He disabled the engine. We have to go on foot. Now's our best shot. Let's get the hell out of here."

"What about Amos?" Zoe asks.

"I hate to bruise your little ego," Layal drawls, "but you won't be any help to Amos. Not against Hadrien. You'll just get yourself and your sister killed. Our best chance of survival is running as fast as we can."

Zoe seems to acquiesce. She squeezes my hand once, her palm damp against mine. "Let's go." We jump from the car: Yazmin first, Zoe next, and me close behind. I pump my legs as hard as I can, thigh muscles burning, frigid air threatening to burst my lungs. We push through walls of foliage, weaving through trees and bushes.

Layal sprawls out on the dirt, her body melting into a puddle of flame-red lava. The lava erupts, morphing and then solidifying into a red fox. Layal takes off, her agile legs easily maneuvering between branches and brush. "Faster, come on, guys," Zoe hisses, but we can't keep up with Layal.

And then she's gone. "Thanks a lot, friend," Zoe mutters under her breath. "We still have each other," she says. "Stay close to me."

Leaves crackle under our feet. An owl hoots. Bang! Bang! Bang! Gunshots ring into the night. I stumble over a tree root, twisting my ankle on the way down. "Ouch." I climb to my feet, limping forward through the pain.

I reach out to touch Zoe, but find a branch instead. The dark is deep and vast, enveloping me with its inky blackness.

Bang! Bang! Bang! Bang! "Zoe? Where are you?" Bang! Bang! Bang! Bang! Something hits me in my thigh. Bang! Bang! Bang! I'm thrown backwards, searing pain burning into my abdomen. I touch my stomach, and find wetness that's soaked through my clothes. "I've been shot," I manage to mumble. I try to get up, but I can't. I can't even move. It's like my legs aren't even attached to my body anymore.

"Yaz? Saria?" I can hear Zoe's frantic voice, but she sounds so far away.

"I'm over here," I yell back. Footsteps grow louder, twigs snapping beneath the footfalls. Someone grabs me by the upper arm, pulling me up from the ground. A flashlight shines in my face. "I've got one of the twins!" An Aurelian soldier dressed in his royal blue uniform smiles like he won a prize.

Another soldier emerges from the shadows. His knife glints as he raises it up high, and then plunges it downwards, straight into my chest. I yelp in agony and gurgle on the blood rising in my throat.

"What'd you do that for?" The soldier holding my arm asks. "Talon wanted her alive."

"I always wanted to know what it feels like to stab a nimwit." The knife-wielding soldier shrugs. "Besides, she was going to die anyway, man. She had a couple more minutes max."

"So how did it feel?" The first soldier asks. Something flutters overhead, its wings beating branches as it passes through. I slip in and out of consciousness. Black fog clouds my vision.

"So good, man, so good. You have to try it." He passes his knife to the other soldier.

The first soldier grins. "Should I go for the neck? Or gouge out her pretty blue eyes?" He traces the air by my eye sockets with the tip of the knife, taunting me. I whimper.

Above us, a branch creaks. Then men look up as Red drops down. Red lands effortlessly on his feet. Red punches a soldier in the face with one hand while snatching his knife with the other. Crack! The soldier falls backwards, letting go of my arm. I hit the ground with a thud.

The other soldier lifts his gun. Before he has a chance to fire it, Red twists his arm. The gun skitters across the dirt. With one quick swipe, Red slices his neck. Blood pours down as the soldier's eyes bulge, his hands to his throat as he keels over.

"Sari." Red kneels by my side. "I got to you as fast as I could. They had us surrounded back there. Sari, Sari, answer me. Sari, please."

I'm dying. I know that as well as I know the woods back home, as well as I know the angles of Red's face. I don't have much longer. A few minutes, an hour at most.

Before I die, I want him to know that I love him. I move my lips, but the words drown in the blood in my throat.

There are hundreds of connections, a maze of pathways, between the brain and the mouth. When you're dying, the wires crisscross and tangle. Words can get lost before they ever reach your tongue.

The black fog closes in. My eyes are heavy, oh so heavy. I'm going, slipping away. I'll never get the chance to tell Red how I feel.

"Sari, don't, please. Sari, open your eyes. Sari, Sari!"

I was a fool, holding back. Don't make the same mistake that I did.

If you love someone, tell them now. Don't wait. It could be your very last chance.

CHAPTER 29

Zoeli

It's so dark that I can't see an inch in front of me. I feel my way forward, branches scraping against my cheek.

Bang! Bang! Bang! Bang! Something slams into my arm. Pain radiates from my bicep to my forearm. "Argh." I clench the bullet wound. "Goddammit. Yaz, Saria, where are you?" I reach into the darkness. "Yaz? Saria?" How did I lose them? Just moments ago, they were right here.

I channel my energy, pulling it from deep in my core and into my hand. A blue orb materializes on my palm, illuminating the night. It'll make it easier for them to find me, but I don't have a choice. I'm wandering blind.

"Yaz? Saria?" I step over rocks and duck under branches. On the other side of a boulder, I can make out the shape of a body on the ground.

I jump over the big rock and fall to my knees. Yaz is face down in the dirt, purple-streaked hair splayed out around her. "Yaz!" Hands trembling, I turn her head. Blood weeps from a circular bullet wound in the center of her forehead. Her brown eyes are still open. "No! No, no, no!" I pull her to me, hold her head against my chest. "Yaz, you're going to be okay. You're going to get through this. You're the strongest person I know." I put my hand to her forehead, pouring healing energy into the wound. I put my other hand on her neck, feeling for a pulse.

She's cold, so cold. Eyes wide open, unblinking. No matter how hard I try, no matter how much healing energy I unleash, her heart does not beat. She's dead. "No! No! No!"

"Zoe?" I startle at Kian's voice. I was so caught up I didn't even hear him approach. "Zoe, I'm so sorry." Kian kneels beside me.

I wail into his chest. "She's dead, Kian."

"I wasn't fast enough. I should've killed them before they could shoot at you."

"Stop that," I say. "If it's anyone's fault, it's mine. We were all running. I lost her in the dark." I choke on my words, sobs erupting from my throat. "Where's everyone else?" I ask.

"I don't know. While Amos was fighting Hadrien, Red and I hid nearby, calculating our next move. We saw you get out of Layal's Jeep and at least a dozen Aurelian soldiers following you," Kian says. "Red and I killed them all. But not in time, apparently."

"Oh my God," I say. "Is Red okay? Did you see Saria?"

"Red and I split up to look for you and Saria. Me by foot, him by air. We're able to cover more ground that way."

I rock back and forth, Yaz's lifeless body crushed between my arms. This has to be a nightmare. This can't be real. When am I going to wake up?

Branches rustle. Pebbles clatter against each other. Kian stands up, fists clenched. "Who's there?"

"Kian?" I recognize Red's voice. "Is that you? I found Sari." My breath rushes out of my body. My sister is alive.

Red steps out from behind a bush, holding Saria like a child. She's limp against his chest, her arms dangling by her sides. "She's not doing well. We need to get her help." He talks fast, like there isn't a minute to spare. "We need a healer."

"I can heal her," I say, even though I'm not too sure that I can. I've already exhausted most of my energy trying to heal Yazmin. God, I'm so stupid.

"You're drained and hurt," Kian says, pointing to my arm. "You shouldn't be healing anyone. You need a healer for yourself."

"Huh?" Blood spills down my arm, caking around my wrist. I honestly forgot that I got shot. My grief is all encompassing: searing every cell in my body with unimaginable pain. I can't tell the difference between a bullet wound and every other part of my body. "Oh, that."

"Edith isn't too far from here. She'll find us a healer. Someone who can be discreet."

I stand, lifting Yaz up in my arms. My knees buckle under the weight, and I crash back down. Yaz's neck flops at an awkward angle to the side.

"Is she—?" Red asks.

"Yes, she's dead!" I cry. "But I won't leave her here! She deserves a proper burial. She deserves—" I choke on words that are too big to come out. Because Yaz deserved so much more. She deserved a chance to grow up. She deserved to sing a million more songs. She deserved adventures and romance and love and a long happy life. I failed her.

"I got her," Kian says, taking Yaz into his arms. "Now let's go. It won't be long before they send more troops."

The walk to Edith's cottage is a blur. It's surreal, like I'm floating through space. Maybe this dream-like state is on purpose, my brain's way of refusing to believe that Yaz is gone, that Saria might be next. If I were to face that reality, really face it, I'd crumble to the ground, unable to go on. I move forward in a stupor, because it's the only way I can keep going right now.

Edith waits on her front porch, barely dressed in a thin nightgown despite the chilly weather. "Come in, come in." She waves us inside with her gnarled hands.

Kian lays Yaz out on the living room floor. Edith crouches beside her. "Oh dear, oh dear." She places her hand on Yaz's forehead over the bullet wound, her eyes closed. "She's at the gate," Edith says. "Before she goes in, she wants to say thank you. Zoe, she wants you to know how much your friendship meant to her, and how much she appreciates you putting your neck on the line for her."

I sob.

"She wants you to know that she's going to be okay, that she sees her grandpa and her cousin Amir on the other side. She won't be alone."

I've never cried like this before. Tears rush down my face, soaking my neck and chin. "Please, Yaz, don't go," I beg.

"She's already gone," Edith says. "She's at peace now." Edith presses Yaz's eyes closed. She looks serene and beautiful, long black lashes still against her cheeks.

"Saria needs a healer. Right away." Red says. "I've been trying to put pressure on her wounds, but she's losing more and more blood."

Edith rolls a blanket out on the floor. "Put her down," she orders.

In the light, I finally understand the severity of my sister's condition. Her skin is ash-gray. Her lips are blue. When Edith lifts her shirt, I gasp. Several bullet wounds pierce through her abdomen. Blood spews from an enormous gash on her chest. Her thigh is soaked in blood, indicating another wound beneath her jeans.

"She's hanging on by a thread," Edith says. "She's got a few minutes left, maybe, tops. Even if I called the most talented healer, she'd be gone long before they arrived, although I doubt that they could help even if they got here in time. This is beyond healing."

I grab Edith by her nightgown, the thin cotton tight in my fist. "You have to do something! Save her! Do something!"

Edith lifts a crooked finger. "There's only one person here who can save her, and it isn't me." She points at Red.

CHAPTER 30

Saria

I'm zooming down a long hallway, light and free. There's no more pain, no more restrictions imposed by gravity. For the very first time, I can fly.

There's a light ahead, glittering and bright, like the sun. I'm pulled towards it like a moth to a flame.

"Sari, drink." Red's voice is so far away, like he's far, far away, at the other end of a tunnel. "Drink," he repeats. Liquid touches my tongue, metallic and spicy, an unusual flavor, but surprisingly good.

The hallway, the light, the glitter, it all fades away. I can feel the floor hard beneath my back, restrained by the laws of gravity again. My lips are wet with the metallic fluid. I'm so damn thirsty. I open my mouth wider, and the yummy drink spills down my throat.

"Is it working?" Zoe asks.

"It's too soon to tell," Red says. "She's still alive, and she's drinking it, but not everyone reacts well to the venom. Only a small number of people survive the transition. We won't know for a few more hours."

Then I remember: the gunshots, the knife plunging into my chest, the unmistakable knowledge of my impending death.

But I'm not going to die. I'm going to start a new life.

I'm going to become a vampire.

Red's venom flows into me, and I suck it down ravenously. The infection breaks into my cells. It adheres to my DNA. And with it comes the heat, a fever like I've never known, a fire scorching inside my skin.

It's going to burn me alive. "Sari, stay with me."

I try to hold on, but the pain is too much to bear.

The darkness overtakes me.

CHAPTER 31

Zoeli

Keisha paces back and forth across Kian's living room. "I should've been there. I thought that the plan was foolproof, and everything was going to be fine."

I curl up in a fetal position on the brown leather couch. Kian enters the room, a mug in his hand. "I made a special tea to help you sleep." Out the window, a streak of orange stretches across the indigo sky.

I shake my head. "I don't want anything right now."

"Zoe, we won't find out about Saria's condition until after sundown. You have to get some rest." He places the cup on the coffee table in front of me.

"You two need to sleep," I say. "Kian, you have work in a couple of hours, and Keisha, I'm not even sure when you sleep. It seems like you and Garth work twenty-four seven."

Keisha yawns. "We get an hour or two here and there. The clock is ticking. Everyone is depending on us to get this bomb done and to get it right. We're almost there."

"How's your arm?" Kian asks, eyeing the gauze wrapped around my bicep. "Do you need pain medication?"

"Whatever Edith gave me seems to be working well enough." I hold the teacup to my nose, breathing in chamomile and lavender scented steam. "Go to bed, you guys. I'll be alright." I'm lying. I won't be alright, probably not ever again. Not when Yaz was supposed to be here tonight. I was so excited to show her my new guitar. I imagined us staying up all night, me strumming, her singing, both of us just happy to be together.

Instead, she's on Kian's garage floor, her muscles stiffening as rigor mortis sets in. "If you need anything, just knock," Keisha says. "I'm a light sleeper."

Kian stands up. "I'll leave my bedroom door open," he says. "Come right in. Even if you just need to talk."

"Thanks," I mumble. The wood floor creaks as they make their way down the hallway and into their respective bedrooms.

I finish the tea in one gulp and lay back down. When I close my eyes, I see Yaz: warm brown eyes, purple waves framing her pretty face. She was the one who encouraged me to write songs, the one who believed in my talent when I didn't even believe in myself. My eyes fly open. Tears flood my vision. I'm not sure how I even have any tears left to cry.

I toss back and forth. My heart thumps in my chest. Blood rushes in my ears. My jugular ticks in my neck. I've never heard silence quite this loud.

Zoe, what the hell did you do? Ugh, I guess I'm so exhausted that my defenses are down again. Whenever he gets a chance, Damian will sneak through.

Yaz is dead.

I heard. What were you thinking? I told you not to do anything stupid.

I was thinking that I needed to save my best friend! Tears of frustration stream down my cheeks. I should've known better than to respond to him.

You should've listened to me.

Fuck off, Damian. I fling my walls back up, thicker and stronger than before, wrapped in barbed wire and steel spikes.

I stand up, enraged. My best friend died, and my "soulmate's" response is "I told you so." How dare he! I'm half tempted to climb up the chimney, climb to the palace, soar through Damian's window and smack that goddamn lopsided grin off his face.

There's no way I'm sleeping now. I clench my hands into fists, fighting the urge to punch a hole in the wall. I want to take the sharpest knife I can find, fly over to Melvin Fox's mansion and— And what? Get myself killed? Get captured by Talon?

My hands tremble. I want to rip a picture off the wall and throw it on the floor. I want to bang my head against the wall. I want to tear someone's face in two with my bare hands.

What the hell am I thinking? I'm losing it. I rake my fingers through my hair.

I tip-toe down the hallway. As promised, Kian's door is wide open, his bedside lamp still on. He sits up when he sees me. "Hey," he says. "Are you okay?" I try to answer, but all that comes out is a squeak. "Come in." He pats on the empty space beside him.

"I feel like I'm losing my mind." I sit next to him, my outer thigh touching his.

Kian puts his arms around my waist. I rest my head on his shoulder. "I'm here for you, whatever you need. If you want to talk or if you just want to be silent, just let me know."

"Silence," I say, grateful for that option. "It hurts too much to talk about it." I focus on Kian's breaths, long and steady, and match mine to his. Just breathe in and breathe out. "I felt like I was going crazy. I don't want to be alone right now."

"You can sleep in here tonight," Kian says, shifting over to make room. "If you want to."

"Okay." I lay down, my head sinking into a satin pillow. Kian moves over until he's on the other side of the bed. He lays inches away from me, our bodies close but not touching. I roll onto my side, facing him, my legs bent. My knees brush against his upper thigh.

He turns his head so his eyes meet mine. "Close your eyes."

I wonder if he's going to kiss me. As soon as my eyes shut, I realize how silly I am. He only meant for me to go to sleep. Kian wouldn't try to kiss me, especially not at a time like this.

I suck in a deep breath. Maybe this whole night was just a bad dream. Maybe I'll wake up and everything will be okay.

I wish life was like a video game, and I'd have a chance for a do-over. If I woke up yesterday and could redo last night, I'd listen to Saria. I should've trusted her intuition in the first place.

Then, I'm back in the woods, running, running, running, Yazmin's hand in mine. "Don't let go, Yaz. Don't let go." I clench her fingers with an iron grip, sprinting up hills and never running out of breath. "We're safe now, Yaz. It's going to be okay." Yaz faces me. A smile spreads wide across her face. It's only then that I notice that something's wrong. Her gums are black, her teeth spotted yellow and brown. The rosy color drains from her cheeks. Her face morphs: pallor white then ash-gray, blue lips shriveling, cheeks sunken in. Her teeth disappear, her mouth a gaping black hole. Her eyes hollow out until she's nothing but a skeleton.

I jerk awake. It's brighter in Kian's room, golden rays streaming in through the window. He's still awake, staring at me, the strangest look on his face. "Are you alright?" He asks.

"No, I'm not alright," I say, my tone angry. "My best friend is dead, and my sister might be, too."

"I'm sorry. It was a stupid question."

For a few minutes, we just stare at each other. There's nothing that either of us can say to make this better. Words will only make it more real, and twist the knife deeper.

"You know, I was always kind of a loner." Kian breaks the silence. "In school, I was the weird kid. No one wanted to hang out with me, but you know what? I didn't care. I was content with my family and animals. I never felt a connection with anyone else, never even wanted to." Kian's brow furrows, like he's deep in thought. "More recently, with me taking on the leadership role within The Resistance, I met people like Stellan, Blossom, Chester, Rubi, Garth, and so many others who I respect and trust, but no one I can say that I truly felt connected to. Not until I met you."

My heart flutters.

Kian goes on. "I'm intimately aware of how much it hurts to lose a family member, but I never understood the pain of losing a friend. But now, if I imagine losing you, I can understand it. And I'm so terribly sorry for your loss." Kian sucks in a deep breath. "What I'm trying to say, Zoeli, is that I think you're my best friend. And I never had a best friend before. Hell, I never even had a friend."

Tears roll down my face. "You have no idea how much that means to me." I fight the urge to touch his cheek. "Thank you, Kian."

"No," he says. "Thank you."

CHAPTER 32

Saria

The eyes I open aren't the same ones I closed.

The world around me is brand new. The woods are a magical place full of life and details that I never noticed before. Even in the dark, I can make out the trees' texture, tiny insects crawling up their bark, and various types of fungi growing along the root crown. I see veins running parallel down a blade of grass, the sparkle of each drop of dew on its surface.

"Wow," I breathe. "I can see so clearly now."

"You have the senses of a predator," Red says. "Your eyes have less cones and more rods than before."

I can sense an animal nearby. I hear its heart beating: thump, thump, thump. I lick my lips.

"You're hungry?" Red asks. I nod. With one swift moment, he grabs a rodent, his fingers tight around its squirming body. The white mouse stares up at me, its black beady eyes wide with terror. Red holds it to my lips.

I bite into it, my fangs easily piercing its flesh. It dies instantly. Warm blood fills my mouth. It's spicy and sweet, and so, so good. I suck it down like a cold drink on a hot day. When I'm done, Red tosses the rodent aside. "I'm so sorry,

Sari," he says. "There wasn't another choice. You were going to die."

"You have nothing to apologize for," I say. "I feel great." I run my hand over my stomach, searching for any evidence of yesterday's gunshot wounds, but find none. Any hint of yesterday's injuries healed as I slept.

"I didn't want this for you," Red says. "I wanted you to grow old and have a family. Not banished from the sun, forever seventeen."

"But I wanted this for me," I say. "I'm stronger than ever before. Year after year, I'll grow even stronger. I won't have to be afraid anymore. I'll be able to defend myself." I look up at the sky. "In astronomy I learned that there are billions of stars, but tonight is the first night that I can see them all. And now I have billions of years, infinite time, to learn and grow and to…" My voice trails off. "And to love you," I say. "And that's the best part of all."

For the first time, I notice that Red's eyes are made of rings of color: periwinkle, cobalt, and sky blue. "Sari." His lips press against mine. Tingles rush from the top of my head to my toes. His tongue slips into my mouth. I'm hot and cold at the same time: fire exploding in my core, goosebumps rising on my arms. "I love you, Sari." I've been waiting so long to hear those words, and it's everything I ever hoped it would be. My heart is so full it might explode. If I wasn't immortal, I might be the first person to die from joy induced spontaneous combustion.

"I love you, Red." I lace my fingers through his hair. He kisses me again.

"Do you want to fly with me?" He asks.

My heart jumps with excitement. I've been dreaming of it ever since Red and I met: the two of us, taking to the skies together. Now that I'm a vampire, I can fly as a bat. "How?" I ask.

"Just imagine it," Red says. "Imagine you're soaring through the sky."

I close my eyes. I can see myself: black wings open wide, wind rustling my fur, the stars racing by.

When I open my eyes, it's real. I flap my wings, lifting higher up into the night sky. Red flutters around me, his blue eyes ablaze with excitement.

It feels so natural, like I've been doing this since the day that I was born.

I would choose this a million times. I would die, over and over again, for one night like this.

CHAPTER 33

Zoeli

Two Weeks Later

In some ways, everything is different. Something inside me is irrevocably broken. Over time, I know that I'll adapt. Eventually, I won't dream about Yaz every night. I won't burst into tears every time I strum my guitar. I'll find ways to move on, but I'll never be the same.

In other ways, nothing has changed at all. After a hearty breakfast, Kian and I work out. Today was leg day, so squats, lunges and deadlifts. Afterwards, we replenish the calories we burned by eating copious amounts of donuts and pastries. When our sugar rush commences, we spend the rest of the day practicing magic and studying spells while Garth and Keisha work on their weapon of mass destruction. I hoped that the bomb would be ready by now, but Keisha and Garth swear that they're almost there. "A few more days," they told me earlier.

I can't see Saria until after sundown, but she slept most days anyway, so it isn't much of a change. She comes over almost every night, arm-in-arm with Red, looking happier than I've ever seen her. Every day, I thank God that she survived the transition.

Last night, as Saria studied pictures of Kian's mom, she commented on her beautiful wardrobe. I echoed her sentiments, also enamored by Kinley Reynold's gothic style. Kian led us to his mother's closet and invited us to "take whatever you want." At first, I hesitated, knowing that Kinley's things have remained untouched since her death. Kian assured me, "She'd want you to have them."

And so, Saria and I raided Kinley's walk-in closet, oohing and aahing over the luxurious fabrics. We tried on outfit after outfit. For a moment, we were normal teenagers again, spinning around the full-length mirror, chatting about fashion. Saria looked like a vampire queen in a black gown with a thigh-high slit and an embroidered neckline. I added new pieces to my wardrobe: a cropped black leather jacket, a satin corset, black jeans, and at least a dozen more.

Saria isn't the only one who almost died that night. Amos and Hadrien fought until both were ready to drop out of sheer exhaustion. There was no clear winner. Badly injured and worn, Amos fled the scene. If he continued on, Amos feared that he would've been dealt a fatal blow, given that he was feeling weak and disoriented. All of his wounds healed during his day's sleep, a perk of being a vampire, but Amos doesn't seem keen on confronting Hadrien again.

No one's heard from Layal since she darted into the woods. I doubt that anyone is going to see her anytime soon. Since Hadrien saw her face, now she's on Talon's most wanted list. I imagine that she's hiding in a foxhole somewhere. All I know is that if she dares to come around here, she has some explaining to do.

Luckily, Hadrien didn't see Kian, and all of the soldiers who did are dead. Next time, we have to be more careful. I'll never underestimate Saria's intuition again.

The biggest change since that night is that I sleep in Kian's bed. Some nights, we lay in silence. Other nights, I ramble on and on, sharing every detail about Yaz, stamping them into my memories, never to be forgotten.

Tonight, I lay on my side, watching him. He turns his head, feeling my stare on him. "What's up?" His lips curve into an awkward smile.

I shrug. He's on the other side of the bed, so careful to never touch me. I inch closer to him. Kian's brow furrows. "What are you doing?"

"I just," I sigh, unsure what to say. "Do you want to cuddle?"

"Cuddle?" Kian repeats it like I'm speaking in a foreign language.

"Cuddle, you know, like a hug?" I look away. "It would just be comforting to me, that's all." God, this is so embarrassing.

"Um, okay, sure," Kian says, surprising me. He rolls onto his side, facing me, and holds out his arms. "Um, come in."

I wriggle over to him. I rest my head on his chest and curl my arm around his back. His arms close around me. Warmth envelops me, like a blanket fresh out of the dryer. I breathe in his scent, spicy soap and aftershave.

It feels so good, but I want to be even closer. I want to crawl inside his skin. I pull him tighter to me, our bodies pressed flush together.

I'm suddenly keenly aware of my pajama's flimsy fabric, and the worn cotton of his gray sweatpants. Two thin pieces of cloth are all that stands between his skin on mine.

I pull back and look up at him, curious if he's having the same reaction as me. His lips dip down to brush against mine. Soft, tentative at first, then faster, harder, desperate. His fingers tangle in my hair. My nails dig into his back. I can feel his body reacting to mine.

Kian is clumsy, fumbling with the buttons on my pajama shirt. "Are you sure that you want to do this?" He asks.

"Yes," I say. My shirt slides off my shoulders as I pull Kian's over his head.

"I've never done this before," Kian says.

"Then I'm the one who should be asking you," I say. "Are you sure that you want to do this?"

"I want to," Kian pauses. "I just wanted you to know because, um, I don't know what I'm doing. I might not be good at it."

I smile at him. "Practice makes perfect."

* * *

Afterwards, I lay across him, my leg wrapped around his knees, my chest against his. I breathe heavily, my heart pounding, tingles still racing down my spine. Moz lays next to us, singing his soulful song.

"I'm not your soulmate," Kian says, staring up at the ceiling.

"Stop it," I murmur. "I don't want to think about him."

"I've studied enough to know that the soulmate connection is relentless. It won't be denied. You'll end up with him in the end."

"I won't," I grumble. "Can you please stop talking about this? I want to enjoy my time with you."

"Okay, I'm sorry." Kian runs his fingers up and down my bare back. "It's just, it's hard not to think about it, you know?"

"I guess I'll have to think of more ways to distract you." I grin devilishly.

Kian raises his brows. "Will you now?"

When we come together, it's more than lust and flesh. It's our souls intertwined, two hearts beating as one. In the throes of passion, I want to tell Kian that he's the one. That the gods got it all wrong. That I never felt this way when I was with Damian. That this isn't my first time, but it's the first time I ever felt like this.

Kian Reynolds? You've got to be shitting me.

I gasp. I didn't even notice my guard coming down. It's none of your business.

Of all people, this is who you choose? Kian Reynolds? He's ugly and weird and—

And more of a man than you'll ever be.

Images fill my mind: Damian punching Kian in the face, over and over again, beating him to a bloody pulp.

Don't you dare.

More images: Kian sprawled out on his back, blood spewing from the knife lodged in his throat.

Leave us alone! I erect my walls, fortifying them with all the strength that I can muster. But it's too late.

Damian knows.

CHAPTER 34

Damian

I pace across my father's office, clenching and unclenching my firsts. Kian Reynolds. I can't believe it. I'm not a fan of Weston, but he should've finished him off when he had the chance.

I turn on the computer and flip the screen until I get to the live footage of employees entering the palace. Kian is due to arrive any minute.

Kian enters the screen, messy white hair sticking out over his too big ears. What the hell does Zoe see in him? He looks like a goddamn albino freak.

I hold a walkie-talkie to my lips. "Sergeant Sterling, this is Prince Damian, over."

There's a blast of static and then Sterling's voice comes through. "Copy."

"I want Kian Reynold's in my father's office. Stat."

"On it."

I crack my knuckles, my pulse twitching in my neck. I sit on the blue velvet throne at the head of the mahogany conference table. My father takes Sundays off, so his office is all mine.

A few minutes later, there's a knock at the door. "Come in," I say.

Sergeant Sterling pushes the door open. "I have Reynolds, your majesty." Kian stands beside him, his gaze on the ground.

I nod. "Leave us," I say.

"Yes, sir." The door closes behind Sterling. Kian stands at the other side of the room, shifting side to side.

"Do you know why you're here?" I ask.

Kian stares at the wall, not saying a word. He's uglier than I remembered: skinny face, pasty skin, gap between his front teeth, crooked nose. A raised pink scar slices his eyebrow. "You're hideous," I say.

Kian lifts his brows. "That's not what Zoe said last night."

That's it. I'm going to rip this kid in two. I raise my hand, aiming at him. A laser-like blast of purple magic shoots from my pointer finger.

Kian opens his palm. In a split second, a golden protective mist swirls around him. The purple blast ricochets off the mist, and boomerangs back into my abdomen. "Argh!" I clutch the point of impact, pain radiating from my stomach to my ribs. Kian smirks.

"You piece of—" I snarl. I stand up and shoot again, harder this time. This time, when it bounces back, I duck in time, avoiding the blow.

I grit my teeth in frustration. Kian's defensive magic is stronger than I imagined. I ball up my fists and take a fighting stance. "Let's do this the old fashioned way. No magic." I'm sure that he's going to refuse. It isn't fair and I know it. I'm bigger, taller and broader. I weigh at least fifty pounds more.

To my surprise, the golden mist dissipates. "Let's go," Kian says, his fists up.

We circle each other like boxers, bouncing on our feet. I swing first. Kian swerves out of the way. His fist comes up from nowhere, an uppercut to my jaw. I wince, hoping that he didn't do any damage to my chin. I'm too handsome to be taking blows to the face.

I growl. "You know what makes me sick? My mother did you a favor. She gave you a job that you're not even qualified for. And what do you do? You go and make a move on my girl. You ungrateful, disloyal, piece of shit." I swing again. This time I don't miss. Crack! Kian stumbles backwards.

I have him up against the wall. It's over. I sock him in the eye. I jab him in the nose. I punch him again and again and again. Kian curls up, his hands blocking blows rather than attempting to fight back. I win.

I step back, panting. "Now you listen to me," I say. "You're going to stay away from my girl. Do you understand me?"

Kian wipes blood from beneath his nose. His left eye is red and puffy. A bruise is already forming on his swollen cheek.

"I said, do you understand me?"

"I understand," Kian mumbles.

"Good," I say. "And you're fired. I wasn't able to find anyone to cover your shifts for today or tomorrow, but after that, you're done. Consider yourself lucky that I don't tell the magistrate to charge you with harboring a fugitive." I point to the door. "Now get out of here. I don't want to ever see you again."

Kian leaves without a word.

* * *

I thought that kicking Kian's ass would make me feel better, and it did. But the satisfaction was short-lived. Less than an hour later, I'm enraged again, pacing around my bedroom like a caged animal.

No matter how badly I hurt Kian, the fact remains: Zoe betrayed me. The only thing that would make me feel better is if she came back to me. Even better, if she begged for forgiveness.

I scroll through my phone, names whizzing by. If I call Caliah, a little sweet talk is all it would take to convince her to come over. I'm sure she'd be willing to do things that help me relax. It's tempting, but my mind-state is so screwed up, I'm not even in the mood.

I call my cousin Colson. Since we were kids, he's been like an older brother to me. He always seems to know what to do. He doesn't answer the phone.

I check the clock. It's still early on a Sunday morning. Colson's probably in bed. I'll just go over there and wake him up.

A few minutes later, I pull into Colson's driveway. I skip up the front steps, remembering playing hopscotch on them when we were kids. As usual, the front door is unlocked. I waltz right in and kick off my Nikes, adding them to the pile of sneakers by the doormat. I pass through the foyer and enter the living room. Cartoons play on the big screen TV. Colson's little brother sits on the carpet, surrounded by toy cars and blocks.

"What up, Atlas?" I lean against the back of the L-shaped sofa.

"Damian!" Atlas jumps up when he sees me. "Look what I can do!" He opens his hand, revealing a chunk of celestite. "Watch me!" He grabs a toy rocket ship and positions it on the coffee table, face up. Celestite clenched in his fist, Atlas's face squishes up in concentration. "Three, two, one, blast off!" The rocket ship takes off, shooting straight up into the ceiling before it crashes back to the floor. Based on all of the marks on the ceiling, this wasn't Atlas's first try.

"Nice job, little man," I say. "You're going to be a world-class sorcerer."

Atlas's whole face lights up, a sparkle in his brown eyes. "Do you want to see more? I can even make my monster truck do tricks."

"Show me later. I need to talk to Colson. Is he in his room?"

"Yeah, he's still sleeping. I yelled for him earlier, and he told me to leave him alone."

Colson's mom enters the room. "Damian, how are you my dear?" She opens her arms.

As we embrace, I have to bend down to kiss her cheek. But it doesn't feel like it was too long ago when she used to scoop me off the ground to tend to my skinned knees. "Hi, Aunt Margie. I'm just coming by to see what Colson's up to."

"It's a good thing you're here. That boy will sleep all day if we let him," Margie grumbles. "When you get him out of bed, tell him to take out the garbage."

"Will do." I head down the hallway towards Colson's bedroom. I try to turn the doorknob, but it won't budge. It's locked. I don't bother to knock. Magic spills from my fingertips, sliding into the keyhole. Another quick jiggle and the door bursts open.

On Colson's king-sized bed, a redhead gasps, scrambling to cover her bare breasts. Colson sits up, scowling. "Damian, what the hell, man? Close the door." I slam the door behind me.

"Sorry, man. I didn't know that she was here."

"No one does," Colson hisses. "So, keep it down man. She snuck in my window last night."

The redhead lays beside Colson, smoothing her messy hair. She pulls the blanket high, covering her nakedness, but I already got an eyeful. She has a nice rack. I notice the crown-shaped mark on her collarbone, my eyebrows raising in surprise. "You're a royal?" I ask.

"I'm Penelope Wolfe," the girl replies. "But call me Penny."

"Penny," I repeat. "How come I don't know you?"

"When I was a baby, my mother was accused of a crime. My parents fled from Aurelia, moved to the human realm, and changed our last name," Penny explains.

I settle into a leather armchair. "Why did you come back? Were the charges dropped?"

Penny's lips spread into a wide, almost disturbing smile. "Now that my great-great-great-great aunt is in power, all of the charges have been dismissed."

"Your aunt?" I repeat, not following.

"Yes, I believe you know her quite well. Licinia Wolfe." Penny says, her tone full of pride. "Talon, Licinia, and my family were all wrongfully expelled from our homeland, and now that we've rightfully returned, it's a new era for Aurelia. Three representatives from the most powerful royal families, Keifer Nightingale, Talon Crowe, and Licinia Wolfe, ruling side-by-side, changing antiquated laws and leading Aurelians to a future more prosperous than we ever imagined." Penny runs her finger along Colson's cheek. "And to think, without this guy right here, none of it would've been possible."

"You give me too much credit," Colson says. "All I did was give a little blood."

"Without your contribution, we wouldn't have been able to breach the portal. None of this would've happened."

"Wait a minute." I shake my head in disbelief. "Are you telling me that Colson's blood was used to open the portal?" I turn to my cousin, eyes narrowed. "Were you complicit in the invasion of Aurelia?"

"Aww, man, don't say it like that," Colson responds. "They were going to find a way in sooner or later. I just ensured when they got in, we'd be safe. I did this for you, man. For all of us with the Nightingale name."

"Did you?" I rest my hands behind my head. "Enlighten me."

"I made a deal. If I gave my blood, they wouldn't kill you or Keifer. They'd even allow you to stay in power."

"Bullshit," I retort. "They allowed us to stay in power for public perception. Most Aurelians love my parents. They were worried about an uprising."

"Not true. Hadrien is strong enough to handle an uprising. They honored the deal I made with them."

I shake my head. "If that's what helps you sleep at night, but you should know that you sound like an idiot."

Colson narrows his eyes. "And you sound like an ungrateful prick. If it wasn't for me, your ass wouldn't even be the prince right now. When I gave my blood, it was under the condition that you would remain the prince. And this is the thanks that I get?"

"Are you serious?" I ask, my fists balled at my sides. "You didn't need to give them your blood to make me the prince. I was already the prince. If they hadn't come into Aurelia, I'd be on my way to becoming the one and only king. Now I'll have to share the throne."

"It's always all about you, isn't it?" Colson scowls. "What about the betterment of Aurelia? What about me? Talon promised me a leadership role, right after I finish college."

"Ah, so that's what this is all about. You wanted more power. You didn't think that I'd offer you a position? You could've been my chief advisor, court magistrate, whatever you wanted, man. You didn't have to do this!"

"It wasn't only about that, man. It's about the Aurelian people. At first I was resistant too, but the more I talked to Penny, the more it made sense. We're superior to humans. I didn't make it that way, it's just a fact. The laws protecting humans and prohibiting their enslavement inhibited the advancement of our kind. It's time that we put our species first."

"You sound like a bigot, man."

"Not long ago, you would have agreed with me. You let that nimwit get into your head."

Is he right? Did I used to sound like this?

I'm not an angel by any means. I'll admit to believing that supernaturals are superior, but never to the extent that I justified slavery. There were at least few times when I witnessed discrimination and even mistreatment of duds, and I turned the other way. I've used slurs more often than I should have, but I never advocated for violence.

That makes me better than them. Right?

CHAPTER 35

Saria

I lean back in Kian's brown leather armchair, my twin sister on the couch across from me, her legs bouncing fast. "I would've told him about my telepathic connection with Damian, but I was sure that he would throw me out of The Resistance. I thought that I could control it..." Zoes voice trails off. "When I apologized, Kian wouldn't even look at me. He doesn't trust easily, but he trusted me, and I ruined that. He's never going to forgive me"

"He will. I think he just needs some time." Blossom sits beside her, one hand on her bulging belly, the other on Zoe's arm. "But I'm worried about his safety. I can't believe that he went to work after that."

"I told him to stay home," Zoe says. "He wouldn't listen." Moz, the dragoni, sprawls out on the rug, belly up. Zoe kneels down and strokes the yellow scales covering his stomach.

I watch the wall clock strike seven pm. Kian should be home any minute now. The doorbell rings. "That must be the pizza delivery," Blossom says, rising from her seat.

Stellan stands up faster than Blossom can. "I'll get it. You need to rest."

Blossom rolls her eyes. "I'm pregnant, not disabled." As Stellan walks ahead of her, Blossom shrugs and sits back down. "If you insist."

A moment later, Stellan reappears holding two pizza boxes. The aroma wafts towards me, and I begin to salivate. It's not fair. If eating food will make me violently ill, why does it have to smell so delicious? Red assured me that over time, I'll stop noticing the appetizing aromas, but I'm not so sure. I think he underestimates how much I love pizza.

As if he can read my thoughts, Red puts his hand on my shoulder. I force a smile, hoping that he can't see the turmoil behind it.

When I dreamed of becoming a vampire, I only thought of the positives: power, immortality, and loving Red for eternity. I never imagined that the downsides would hit me as hard as they have.

Last night, I had a breakdown. The words spilled faster than my tears. I lamented over all of the things I'll miss: sunbathing on the beach, finishing high school, throwing my cap in the air at graduation, going to college, birdwatching during daylight hours when the most beautiful species are active.

As soon as my thoughts escaped my lips, I regretted saying them. Seeing the despair on Red's face, I knew that I should've kept them to myself. Since then, I keep pretending that I've never been happier, but I can tell that he sees right through me.

It's an adjustment, but I'll be okay. I'll get used to it.

Stellan sits beside his wife, his hand on her belly. "Do you feel that? She just kicked!" His voice brims with excitement.

Blossom giggles. "Of course I felt it. She almost broke my rib."

I swallow hard. I'm only seventeen, so I don't want children anytime soon, but I always imagined that I would. When I envision my future, I imagine myself with a baby in my arms, a toddler waddling around and calling me mommy. That picture dissipates. I'll never be a mother now.

Red studies me, his gaze shifting from Blossom's belly back to me, concern etched into his forehead. I take his hand, smiling wider than before. His worry lines grow deeper.

The front door opens and shuts. Kian walks into the room. My hand flies to my mouth. His left eye is half-shut from swelling, a black bruise encircling its socket. He has a split lip, blood caking in the cut. His cheeks are red and swollen.

"Oh my God. What happened?" Zoe asks.

"What do you think happened?" Kian responds, his tone sharp.

"Do you need a healer?" Blossom asks.

"No, but I need a job," Kian retorts. "I'm fired. Tuesday is my last day."

Zoe gasps. "He can't do that."

"He can and he did."

"I'm so sorry, Kian." Zoe reaches out to him, but Kian moves aside, avoiding her touch.

The doorbell rings. "Who's that?" Red asks.

Kian freezes.

"Are you expecting someone?" Blossom asks.

Kian shakes his head. Ding-dong. Ding-dong. Kian pulls the curtain aside, peeking out the window. "I don't believe it," he says.

"Who is it?" I ask.

"It's the queen." The doorbell sounds again. Kian points to me and then Zoe. "You two stay hidden. Nobody else moves. I'm going to see what she wants."

Zoe and I duck into the hallway closet, our ears pressed to the door.

We hear the front door squeal open. "Good evening, your majesty. To what do I owe the pleasure of your call?"

"Kian, oh my gosh, what's happened to you?" The queen sounds horrified.

"I didn't have the best day at work," Kian grumbles.

"I heard that you were fired," Taya says. "That's why I'm here. I want to offer you another job."

"You do?" Kian seems skeptical. "Have you discussed it with the rest of your family? Because I don't think they're going to approve."

"This is a private offer. Just between me and you."

"Um, ok." Kian sounds bewildered. "What is it?"

"I want to hire you to kill Hadrien."

CHAPTER 36

Zoeli

I never thought we'd see that day that Queen Taya would join The Resistance, but here we are. Taya follows us around the basement as we show her all of the stations, explaining our battle plan. When we're done, we all sit in metal folding chairs facing a map of Aurelia.

"This is quite the plan," Taya says, smoothing her wavy brown hair. "But I'm not sure that I understand how you intend to defeat Hadrien."

"We created a bomb," Keisha says. "We plan to drop it during the day while Hadrien sleeps. It will demolish the palace and everyone inside."

"Everyone?" Taya's brows raise in alarm. "Including my son and daughter? Including me?"

"No, not necessarily," Garth responds. "We've designed a magical system that can identify and spare innocent lives."

Taya's eyes widen. "Well, that's quite impressive. How exactly would an innocent person be distinguished from others?"

"Within a split second, the magic will study each person's psyche, measuring their loyalty to Talon. If the assessment determines that a person has little or no allegiance to Talon, another form of magic will be injected into their veins, a magic that will afford them invincibility, if only for the thirty seconds it will take for the castle to collapse."

"That's incredible," Taya responds. "But it's not foolproof. What about those who have goodness in their hearts but have lost their way? Many impressionable minds have been brainwashed by misinformation, and may only need a break from the propaganda and biased media coverage in order to find the right path. Would they all be killed?"

"Unfortunately, there's no reliable method to measure goodness in one's heart. Each and every one of us has goodness in our hearts. It's our actions, our allegiances, and our behaviors that determine who we are," Garth responds.

"And what about those who are simply uneducated or uninformed? It isn't their fault that they don't know any better. And what about young people who are still figuring out who they are? Would they be killed too?"

"Queen Taya, I hear what you're saying, but there's no way for us to measure who someone might become in the future. The purpose of our assessment is to determine who is a threat, and eliminate that threat immediately."

"I think I have a better way. I was considering doing it myself, but I'll feel more confident if I have some help. My way helps preserve innocent life and also the palace. We may have been infiltrated by malevolent leaders, but the palace itself is an architectural masterpiece and a symbol of our homeland."

Kian folds his arms across his chest. "Before I consider your proposition, I must know, what do you plan on doing after Hadrien is killed?"

"Without Hadrien in the picture, Keifer won't be afraid to stand up to Talon and Licinia. We'll throw them out of the palace, and life will continue as before."

Kian shakes his head. "That's not going to work for me. Things may be worse now, but they were bad before. Keifer isn't fit to be king, and you know it. And neither is your son." His tone takes on a harsher edge when he says *your son.*

"Then who do you suggest should be king?" Taya asks.

"I believe that we should enact a democracy. Every Aurelian citizen should have the opportunity to vote for their leader. That includes duds, half-breeds, and even humans should they decide to immigrate here."

Taya cocks her head, considering. A moment later, she extends her hand. "You have a deal."

Kian takes her hand, and they shake on it.

CHAPTER 37

Zoeli

It's the night before the big day, and I can't sleep. We spent most of the evening with Taya, ironing out the details. Our plan is solid, but I still worry that something could go wrong. I thought we had it all figured out last time, and look how it ended up. I blink away tears thinking about that night. "I miss you Yaz," I whisper to the dark room. "They're going to pay for what they did to you. I'm going to make sure of it."

I can't seem to get comfortable on the living room couch. I try laying on my side, and then stretching out on my back, but nothing feels right. I'm half-tempted to walk down the hallway and slide into Kian's bed, but I probably shouldn't push my luck.

My conversations with Kian have been limited to logistics and strategy. Since we need to get this done before Kian's official termination of employment, we've been working at a break-neck pace. Besides mapping out Hadrien's assassination, we had to contact the other faction leaders to corroborate the battle plan. Not long after Hadrien is killed, we'll officially declare war.

With everything going on, I haven't had time to bring up what happened with Damian, but I'm not sure what else I would say. I already told him that I'm sorry. I'll apologize again and again if he needs me to.

I glance at the clock. It's almost two in the morning. I sigh. I've been cooped up in the house all day. Maybe some fresh air will help me get some sleep.

I rise up out of the chimney, and soar across the starry sky. I flap my wings against the wind, zooming over the Elysian Forest and towards the Azula Sea. I perch on the edge of a branch, watching the smooth, glossy water.

There she is, stretched out on a rock like all of the times I spotted her before. The mermaid turns around, droplets spraying from her shimmery green tail. Her purple eyes meet mine. For a few moments, we just stare at each other.

Finally, she speaks. "What is it that you want, witch? Do you wish to harm me?" Her voice drips with venom.

Is that what she thinks? That I want to hurt her? I watch her because she captivates me. I'm mesmerized by her beauty, and in awe of her existence.

I should probably just leave. Witches and merkind are sworn enemies. A few kind words won't erase a hundred years of tension. She'll probably tell me to go to hell.

Yet, I'm compelled to speak to her. Blue ribbons of magic swirl around me as I fly to the ground. By the time I land, I've shifted to human form.

The mermaid gasps. "If you come any closer, I will attack. I will not stop until you are dead."

"Whoa," I say. "I don't want to fight you."

"Why are you here? This is our territory. It's the last thing we have that's our own. You've taken everything else from us," she hisses. "You don't know what it's like to have your rights stripped from you, to have your natural born right to use both your tail and your legs taken from you."

"Actually, I know more than you think," I say.

The mermaid's purple eyes blaze with anger. "What do you know about being trapped in an underwater prison? Besides the mental anguish we've suffered, our underwater existence has wreaked havoc on our bodies. Mermaids were meant to live equally on the land and in the sea. We were built with both lungs and gills, and daily oxygen is essential for our health. Yet, most modern merkind are so fearful of coming to the surface that they have never taken a breath of air. Our bodies require a diet from both land and sea, yet we survive only on sea creatures. We're dying in record numbers, day after day. Young merkind are developing rare forms of cancer and organ failure. Most of us struggle with infertility. Sooner or later, possibly sooner, we'll be extinct."

"I'm sorry to hear that." I shuffle from foot to foot. "There are some of us who want to do the right thing. We want to free you."

The mermaid snorts. "I'll believe it when I see it."

"I can understand why you'd feel that way," I say. "And I'll understand if you don't believe me, but I promise you, I'm going to try."

For the first time, the mermaid's expression softens. "You better get out of here. If my brother sees you, he won't ask any questions. He'll shoot to kill."

I nod. "Thanks. By the way, what's your name?"

She doesn't answer.

"That's okay, you don't have to tell me. I'm Zoeli. And, um, I'm sorry I disturbed you." I turn to walk away.

"Isla."

I spin back around. "What's that?"

"My name is Isla."

My lips curve into a small smile. "It was nice to meet you, Isla."

With a quick nod, Isla slides off the rock and into the water. There's a splash, a ripple of waves, and then she's gone.

CHAPTER 38

Zoeli

When I wake up, there's a fresh cup of coffee and a donut at the table where I usually sit. Heat radiates in my chest, and a goofy grin spreads across my face. Maybe this means that Kian forgives me. At the very least, we're headed in the right direction.

Kian walks in, wearing his royal blue guard uniform. "It's time to go."

I gulp down the rest of my coffee. "I'm ready."

A few minutes later, I duck down in the passenger seat of Kian's car. The engine roars to life, and Kian backs out of the driveway. "Late last night, when Hadrien wasn't looking, Taya slipped the potion into his glass of blood. He drank the whole thing," Kian says.

"And she's sure that will make him sleep?"

"As sure as we can be. Hadrien's an anomaly. As far as we know, there's no one else like him. But this also isn't an ordinary sleep potion. This is a weapon of war, mixed and chanted over by more than fifty talented witches, then stored in a container made from demonite to ensure optimal preservation.

"To test it out, Taya put one droplet on her tongue. She was out cold for over twenty-four hours. We're confident it should knock him out. Even if he wakes up, he'll be weak and disoriented, and it'll be three-on-one."

"We make a good team. We got this." I suck in a deep breath. "Kian, about the other night, I am so sorry. I—"

"Forget about it," Kian says. "I'm sorry that I overreacted. It was just shocking, that's all."

"I should've told you about the telepathic connection. I thought that I'd completely blocked him out. That night, well, I lost control, slipped into oblivion or something."

Kian raises one brow, his lips curving into a satisfied smile. "I was that good, huh?"

"The best I've ever had."

"Really?" Kian stops at a red light. He turns to me, his eyes wide with disbelief.

"Not even close." I gaze into his eyes, irises so pale they fade into the whites, but this close, I can make out the faintest color blue. His left eye is still swollen, the pale skin around it violet and green.

The car behind us honks. I startle. The traffic light turned green, but neither of us noticed. Kian hits the gas. I can see the palace in the distance, looming over us in the brightly colored sky.

Kian reaches over and takes my hand in his. His fingers are long and slender, curled around mine. And suddenly, I'm not scared anymore. Everything is going to be alright.

* * *

As Kian pulls into the employee parking lot, blue tendrils swirl around my limbs. I trade hair for feathers, then arms for wings. A moment later, the transition is complete. I am a crow.

Kian parks his car, turns off the engine and unbuttons the top half of his work shirt. "Come on in," he says.

I wriggle inside his shirt, laying as flat as I can against his abdomen. Kian refastens his buttons. "Can you breathe in there? One peck for yes, two pecks for no." I poke his belly with my beak once. "Okay, if you can't breathe, give me another poke," he says. "It shouldn't be long. Taya is coming to get me right away."

I cling to him, careful to remain still as possible as his boots thud against the pavement. He digs inside his pocket. A moment later there's a beep as his employee card opens the back door. I can feel Kian's heartbeat, vibrating against my feathers.

"Reynolds! What happened to your face, man? Is what I heard true? Did you scuffle with the prince?"

"I'll tell you about it on my break." Kian keeps on walking. As he moves down the dungeon hallways, I recognize the tinny echo of the guard's footsteps, the familiar howl of an old, wretched prisoner named Helen. Suddenly, I'm back in my old cell, shivering on the stone floor. A guard with strange eyes watches me from the other side. He pushes a thick comforter through the bars, risking his job to keep me warm.

"Reynolds, there you are." A male voice brings me back to the present. "The queen is looking for you. She asked that you meet her in her private office up on the third floor. Do you know where that is?"

"Yes, sir," Kian responds. "Do you have someone to cover my post?"

"Nilson is going to stay on until you get back."

"I'm on my way."

I stay flush against Kian's stomach, hoping that no one notices the bump beneath his shirt. Hopefully they'll just think that he's bloated. With all the donuts we inhale, it's hard to believe that his stomach is as flat as it is.

We're in the main part of the castle now, weaving through a labyrinth of hallways. "What is your business here?" A new voice asks.

"Officer Reynolds, sir. The queen asked to see me."

"Alright. Go ahead."

With every step that Kian takes, I bounce from side to side. A door opens and shuts. Finally, I hear Taya's voice. "Are you ready?"

"Ready as I'll ever be." Kian unbuttons his top button and looks inside his shirt. "Zoe, are you?"

I pop my head out the top of his shirt. "Hey, Zoe." Taya is dressed in business-casual attire: a collared shirt, khaki pants and brown loafers. Her hair is tied up in a tight bun. "Very few have access to the hallways that lead to Hadrien's sleeping quarters. She holds up a black keycard. Even I don't. But my husband's card permits access to the entirety of the palace. I took it from his wallet when he was sleeping. I doubt he'll even notice it's missing. Servants race to unlock doors for him before he ever has to use it.

"When we approach the final doorway, two highly trained knights will be guarding the entrance. Zoe, you stay out of sight. Kian, let me do the talking. You got it?"

"Got it," Kian says. I bob my head in agreement.

Taya picks up a beige leather tote bag from the floor. "This is going to get messy, so I brought a change of clothes for everyone. To ensure that Hadrien stays dead, we'll have to decapitate him and then cut out his heart. Afterwards, his head and his heart need to be incinerated, and the ashes buried at least six-feet deep in separate locations. I'll take care of that part.

"Once the deed is done, we need to disappear. There will be eye witness accounts and video footage of us entering the room. For Hadrien's privacy, there aren't any cameras inside his bedroom, but once they find his remains, it won't be hard for them to figure out what happened. Kian, make sure that everyone is gone from your house. SWAT teams will be surrounding your place. There's going to be hundreds, if not thousands, of soldiers out looking for you."

"Understood," Kian said. "But I'm not going into hiding. I'm going to meet up with my troops, and we're going to war."

Taya spreads open her tote bag. "Zoe, you're less likely to be spotted inside my bag."

As much as I love being close to Kian, I have to admit Taya's right. Besides, it was getting stuffy in his shirt.

Taya wraps me up in a soft t-shirt, then places me inside her bag. "Okay, let's do this." She hangs the bag over her shoulder.

I can't see anything other than the t-shirt's green fabric in front of my eyes. With every stride, I'm jostled around the bag, making it even more difficult to keep track of where we are.

We stop for a moment. I hear the beep that proceeds the swipe of a keycard. Then, we're moving again.

As we walk, I hear the regular hustle and bustle of the palace: the clattering of dishes, a lively conversation, a maid's vacuum, laughter echoing down the corridor. The further we walk, the quieter it becomes.

Beep. Beep. We enter another restricted area. All I hear now is the tap of footsteps against the tiles: Kian's thump followed by Taya's clack.

"Your majesty," A male voice rings out. "What brings you here?"

"I need to speak to Hadrien."

"He's asleep." I hear another male voice. "He asks not to be bothered during these hours."

"Sir Charles, this is an urgent matter," Taya responds. "My husband asked me and Officer Reynolds to speak to Hadrien immediately."

"We haven't been notified of an emergency," one of the knights says.

"It's a very sensitive matter. We're trying to keep it quiet," Taya says. "So as not to alarm the public."

"Hey, wasn't he fired? I heard he got in a fight with the prince."

"You shouldn't believe everything you hear," Taya scoffs. "Most of the time rumors are simply untrue. Now, will you please move aside so I can handle my business?"

"Um, your majesty, we're under strict orders to not let anyone inside without explicit permission from the high ruler or the king."

"With all due respect, I'm not 'anyone,' Sir Walter. Shall I call my husband and let him know that you're defying my orders?"

"Um, I mean—"

"It's fine," the other knight cuts him off. "She's the queen, man. The rules don't apply to her."

And we're in.

CHAPTER 39

Zoeli

As soon as the door shuts behind us, I peek out the top of the tote bag. It's pitch black inside Hadrien's bedroom. An orange flame, like a candle, rises from Taya's fingertip, illuminating the room with a soft glow.

Cavernous walls are painted blood-red. Thick black fabric covers the windows, blocking out any daylight. A four poster king-sized bed is dwarfed by the enormity of the room. The four vertical posts are intricately carved, lifelike skulls perched on top.

Hadrien lays across black velvet covers, his eyes closed. I hold my breath, worried that the slightest noise could wake him up.

Taya digs inside her tote bag. She holds a short sword, its ruby handle glinting in the light. It appears handmade, curved teeth poking out from both sides to create a unique shape almost like a flame. "This is for the head." She hands the blade to Kian.

She sifts through the bag and grabs a golden dagger. Diamonds and sapphires encircle its handle, a nightingale etched into the blade. "And this is for the heart."

Blue beams swirl around me, lacing through my feathers. A moment later, my feet are planted on the glossy wood floors, my talons replaced by hands and fingernails. "I'll do the honors," I say, my hand outstretched.

Last night, Taya told us that she's never taken a life before. She thought she might faint if she did the stabbing. Kian and I were happy to take that burden off her hands. While I'm not a killer, I don't feel any remorse in this case. Hadrien is the embodiment of evil, and eliminating him means saving thousands of people from death and suffering.

We tiptoe over to the bed. The dagger is cold against my palm. My heart must be beating a thousand times per minute. Hadrien is motionless, his legs sprawled apart, his hands by his side. This almost seems too easy.

I hold the dagger overhead, aiming straight for his chest. Sweat beads along my hairline. One swift motion and he's done. I got this. I count in my head: One, two—

Hadrien's eyes pop open. Before I can say a word, his fingers are around my throat. I can't breathe. He clenches harder. My vision blurs.

Kian's sword falls on Hadrien's neck. It slices off his head in one clean swipe. Blood spews like a geyser from the severed arteries. Hadrien releases me, his hand dropping back on the bed. I suck air in, filling up my oxygen-deprived lungs. "Are you okay?" Kian asks.

With one forceful thrust, I plunge the dagger deep into Hadrien's heart. "I am now."

Even with a blade lodged in his chest, his heart continues to beat. I remove the blade and stab him again and again. The heart still beats.

"Take it out," Taya says.

I slip my fingers inside the wound. I rip his heart from his body. It throbs in my bare hands. My hands and arms are soaked in blood. I can taste it in my mouth. Bile rises in my throat.

Taya holds her tote bag open. I drop the beating heart inside, right next to the severed head. "Now go clean yourself up. We have to go."

In the adjoining bathroom, I rinse my face and change into clean clothes. There's so much blood. No matter how much I scrub, I can still smell it.

I leave my bloodstained clothes on the bathroom floor. Back in the bedroom, Taya stands in front of a bookshelf, laser-focused as she runs her fingers along the spines of the books. "I found it." Taya presses a black book with gold lettering. Click. The bookshelf swings open, revealing the hallway hidden behind it. Taya swings her blood-soaked tote bag over her shoulder. "Let's get out of here."

I look back once. Rivers of blood roll down the sides of the bed. Hadrien's decapitated body is unmoving, but until we burn and bury his head and heart, it's possible that someone could put him back together again.

Taya leads us through secret passageways, down dirt stairs and into a maze of underground tunnels. We sprint through the darkness, the flame from Taya's hand our only light source. We turn left, then right, then right and left again. I'm panting from the exertion, sure that we must be lost.

The ceiling gets lower and lower, until we're forced to crawl, hands and knees dragging through the mud. Sweat drips down my back. My heart races like a jackhammer.

"We're here," Taya says, pushing open an overhead latch. Sunlight shines in from above me. I squirm out of the hole and roll onto the ground, tempted to kiss the grass.

"We did it!" I jump to my feet. We're out in the woods, at least a half-mile from the palace. I stretch my arms out, wrapping Kian and Taya both into a hug. "We actually did it!" I jump up and down, and both Kian and Taya join in.

It's a moment to celebrate, that's for sure.

But it's far from over.

We may have won the battle, but we still have to fight the war.

CHAPTER 40

Zoeli

"The troops are lined up," Kian says. "Are you ready to go?" He wears a bulletproof vest over his camouflage tactical gear. A machine gun hangs from a strap on his shoulder. The sword he used to behead Hadrien is tucked into his belt.

Wind whistles through the trees. A thin layer of snow covers the ground. Snowflakes drift through the air. I shiver.

Keisha twists her black curls up into a tight bun. "I'm ready to slay them all."

"That's the spirit." Kian pats her shoulder.

I swallow hard. "So, you'll be on the ground, and I'll be in the air." My gaze shifts from Keisha to Kian. I might never see them again.

"That's the strategy," Kian says.

Keisha wraps me in a hug. "Good luck up there," she says.

"Take care of yourself," I say, squeezing her back. Keisha walks away, leaving me and Kian alone. Behind me, a bush rustles. I spin around, fists raised. A gray rabbit runs past, kicking up snow in its wake.

"Relax," Kian says. "My friends would let me know if the enemy found us."

"Friends?" I raise my brows. "Your advisors?"

"They're some of the best friends that I've got."

"Better than me?" I ask.

The snow falls faster now. Snowflakes cling to Kian's eyelashes. "No," he says. "Not even close." His thumb caresses my cheek. "Zoe—"

"Reynolds, where are you?" A voice interrupts whatever Kian was about to say. Josiah, one of the other faction leaders, steps between the trees. "There you are, man. All of my guys are ready. What's the hold up?"

Kian's hand falls to his side. "I'll see you later," he says.

"Later," I say. As he walks away, I bring my hand to my cheek. My skin still tingles from his touch.

* * *

The war rages, bloodier than I ever imagined. I perch on the edge of a stone turret, one of the highest points of the palace. On the ground, I see Kian's golden mist, protecting his soldiers. Keisha pops out from behind a tree, throws a knife into an enemy's chest, then ducks to avoid bullets whizzing overhead.

About a dozen Aurelian soldiers approach Kian and his troop, their guns pointed straight ahead. I shoot a blue orb from my talon. It lands beside the Aurelian soldiers, and then explodes, detonating like a grenade. When the blue mist dissipates, the whole group of Aurelian soldiers are on the ground. I hold my head up high. Kian must be proud, too. We've been working really hard on that one.

A large crow beats its wings, soaring through the color-streaked sky. From this distance, I can't tell who it is: friend, foe, or ordinary crow. A smaller crow follows behind it, zooming over the setting sun, an orange half-circle dipping below the horizon.

They fly closer and closer. I squint, trying to figure out who they are. The larger crow lands on the turret, just a few feet away from me. The smaller one lands right beside it, watching me with turquoise eyes. There's no mistaking my cousin Caliah's eyes. I stare at the larger crow, recognition dawning on me. It has the stout frame and beaklike nose of my Aunt Gwenna.

But what are they doing here? Which side are they fighting for? With my Aunt Gwenna, it's hard to tell. Even though she's family, she's made her disdain for humans and half-breeds clear. I always thought that Caliah was a good person, but after what Kian told me, I'm not so sure.

I don't want to fight my cousin or my aunt, but I'll do whatever's necessary.

A blast of magic shoots from my aunt's talons, knocking several Aurelian soldiers down. Caliah launches a cannon-like projectile at another group of soldiers dressed in royal blue.

Hell yeah! I release a celebratory caw. With my aunt and cousin by my side, we're going to snipe down all of these bastards. Every last one until Aurelia is free.

CHAPTER 41

Saria

As soon as my eyes open, I'm on my way to battle. Well, maybe not that exact moment. Don't forget that I sleep six feet underground now. First, I had to dig my way out of the grave.

Red slips his fingers through mine. "Try not to get too close to anyone, and no matter what you do, protect your chest. Remember, you're immortal now. Gunshots may hurt, but not enough to slow you down. The only thing you have to fear is a wooden stake to the heart."

"Got it." My heart doesn't pound in my chest because my heart doesn't beat at all. It's amazing how much easier it is to think clearly when I'm not suffering with the physical manifestations of anxiety. Another unexpected benefit of vampirism.

The closer we get to the warzone, the more dead bodies we find. Young and old, men and women, so many lives lost. They won't get a second chance. They're not as lucky as I am.

Red and I duck behind a boulder. He peeks out from behind the rock, spotting two enemy soldiers. Blue beams shoot from Red's palm, thrusting both soldiers to the ground.

"Did you kill them?" I whisper.

"Nah, I just put them to sleep to prevent them from hurting anyone else," Red says. "If they're just following orders, I can't justify murdering them. I'll only kill someone if I know they're evil or my own life is in danger. Hopefully, by the time they wake up, Talon won't be in power."

I scan the battlefield. "Speaking of someone who we know is evil," I say. Licinia moves across the palace lawn, her platinum blonde waves flying loose behind her. She jump-kicks a soldier from our side in the chest. He crumples to the ground as she punches another soldier in the throat. I can hear the crack of his trachea from here.

Licinia is undeterred by the bullets piercing her skin. With a quick wave of her hand, she redirects a blast of offensive magic shooting in her direction.

"Should we?" I ask.

"Let's get her," Red says.

We slither out from behind the boulder, staying low to the ground. We slink up behind her. I clench a wooden stake in my fist.

Licinia spins around. When she sees us, she throws her head back. Cackles escape from her throat. "You two really think you can take me? Do you not understand that I'm both witch and vampire? I possess power that you could never imagine."

"I also have the power of both, Licinia," I say. "Just like you."

"Not quite." Licinia raises one brow in amusement. "I was a full-blooded witch, not a dirty half-breed. Besides, what are you? A day old?" She cackles again.

"Rather than all this talk, let's see what you got," Red says.

"You asked for it." Licinia smirks. She curls her lip, and I'm struck in the chest with a sharp pain, like a knife twisting in my ribcage. My knees buckle as I fall to the ground, writhing in agony. Licinia shrieks with laughter.

"Stop hurting her," Red demands. Blue lasers shoot from his palms. Licinia ducks, avoiding the blows.

Red and Licinia circle each other. His eyes like blue flames, hers like black coal. Red shoots again, this time an explosion of blue, like a rocket into her chest.

Licinia flies backwards, landing in the snow with a thud. Red straddles her, wooden stake aiming for her chest. Licinia grabs hold of his wrists. Veins bulge in Red's neck, his face squished up in concentration as they both struggle for control.

The pain in my chest is still unbearable. I try to move, but I can't. It feels like there's a thousand pound weight on my legs.

I watch helplessly as Licinia manages to twist Red's arm around, so that the stake he holds points at his own heart. Licinia's lips spread into a maniacal grin. "You chose the wrong side, Redvers. You should've known better."

"No!" I shout. I can't let Red die. I remember the night we met on the streets of New York City, his fluorescent blue eyes glowing brighter than the streetlights. I can see us now: twirling around the dance floor, the music pulsing in his nightclub. I think of all the late nights awake on the phone, how he listened, *really* listened, when I needed someone to talk to. I can feel his lips on mine the first time we kissed, how he climbed on top of me, the ecstasy when his fangs pierced my neck. My power flows hot in my veins.

I can't lose Red. Something explodes inside of me. I convulse from the impact. And then I can move again. I jump to my feet, sprint and lunge forward. I slam the stake into Licinia's heart. Poof, and she's gone. All that's left of Licinia is a pile of black ashes.

"You did it," Red says, blue eyes wide. "You killed Licinia."

"We did it."

CHAPTER 42

Zoeli

Red blood is splattered everywhere on the white snow. There are so many bodies, and no end in sight. How much longer must this go on? How many lives will be lost?

The snow is heavier than before, coming down in sheets. I've lost sight of Kian and Keisha. I don't even know if they're alive. Every time I hear a scream, I wonder if it's one of them. I worry less about my sister. As a vampire, Saria has a greater chance of survival than the rest of us.

All of a sudden, everything goes dark. All the streetlights go out. Every light in the palace shuts off. The buildings in the distance turn dark. But it's more than a blackout. Even the stars disappear from the sky. The ribbons of color that originate from the Rock of Vitality are gone. It's pitch black. What the hell is going on?

Violet eyes materialize up above, big enough to take up the whole sky. "Enough is enough!" The woman's voice shakes the ground. "This magical world was created for my son, Zamus. This is where he married his beautiful wife Aurelia and raised their many children. This land was filled with love, kindliness and joy. Since his death, the land named after his wife has been inhabited by their descendants. And now look at what it has become! Zamus would never allow this barbarism to exist in his wife's name!"

Red lava spews from Mount Zamus' mouth, shooting at least a thousand feet into the air before crashing down like a tsunami. Lava spills over the land, rushing across the snow. Beneath my feet, the palace begins to crumble. I fly off the wall just as the stones tumble down, descending into a cloud of dust.

"Evacuate now!" Astrid shouts. "Everyone get out! You don't deserve this place!" Boom! Mount Zamus erupts again. Another enormous wave of lava slams into the earth. "If your heart is full of hate, the lava will eat you alive. If you're a benevolent person, you have nothing to fear. The lava will do you no harm. Still, everyone must leave! Aurelia will be no more!"

I swoop down lower, searching for my friends amongst the chaos. Red lava surges across the ground. A soldier runs, the lava just a few feet behind him. He doesn't run fast enough. The lava catches up, lapping over his feet. It sucks him down like quicksand. The man's screams are cut short as it swallows him whole.

I sail over the crowd, scanning until I see his white-blonde hair. Oh, thank God. I descend further, landing on his wrist. "Zoe!" Kian says, relief written all over his face. "I've been looking for you. You're alright."

Lava sloshes over his combat boots, but Kian is just fine. A soft blue glow cloaks my feathers as I switch bodies. I throw my arms around Kian's neck. "You're alive!"

He smiles at me. "So are you."

I look down at the lava, rushing over my shoes like a shallow river. "Astrid did it. She ended the war."

Kian frowns. "She's also destroying Aurelia. I've received word from the suburbs. All of the houses are collapsing. She wants us all out." Kian gaze fixes on something behind me, his eyes widening. "Look." He points.

Hundreds of half-naked people walk across the lava, most of them exposed from the waist down. Towards the front, I recognize Isla, long white hair draped across her body to cover her private parts. I stare at her legs, tears welling in my eyes.

Isla lifts her hands up. "What should we do?" She shouts to the sky.

"Get out of here," Astrid responds. "Aurelia will be no more. Go start a new life in the human realm. There are many oceans and uninhabited islands that you will enjoy."

"Zoe, what's happening to me?" Kian studies his arm, his brow furrowing. His camo jacket fades before my eyes, blending into the background, like he's disappearing into thin air.

I stare at my own hand. It blurs around the edges, like it's dissolving into space. "The same thing is happening to me."

And then I'm gone.

CHAPTER 43

Saria

"How did we get here?" A moment ago, Red and I were in the midst of pandemonium, watching our enemies get swallowed up by lava. A moment later, we're miles away from the war site, somewhere in the Elysian Forest.

"I have no idea," Red says, his expression just as baffled as I am.

"What just happened?" Zoe's voice comes out of nowhere.

"Zoe!" My sister wasn't there a second ago, but I don't even question it. I just throw my arms around her. Zoe squeezes me so tight she might break one of my ribs. Tears stream down my face. "You're alive. I'm alive. We're going home." She clings to me, both of us sobbing.

"Where are we?" I jump when I hear Kian's voice. Where the hell did he come from?

"I believe that we're in the Elysian Forest," Red says. "The better question is: how did we get here?"

"I summoned you." Astrid appears, a ghostly figure drifting between the trees. "Throughout this entire ordeal, the four of you have exhibited extraordinary bravery, integrity and a fierce desire to protect not only your people, but all people. Your kindness, determination, and courage in the face of grave danger has inspired me. You deserve to be rewarded. I will grant you one wish each." Her purple eyes shine like amethysts.

"A wish?" I ask, dumbfounded. "Any wish?"

"There are certain limitations. I cannot change the past. I cannot bring someone back from the dead," Astrid says.

"Can you change someone back from a vampire?" Red asks.

"I can do that, yes."

"Then I know what my wish will be," Red says.

I gasp. "Red! Why would you do that? You love being a vampire."

"Yes, but I love you more," Red says, taking my hand. His eyes meet mine. "I want to sunbathe with you on the beach. I want to eat pizza with you. I want to birdwatch with you during the day when your favorite birds are most active." Red takes a deep breath. "And when we're older, I want to raise a family with you."

"Red." I gaze into his eyes, wondering how I got so lucky.

"Do you want that too? Be honest, Sari."

"Yes," I croak. "I do, more than anything."

"I'll miss having magic," Red says. "Remember, I'm not like you. I'm just a mere human."

"What did you say?" Astrid's laughter sounds like wind chimes. "Red, you really don't know?"

"Know what?" Red's brow furrows.

"Of course," Astrid says, her expression turning serious. "How could you? I just kind of assumed you figured it out, what with all that blue magic shooting from your hands and eyes all the time."

"That's not from being a vampire?"

Astrid shakes her head, her long brown waves swaying behind her. "Hadn't you noticed how much more powerful you are compared to other vampires? Even vampires older than you?"

"I don't understand. What are you trying to say?" Red asks.

"Your mother was a witch during a time when it was very dangerous to be one. Tensions between vampires and witches were at an all-time high. Many of her friends and family members were viciously murdered by packs of rogue vampires, further cementing her fears.

"After she met your father, she decided that it would be safer to assimilate to human culture. She concealed her identity from everyone, including her own children. Since your father was a human, she mistakenly thought that her children wouldn't inherit any magic.

"She managed to stay hidden for many years. Until one evening, she was walking along the sidewalk when a group of vampires recognized her. They followed her home, and well, you know what happened next. Her worst nightmares came true."

Red's jaw hangs open. "What you're saying is that my mother was a witch and my father was human."

"Like me!" I say, squeezing his hand. "You're a half-breed."

Zoe laughs. "Don't worry, Red. We won't call you a nimwit."

"So, if I wish to not be a vampire anymore, I'll still have magic?" Red asks.

"That's right," Astrid says, her cherry red lips curving into a smile. "Is that your wish?"

"One hundred percent," Red says.

"You must say it," Astrid responds. "Say my name first, and then your wish."

Red clears his throat. "Astrid, I wish to not be a vampire."

A white spotlight shines down on Red. I hold my breath. A moment later, the light fades.

"That's it?" I ask.

Red turns to me, tears pouring down his face. He pulls me into his arms. He's warmer than he was before, his breath hot against my cheek. I put my head on his chest. His heart beats: lub-lub, lub-lub. "You're alive," I breathe.

"Saria, you're next," Astrid says. "I assume I know what your wish will be."

"Yes," I say, facing Astrid. "Astrid, I wish to not be a vampire."

The spotlight shines down on me, and the future is oh so bright.

CHAPTER 44

Zoeli

"Zoeli, you're up," Astrid says. "What do you wish for?"

My mind races. What is the one thing that I want the most? More importantly, what is the one thing I want the most that I cannot achieve on my own? "I want the freedom to choose who I love. I want you to sever the soulmate connection I have with Damian."

Astrid shakes her head. "Zoeli, I can't do that."

My hands clench at my sides. "I'm not asking you to change the past or bring someone back from the dead. What's your issue?"

"There are things that you don't understand."

"Then explain them to me!'

"I already told you. In the future, you and Damian will have a child. That child—"

"Are you telling me that I can't choose who I procreate with?" I ask louder than I intended. My face is red hot.

"Damian will grow up and mature. At some point, you will choose him."

"If you're so confident about that, then what's the problem? If you destroy the soulmate connection, I'll still choose him, right?"

Astrid hesitates. "Most likely, but I can't risk—"

"Then you are taking away my free will!"

"Zoeli, it isn't that simple. Unfortunately, this war will not be the last one. There will be a period of peace, but evil forces will emerge again. By that time, you'll be too old to fight. Your child, the one you bear from Damian's seed, is the hero of our future."

"It's my life!" I shout. "You can't tell me that I need to create a person who doesn't even exist yet. Let someone else be a hero."

"I'm not sure if you understand the magnitude of what I'm saying. If you don't have this child, the world is doomed. Evil will prevail."

I groan, taking it all in. "Isn't there another option? This is the age of modern medicine. There's egg freezing, IVF and surrogacy."

"IVF?" Astrid's eyes grow large.

"In vitro fertilization," I explain. "I don't have to be with Damian to have a child who is biologically his. With a surrogate, I don't even have to carry the child."

"I see," Astrid says, considering. "I suppose, as long as the child is born, it doesn't matter how they are conceived."

"But let me be clear: I would prefer that you find another hero. It would make things a lot less complicated."

Astrid glides back and forth, pacing between a bush and a boulder. "If you want me to do this for you, we need to make a deal. Ten years from now, I will come find you. If you aren't married to Damian, you agree to do this whole," Astrid waves her hand. "IVF thing."

"Deal," I say.

Astrid sighs. "Alright. Against my better judgment, I will grant your wish. Go ahead."

"Astrid, I wish that Damian Nightingale was not my soulmate."

The spotlight appears, basking me in white light. A moment later, it's gone. "Is it done?" I ask. Astrid gives me a curt nod. I jump in the air.

"Kian, it's your turn. What is your wish?"

Kian shifts from side to side. "I wish to stay here in Aurelia."

"That's impossible. When Mount Zamus is done, there will be nothing left."

"I don't need anything other than the land," Kian says. "Aurelia is my home."

"It's a wasteland. Completely uninhabitable. Your home is a pile of wood."

"I'll pitch a tent," Kian says. "And then I'll rebuild my country. However long it takes."

"Your determination is admirable." Astrid pauses. "But a place with so much hate and violence should not exist."

"I agree," Kian says. " But Aurelia does not have to be that way. This will be brand new Aurelia, an Aurelia where everyone is welcome and treated with respect. An Aurelia where everyone has the same rights, no matter your family background or magical abilities. An Aurelia where our leaders are voted for in elections, and laws are written by representatives of the common person. An Aurelia that stands for the values that your son and his wife held dear. A true and fair democracy."

"That would be quite the feat," Astrid says. "And it will take much more than magic to accomplish. It will take years of hard labor, strong leadership, and impeccable organization."

"I'll put in the work," Kian says. "Please just let me try."

Astrid snaps her fingers. Her golden gown ripples in the wind. "Your home has been restored. It is the only one standing amongst the wreckage. For the rest, you're on your own. I'll return in one year to check on your progress. If evil has taken over again, your project is done. You must leave. Do you understand?"

"I won't let you down." Kian says. "Thank you, Astrid."

And the goddess fades into the night.

CHAPTER 45

Zoeli

Six Months Later

I've been driving for over two hours when I finally pull to the side of the road. From the driver's seat, I double check the address on my phone. 13 Sunny Hope Lane. I'm here.

The lawn is freshly mowed. I study the house: peach siding, white trim, a wrap-around porch. There's nothing to differentiate it from any other ordinary house in the neighborhood.

I look at the website again. *Our shelter on Sunny Hope Lane offers refuge for LGBTQ youth. We provide home-cooked meals, educational opportunities and mental health services for homeless teens.*

I scroll through the pictures until I find the one. My breath hitches when I see her face. After months of deep diving the internet, I think I finally found her.

I walk up the front steps, wiping sweaty palms on my jeans. I stand at the front door, heart drumming against my rib cage. I press the doorbell. Ding-dong. I step back, my hands stuffed inside my pockets.

I hear footsteps, someone jangling the doorknob on the other side. The door creaks open. A woman in a floral sundress offers a warm smile. "Hi, how can I help you?"

"I'm, um, looking for, um, Sam Reynolds," I say.

"Sam wasn't expecting any visitors." A crease materializes between the woman's brows. "May I ask your name?"

"Zoe," I say. "Can you tell her that I know her brother?"

"I think you have the wrong person," the woman says. "Sam doesn't have any siblings." She starts to close the door.

I thrust my arm straight out, preventing the door from shutting. "Can you tell her that I know Kian?" The woman stares at me. "Please," I say. "It's really important. Tell her that I know Kian. If she doesn't want to see me, I'll leave." I hold my breath, waiting.

Finally, the woman nods. "Sit." She gestures to a wicker couch on the front porch. "I'll be right back."

A few minutes later, the girl riding the dragon on Kian's arm steps onto the porch. Older with shorter hair, but unmistakably her. She wears baggy jeans, a rainbow t-shirt, and scuffed sneakers. "How do you know Kian?"

"Do you have some time?" I ask. "This is going to take a while."

Sam sits cross-legged on the porch swing across from me. I start from the very beginning when I was a prisoner in Nightingale Dungeon, and Kian was the kind guard who smuggled in a blanket for me. I tell her about DOX, Talon's invasion, and how Kian created The Resistance. I tell her about the final battle, the eruption of Mount Zamus and subsequent destruction of the palace, and how Astrid expelled all of us from Aurelia. And finally, Kian's insistence on staying behind when everyone else evacuated, how he and just a few others remained, intent on rebuilding their homeland.

When I finish, her eyes are wet. "I'm so proud of him."

"Kian loves you," I say. "And he misses you."

"I love him, too. That's why I left. I almost got him killed."

"You can't blame yourself for that," I say.

"He wouldn't have confronted Weston if it wasn't for me." Sam wrings her hands in her lap. "And that wasn't the first time he had to defend me. It's not easy having a lesbian dud sister."

The woman from earlier pokes her head out the front door. "Sam, it's time for dinner."

"Okay, I'll be right in." Sam stands up.

"Wait." I hand her an invitation. "We're having a birthday party for our friend and um, it's kind of special because he hasn't had a birthday party in a very long time. Kian is coming in for the occasion. I'm sure he'd love to see you."

Sam looks at the card in her hand. "Redvers' birthday," she reads aloud.

"It's at my house," I say. "The address and date are at the bottom."

"I'll see if I can make it," Sam says. "Um, is it okay if I bring my girlfriend?"

"Of course."

"Thanks for coming, Zoe." She gives a quick wave as the door shuts behind her.

CHAPTER 46

Saria

I've always loved summer nights, but they're so much more special now. I spread my wings, wind rushing through my black feathers.

Zoe zooms past, challenging me to a competition. I race her across the moon, flapping as fast as I can, leaving her in the dust. I was born to fly.

I circle back around, returning to the crows I left behind. My mother caws, a happy song. My sister and I join in, adding our voices to her melody.

It feels like the perfect night. But tomorrow might be even better.

As soon as the sun comes up, Red and I are going to the beach. We'll spend the day sunbathing, swimming and building sandcastles. When the sun goes down, we'll go out to dinner at my favorite pizza restaurant.

Afterwards, when we head back to his apartment, I might even let him bite my neck.

CHAPTER 47

Damian

I slide my key into the door of my new home. I twist, but the door won't budge. It's jammed again. Goddamn it. I use all of my might, my knuckles white on the rusty doorknob.

I pry the door open, sweat beading on my brow. It's a far cry from my old life, when butlers held open the opulent palace doors, bowing before me as I entered. Now, I let myself inside a cramped three-bedroom apartment.

When the lava swallowed up Nightingale palace, all of our furniture and riches were taken with it. I collapse on the old musty couch we bought from a second-hand store. From the other side of the couch, Fallon wrinkles her nose. "You stink," she says.

I lift my armpit and take a whiff. Fallon's right. "You try working a double shift at a fast food restaurant and see how good you smell," I say.

"I would never." Fallon's face squishes up in disgust.

"Well, you need to get a job." Even though Alaina helped Mom get a job at Mountainside Hospital, our rent's higher than her pay. We're barely getting by. "We can hardly afford groceries," I say.

"I'll starve before I work at a fast food joint," Fallon mutters. My sister still hasn't faced reality. She isn't a princess anymore. In one moment, our lives were stolen from us. I'll never forget that moment. It's emblazoned in my mind, a scar so deep that it became part of my soul.

Every night, I relive it in my dreams: the roar of a volcanic tidal wave, the clamor as the palace fell, windows shattering, bricks cracking open, a sound like thunder exploding in my eardrums. I remember it all in vivid detail: my sister's scream, my mom's eyes widening in horror, my father pulling my mom close for the last time.

When the dust settled, I was knee deep in a pile of debris, but somehow unscathed while the palace crumbled around me. My mom threw her arms around me, tears pouring down her cheeks. Fallon wandered the wreckage, calling for my father. It took us days to accept the truth. He was gone, his remains mixed amongst the rubble. Eventually we found a blackened finger, identified as his only by the wedding band.

"Mom can't afford the bills on her own, Fallon," I say.

"I don't understand why that means I have to work. One little blast of magic, and the pathetic human vermin will open up their wallets, none the wiser."

"Mom said we're not allowed to use magic on the humans." Part of me doesn't entirely disagree with Fallon. It would be a lot easier than working this fast food job. But, I'm trying to do the right thing. In my past, I made some really bad decisions, and I lost everything for it. Now, I'm determined to do better. I just hope that I can keep it up. "Besides, that would be stealing."

"Whatever." Fallon grumbles. "Colson told me that he made one thousand dollars last week—"

I hold up my palm. "I don't want to hear about Colson's latest scam." My cousin Colson managed to escape to the human realm before the lava could reach him. I often wonder if the lava would've spared or incinerated him. I guess we'll never know. He's one lucky bastard.

"You two need to make amends, Damian. You were like brothers. Colson misses you."

I shake my head. "I'm trying to prove to someone that I've changed. Hanging around connivers like Colson isn't going to earn me any points."

Fallon's brows raise in interest. "Who are you trying to win over? Your baby mama?" She giggles.

Even though Zoeli refuses to speak to me, my mom talks to her mom almost every day. Alaina told Mom about what happened with Astrid, and the importance of the child that Zoe and I were destined to conceive.

In ten years, Astrid is supposed to check in on us. And if she demands it, I'm going to have to create a child with a woman who despises me.

Ten years is a long time from now. Who knows what could happen between now and then? Part of me wonders if Zoeli and I will end up together after all. She's an extraordinary woman: wickedly smart, strikingly beautiful, and immensely strong. I had some nerve looking down on her. The truth is, I never deserved her. She was right to leave me when she did. She's an incredible woman, and she deserves a man much better than me.

But as much as I admire Zoeli, ever since Astrid severed our soulmate connection, my feelings have changed. I don't obsess over where she is or who she's been with. I don't dream about her at night, or wake up thinking of her in the morning. As time goes on, I find myself thinking of her less and less. Lately, she barely ever runs through my thoughts.

But there's someone else who I can't seem to get off my mind. My phone buzzes in my pocket. When I see the name on the screen, my lips curve into a smile. I slip into my bedroom to answer the phone.

"Hey, Cali." I say.

"Hey, Damian. I just wanted to check in and see how you're doing." Cali is the only one who seems to understand how it feels to lose a parent. Even though my father was an asshole, he was still my father, and losing him hurts.

In seventh grade, after Cali's father died unexpectedly of a heart attack, she cried on my shoulder. Now, she repays the favor. Even though she has every right to hate me for the way I treated her, she's here for me.

"I'm alright," I say. "I just got home from work. I'm going to use most of my paycheck to help my mom pay the bills."

"I admire how you're stepping up," Caliah says. "I'm proud of you."

"Um, thanks," I mumble. "I have a few dollars left over. Maybe enough to go to the movies, if, um, you want to go with me?"

There's a long pause. "Like a date?" Cali asks.

"Um, yeah," I say, my heart beating overtime. There was a time when Cali would jump on the opportunity to go on a date with me. She would stare up at me, her turquoise eyes twinkling, her cheeks rosy with excitement. That was before I broke her trust.

I wonder if she'll ever look at me that way again. I'm such a goddamn idiot.

"I don't know if that's a good idea, Damian," Caliah says.

My heart drops. There was a time when no matter how badly I treated her, Cali would come running back. I guess I'm not the only one who's done some growing.

"I understand," I mumble. The old Damian wouldn't take no for an answer. He'd lie, connive and coerce until he got his way.

That isn't me anymore. I'm going to respect her wishes. Over time, I'll show her that I've changed. Even more importantly, I'll show myself that I can change.

"I still have feelings for you," Caliah says. Warmth surges through my chest. "I'm just not ready to jump back in." She takes a deep breath. "Yet."

"Yet." I repeat. It's the most beautiful word I've ever heard. Yet means that there's still a chance. Yet means that there's hope. And if she ever gives me another shot, I sure as hell won't screw it up again.

CHAPTER 48

Zoeli

I blow up the last balloon and pin it to the ballroom arch assembled in our backyard. Saria hangs the banner, *Happy 18th Birthday, Red!*

"I think we're all set up," I say, checking the clock again. He said he was going to be here early. I sit on a chair, my leg shaking. What if he changed his mind? What if he forgot? I've barely heard from him in months.

My cat, Batman, jumps into my lap. I stroke his soft fur and think of Moz. I wonder how he's doing. Batman purrs, his yellow eyes half-shut.

He peers around the side of the house, his white hair shining in the sunlight. He wears a button-down shirt and pressed jeans. Our eyes lock. He half-waves from across the yard. I forget that I'm mad at him for not staying in touch.

I run into his arms, nearly knocking him over from the impact. "Kian!"

His skin is pink and splotchy, a bashful smile tugging on the corners of his lips. "Hey," he says. I look up at the face I've dreamed of every night. He's just as handsome as I remembered.

"Thanks for coming," I say. "I have a surprise for you. Come inside."

I slide open the glass patio doors and lead him into the kitchen. A coffee and a donut wait on the table. Kian picks up the donut and takes a bite. "This is a great surprise."

"That's not all. Follow me." I walk into the living room, Kian a step behind me. Sam sits on the couch, dressed in basketball shorts and an oversized t-shirt. Sam's girlfriend, Olivia, is beside her, twisting the ends of her long brown hair.

"Sam." Kian's jaw falls open. His eyes turn watery, and then a tear slides out. Sam stands up, and then they're hugging, arms tight around each other.

"I think we should give them some time," I whisper to Olivia. She nods in agreement.

When we tiptoe out of the room, they still haven't let go.

* * *

"Happy birthday to you! Happy birthday dear Red!" Red sits behind his birthday cake, the candlelight dancing in his eyes. "Happy birthday to you!" He blows out the candles.

"Did you make a wish?" Saria asks.

"My dear Sari, all of my wishes have already come true," Red says.

"Aww," I say. "You two are so freaking cute."

"You're finally eighteen," Keisha comments. "A full grown adult."

"Nah, not yet," Red responds. "The human brain doesn't fully develop until at least age twenty-five. In some cases, the prefrontal cortex doesn't mature until age thirty."

Saria grins. "You still have an excuse to make bad decisions. At least for a few more years."

"I'll help you cut the cake," Giselle says, picking up a knife. Giselle and I work quickly, cutting the sheet cake into squares and putting each portion on a festive paper plate.

Kian's voice comes from behind me. "Can I help?"

I hand him a piece of cake. "You can help by eating this."

"Happy to be of assistance."

We sit down at the picnic table, Sam and Olivia across from us. "Are you guys having fun?" I ask.

"We're having a great time," Sam says, but she isn't looking at me. I follow her gaze to the other table. Jasleidy is on Logan's lap, his arms around her waist. The two of them hit it off during the time he was hiding in her family's attic. Caliah sits across from them, looking beautiful as ever with her strawberry-blonde ringlets and twinkling turquoise eyes.

"Oh," I say, realization dawning on me. "I'm sorry. I hope seeing Caliah doesn't upset you."

Sam shrugs. "It was a long time ago. I'm over it, but I really should apologize to her."

"Apologize?" Kian asks. "What for? She dropped you as a friend."

Sam shakes her head. "That's not how it happened."

Kian raises his brows. "What do you mean?"

"I caught feelings for her. It became too hard for me to be around her, knowing that she wasn't gay."

"That's not what you told me," Kian says.

"You asked me why we weren't friends anymore, and I didn't know what to say. I was embarrassed," Sam says.

"The truth is that I ghosted her, and I never even gave her an explanation. It was wrong of me."

"You did what you felt you had to do to protect your heart," I say. "Don't be so hard on yourself."

"Zoe!" I spin around at the familiar voice.

A young woman walks across the lawn, a long braid draped over her shoulder. A child tottles beside her and then squats, plucking a dandelion from the grass. "Rosa! I'm so glad you made it."

"Sorry we're late," Rosa says. "My boss kept me after hours."

"They better compensate you for that," I say.

"For overtime, they pay time and a half. They also provide phenomenal health insurance. Don't worry. They're taking good care of me. Unlike my ex-employer."

Theo walks up behind her. "Hey, Zoe," he says.

"How are you feeling?" I ask. "Is the new treatment regimen your doctor prescribed going well for you?"

"So far, so good," Theo says.

"Zoe! Look! Pretty flower!" Ivy waves the dandelion in the air.

I smile at her. "A pretty flower for a pretty girl."

As the sun goes down, Logan sparks up the fire pit. "I can't wait for senior year," Giselle says.

"It's going to be our first time going to school in the human realm," Jasleidy says, her finger moving back and forth between herself and Caliah. "What should we expect?"

"There won't be any lessons on spellcasting or potions," Saria says. "But there's so much to look forward to."

As Saria and Giselle babble on and on about all of the senior festivities, Caliah and Jasleidy hang onto every word. I smile and nod, but I just can't bring myself to care about homecoming, prom, or senior prank day.

The only event I was looking forward to was The Battle of the Bands, but I won't be participating this year. There's no band without Yazmin. I swallow back tears. My heart still breaks every time I think of her.

* * *

"I had a good time. Thanks for inviting me," Kian says. We're standing in the entryway, saying goodbye. "Thank you so much for finding my sister. I can't even put in words how much that meant to me."

"I'm so happy for both of you."

He leans down and gives me a quick hug. "Goodbye, Zoe."

"Goodbye, Kian." I watch him walk out the front door.

I sprint upstairs, taking the steps two at a time. Before I can lose my nerve, I grab the suitcase from my bedroom closet, and then race back downstairs. "Wait!" I yell, my suitcase rolling behind me. Kian is only a few feet from my front porch. I run to him. "I have another surprise for you."

Kian stares at the suitcase on the ground beside me. "What are you doing?"

"I'm going with you to Aurelia," I say. "I'm running away."

"What?" Kian's brow furrows. "It's your senior year. You have to go to dances and pep rallies and all that fun stuff."

I shake my head. "I don't care about any of that."

"Maybe you don't care right now, but one day you will when you look back on everything you missed."

I fold my arms across my chest. Of all the times I imagined this conversation, it never went like this. "I've made up my mind. I'm coming whether you want me to or not. If you don't want to hang out with me or you're seeing someone else, that's fine. I won't bother you."

"Seeing someone else?" Kian laughs.

I shrug. "I don't know. You don't want me to come with you. You've called me twice in the past three months. I figured that could be the reason."

"If I was seeing someone, I'd have a pretty hard time explaining this." He begins to unbutton his shirt. I wrinkle my brow. What is he doing? He pulls his shirt open, revealing his chest.

My jaw drops. There I am, stamped right over his heart. In his soul mark, I'm a human with crow wings. My blue eyes shine, black hair blowing back behind me. If it wasn't already obvious, my name is written in script, *Zoeli*

"Whoa," I say. I reach out and touch his skin, tracing the lines of the illustration, so much like a tattoo but it's not.

"There's no one else, Zoe. Only you."

I run my finger along my name on his chest. The line at the end of my name extends, stretching over my fingers, and wrapping around my wrist. I watch it loop and swirl, creating letters, *Kian*

Kian stares, his mouth open. "I have no idea how that happened."

I hold up my wrist. "It's like a bracelet. I love it."

Kian pulls me hard against him. His mouth crushes against mine. We kiss, again and again, fire shooting down my spine. His hand slips under my shirt, touching the small of my back. I run my hands through his hair, the strands like silk between my fingers. "There's still a few weeks left of summer. Stay with me until it's time to go back to school. I know you, Zoe. I know that finishing high school is important to you."

"It is, but so is Aurelia. I can always get my GED."

"I'll take care of Aurelia. You can come back after graduation."

Tears spring into my eyes. "But…. senior year isn't going to be the same without Yaz."

Kian wraps his arms tighter around me. "I know it's hard, Zoe, but Yaz wouldn't want you to drop out because of her. She'd want you to achieve all of your goals."

"I guess you're right," I murmur. "But I hate being away from you."

"I'll come visit," Kian says. "I'll come every weekend."

"But you didn't," I say. "I kept hoping you'd come, but you never did."

"I thought about it all the time, Zoe, but I didn't want to impose. I'm not part of your life here. I kinda figured that you forgot about me, that maybe you and Damian were—"

"You can't be serious! First of all, delete that name from your vocabulary. I already have. Second of all, I could never forget about you. I've missed you every day."

"I'm an idiot." Kian shakes his head. "If you wanted me to come, why didn't you ask?"

"I know that you're busy with an important mission. I didn't want to bother you."

"Then we're both idiots." Kian grins. "Because you could never bother me."

"Meow!" Batman circles my feet, rubbing his cheek against my leg and then my suitcase.

"Hey Batman." I bend down to scratch his head. "I'm going to miss you buddy."

"Meow! Meow!"

"He's upset that you're leaving," Kian says. "He's sad when you're away."

"Is that what he's trying to say?"

"He can come with us. Moz could use a friend."

"Zoeli McKinney-Crowe!" My mom stomps outside, arms folded across her chest. "Just where do you think you're going with that suitcase?"

"Mom, um," I stammer. "I was just going to ask you. Can I stay with Kian for the rest of the summer? I want to help clean up Aurelia. Our homeland."

The front door opens and shuts. My dad and sister join my mom on the front porch. "What's going on here?" Dad asks.

"Zoeli wants to volunteer in Aurelia for a few weeks." My mom slides her hands in her jean's pockets. "I don't have a problem with it. What do you think, John?"

"I'll take good care of your daughter, sir," Kian says.

"I know you will," Dad says. "You took good care of them before, too. I don't know where my girls would be if it wasn't for you taking them in." Dad leans against the porch railing. "You'll be back by Labor Day? I don't want you missing any school."

"I promise." I stretch my arms out to hug them both. "Thank you both so much."

"I'm so proud of you," Mom says. "Text me when you get there." My dad holds the door open for my mom, and they both slip inside.

"I'm going to miss you," Saria says.

"No matter the time or the distance, nothing will ever change between us," I say. "Looking back, the only regret I have is letting jealousy, resentment and other people come between us. Never again. You're my other half, my twin flame."

"Always." Saria wraps me in a hug. "Send lots of pictures."

"Will do." With one last squeeze, I let Saria go. "See you in a few weeks." I skip over to Kian.

"There's one more thing before we go," Kian says.

"What's that?" I lift my eyes to meet his.

He leans down so that his forehead touches mine. "When my mother was alive, I asked her why it was so hard for me to connect with people. I wanted her to tell me what I was doing wrong. She just said that someday, when I least expected it, I'd meet someone, and it would just come easy. I didn't believe her, but now I know that she was right. That person, Zoeli, is you." His lips brush against mine, soft and gentle. "I love you, Zoeli." Euphoria surges through me.

"I love you, Kian," I say. His lips brush against mine, again and again.

The magic of Aurelia isn't in its crystals, castles or gemstone walkways. It runs much deeper than that. Even though their love was forbidden, Zamus and Aurelia risked everything to be together. Against all odds, they built an empire.

Their magic lives on in the rest of us: those of us willing to stand up for what's right, those of us who know that love trumps hate every time.

I was torn down. I faced the lowest of lows, but I came back stronger in the end. Sometimes, one thing is destroyed so that something better can be built in its place.

Aurelia isn't going to be as good as it once was. It's going to be better than it ever was. I'll make sure of it.

"Meow!" Batman stands on his hind legs, his paws on my thigh.

"I'm not forgetting you, I promise." I pick up my cat.

"Shall we?" Kian asks, reaching for my free hand.

With one hand around my cat and the other laced through Kian's, we're off to our next adventure. "Let's go."

Did you love The Crowe Sisters Trilogy by Faith Prince?

Keep reading for a free sample of Prince's stand-alone YA fantasy romance novel, Wild Souls.

Chapter 1

Soul Seer

Ethan

Everyone can see Kira and Luke standing in the classroom doorway, but only I can see the boa constrictor taut around her neck. As Luke pulls her closer, a shadow shrouds her light. His hand moves through her hair. Snake-like creatures erupt from his fingertips and slither across her scalp. I stand up at our lab table, fists clenched at my sides.

The bell rings. "See you later," she says and kisses him. As they separate, the snake unravels from her neck and glides back to Luke, coiling around his wrist.

"Later, babe." Luke walks away, a mass of dark scribbles and reptilian varmints following him. Kira glows like gold again. She slides into the seat beside me.

Ms. Anderson stands in front of the class. "It's time to get to work. Everyone should be finishing up the lab we started yesterday. If you have any questions, let me know."

I put my safety glasses on and pour the solution into the beaker. "So, um, what's going on with you and Luke?"

"He's my boyfriend." Kira smiles. "We've been hanging out for a few weeks, but we just made it official over the weekend."

"Oh." I pause. "I'm surprised."

"Me, too. He can have any girl he wants. I'm not sure how I got so lucky."

I shake my head. "That's not what I meant. You're way too good for him."

She laughs. "Yeah, right."

"I'm serious. You should stay away from him."

Kira's brows move together. "I don't understand. He's the class president. He'll probably be valedictorian. And he's gorgeous. What's the problem?"

The snakes. The darkness. The dread that wriggles up my spine whenever he's near. I can't say any of that out loud. She'll think I'm insane.

Kira drums her fingers on the table. "Ethan," she pauses. "I hope I haven't given you the wrong idea. You're not jealous, are you?"

"No, it's not like that," I say. "I appreciate that you're nice to me, and that we're…" I pause, trying to think of how to describe our relationship. We chat during class, but it's not like we hang out outside of school.

"Friends," Kira finishes for me.

"Friends," I repeat after her. It feels weird coming off my tongue. I'm not used to saying it. "As a friend, I have to tell you. He's not a good person."

"How do you know? Have you ever even spoken to him?"

"No," I admit. I barely talk to anyone. Kira knows that. "But you have to trust me." I glance over at her. Apart from Luke, she's luminous as the sun, long golden tendrils stretching up towards the ceiling. A burgundy sparrow is perched on her shoulder, watching me through narrowed green eyes. She'll put up a good fight, that's for sure, but ultimately: snake food. "He'll pollute your soul," I say. "He'll destroy you."

She looks down at her notes. I sense the shift in her immediately. I took it too far. Now she thinks I belong in an asylum. Just like everyone else. We complete the lab in silence.

When the lunch bell rings, she doesn't say goodbye. She leaves the classroom without a word. I wait for the hallways to clear before I head outside. I walk into the woods, weaving through the trees until I reach my spot: a decrepit picnic table under a canopy of multi-colored leaves.

It's Friday, so Alex joins me. Most days, I eat alone. He plops down on the bench across from me, his brown bag crinkling as he digs inside of it. "Good afternoon, Ethan. It's a pleasure to see you again." Alex uses a script we learned seven years ago when our parents signed us up for the same social skills group. Even after my mom threw away a fortune on doctors and therapists, I'm still a mess, but at least I found my first friend in Alex. "How are you today?" Alex asks, his voice flat. No matter how hard our therapist tried, Alex never grasped using inflection in speech.

"Okay, I guess. What's new with you?" I'm careful not to make direct eye contact. As usual, Alex is encompassed by predictable patterns: geometric figures lined up in order of complexity, color wheels spinning in sync, twice counter-clockwise and once in reverse. Lights blink methodically, a complex code that I can't decipher.

"I'm creating a new app in Computer Science class."

"What kind of app?"

"It's a virtual experience app that uses technology similar to Mind-Reel. You know how when you use Mind-Reel, you're transported into someone else's perspective?"

I nod.

"Well, with my app, you can experience anywhere in the world: sights, sounds and sensations, as though you're really there."

My brow furrows. "How is that different from Mind-Reel? When I plugged into a guy's reel from Italy, I walked through the colosseum and touched the limestone walls. I even felt the sweat rolling down my back."

"No." Alex shakes his head. "You felt the sweat rolling down HIS back. You were inside his perspective, experiencing a scene he already lived. You weren't able to alter his past experience or make conscious choices. In my app, you virtually go somewhere as yourself, and are able to control your experience."

"That's really cool."

"Yes, but there's challenges too. Like Mind-Reel, the session maxes out at five minutes. Any longer and users risk permanent brain damage."

"You can market it to people who want a more interactive way to scope out potential vacation spots." I take a bite of my sandwich.

"I think I'll call it Mind-Travel." As he goes on about the programming involved, I finish my lunch. "You're quiet," Alex observes.

"I lost a friend today."

"Who?"

"Kira Barner."

"Where did you lose her?" Alex asks.

"No, she's not missing. She just doesn't want to be my friend anymore."

"I should've known that." Alex's cheeks turn red. As brilliant as Alex is, he struggles to understand idioms. He's told me that when he messes up, he feels like an idiot. He shouldn't. I understand better than anyone that all brains aren't wired the same. "Why is she mad at you?"

I shrug. "It's kind of hard to explain." I don't tell anyone I can see souls anymore. No one ever believed me. I check my watch. "We should head back."

I keep my hoodie pulled low over my eyes. I focus on avoiding seeing souls and soul-animals for the rest of the day. Evil often lurks where I least expect it. Nowhere is safe.

When the final bell rings, I slip inside the library and hunker down at a back table. I can't enter that crowded hallway. Mobs are unbearable for me. This condition requires that I strategize my every move. Sometimes my life feels like an endless chess match.

When the building seems quiet, I walk to my locker, my footsteps echoing in the empty hallway. As I turn my lock, a familiar dread slithers up my spine. Luke is nearby. I keep my head inside my locker, hoping he'll pass by and not notice me.

"Ethan," he says.

My back is still to him. "What?" I dig inside my locker until I find my math textbook.

"Turn around," he says.

I don't. "What do you want?"

"I want to talk to you. Turn around."

In my peripheral vision, I see the snakes. One hisses in my ear. I drop my gaze to the floor. That usually helps block out the visions. But not now, not when Luke is in such close proximity, not when his rage is directed at me. Snakes circle my feet, staring up at me with red eyes. They're ready for a feast.

"I said turn around asshole."

My heart is pounding. I take a deep breath and spin around. "I don't know what your problem is—" I'm cut off by a blow to my stomach that knocks the wind out of me.

"That's for talking shit about me to my girl." He hits me again. "That's for being such a freak." Snakes coil around my wrists and pin me to the wall. I lurch against the restraints. I use all of my strength, but I can't break free. I'm helpless. His fist pounds into my rib cage. "And that's for even talking to my girl at all."

A snake sinks its fangs into my shoulder. Another tears into my leg. I shout and writhe in pain. The agony inflicted by my visions is as real to me as the physical punches.

You'd think he'd stop. I'm not fighting back. That only seems to incense him more. "And that's for being such a pussy!" He pummels my chest. I wonder if I'm going to be beat to death in the school hallway. Of all the ways I imagined I'd go, this isn't one of them.

The girl comes out of nowhere. She shoves him—hard. "What the hell are you doing?" Shades of orange contour her frame, stretching into swirls of blue and violet. Luke's snakes move towards her, their fangs bared. Stars light up all around her, glittering against her purple waves. The snakes pause, almost like they're startled by her brightness. "What's your problem?"

"Mind your business," Luke says.

"I'm nosy!" The girl shouts. She pushes him again.

"YOU STUPID BITCH!" Luke's mass of darkness grows. Fury surges from him. The snakes hiss; their moment of hesitation is over. They spring towards the girl.

"Hey! What's going on here?" Austin Miller jogs down the hallway, his track t-shirt stained with sweat.

"She attacked me!" Luke says.

"Come on, don't yell at a girl. That's not like you," Austin says.

Luke's expression changes. Suddenly he's calm and composed, the demeanor that everyone else sees, the mask that's made him one of the most well-liked guys in our class. I still see the snakes. But I might be the only one. "You're right, man." He faces the girl. "I think we had a misunderstanding."

The girl squares on him. "I didn't misunderstand anything."

"Listen, I know you're upset," Luke says, his tone compassionate. "Maybe we can talk this out tomorrow when you're feeling more rational." He slaps Austin on the back. "See you later, man." And then he walks away.

The girl turns to me. "Are you okay?" she asks.

My body hurts like hell, but I nod. Her stars glisten among her vibrant colors. Her soul has its own pulse, a soft rumble that vibrates gently in my ears. I stare, speechless. She's beautiful. Jolts zig-zag down my spine.

The bell rings. If I don't make it out in time, I'll miss the late bus. "I've, um, gotta go," I say.

As I'm walking away, I realize that I never said thank you. I'm such an idiot. I look over my shoulder. Austin leans against the lockers, smiling as he talks to the girl. She's looking up at him, laughing. They're probably making fun of me. I turn back around.

As I head outside, Taylor Powell whizzes by, her brow tightly creased. Laser-like spikes poke through her skin and shoot into space. I duck to avoid being hit. On the sidewalk, Julien Acosta is encased within an enormous clock. He bites his lip, the clock's hands spinning erratically as the ticking grows louder and louder.

At the bus stop, a group waits. The mixture of souls overwhelms my senses. Neon colors, pastels, neutrals and gray meld together until they're all one vomit-like mixture. Soul-sounds collide until the thrum of a lullaby shifts into a piercing cry. A malevolent soul hides amidst the innocent faces. Red-eyed demons circle me, closing in.

I lower my chin and stare at the cracks on the sidewalk. The images subside. Luckily. Otherwise, I'd be wheeled away in a gurney, like all of the other times before.

People say there's good in everyone. They say good trumps evil. But they can't see what I see. They haven't watched virtue and good intentions get sucked into a vortex of malice and envy, swirling and intertwining, bumping against jagged edges and tearing open, spilling all over each other until you can't tell which is what anymore.

When I was younger and naive, I told doctors and therapists that I can see souls, thinking they could help me. I told them that although I've seen some beautiful souls, the ones that haunt me are vile and terrifying.

They all said that I'm crazy. Delusional. Suffering from hallucinations. That the grotesque and horrid images I see can't be real.

Sometimes, for the world's sake, I hope they're right.

"A heart-warming story with incredible character development, Wild Souls isn't just about falling in love. It's about finding someone loves you for who you truly are, regardless of who the world perceives you to be. It's about overcoming your fears and facing your inner demons. Deep, meaningful, well-written, and at times laugh-out-loud funny,
Wild Souls is a must-read for all ages."

Ethan sees right through skin and bone, his visions exposing the true nature of each person he meets. In his town, he's known as a freak and a liar. Completely ostracized, he keeps his head down and avoids people. After all, there's no point in uncovering the truth about people if no one believes you anyway. Everyone says he's insane. Yet, Jenna likes him.

Jenna has no idea that Ethan can see straight through to her soul. She doesn't know why he accuses upstanding citizens of heinous crimes—spurring hatred towards him throughout their small town. All Jenna knows is that he gets her offbeat humor and fascination with the paranormal. Spending time with Ethan is a welcome escape from wondering why her dad won't answer her calls...

Until Ethan's sixth-sense opens a gate to their souls—literally. As they face their inner-most demons, they could either fall apart or fall deeper in love than they ever imagined...

Pick up your copy today! Available at Amazon, Kindle Unlimited, Audible, Barnes and Noble and many other online retailers worldwide.

https://www.amazon.com/dp/B0B8NVNXZL

Faith Prince is the author of The Crowe Sisters Trilogy (Where Magic Begins, Magic Coming Undone, Twin Flames) and the stand-alone novel Wild Souls.

Besides writing, some of Faith's favorite things include: spending time with her family, reading, country music, cats, chocolate, coffee, traveling, and concerts, in that order.

Visit Faith's YouTube channel at
https://www.youtube.com/c/FaithPrinceAuthor

Signed paperbacks are available for purchase on my website.
www.faithprinceauthor.com

Follow me!

Instagram: https://www.instagram.com/faithprincewrites
Twitter: https://twitter.com/FaithPrinceAuth
TikTok: https://www.tiktok.com/@faithprinceauthor
Amazon: https://www.amazon.com/author/faithprince